Sweet

Landry Family Series, #6

Adriana Locke

To those of us that get scared sometimes.
It's okay to be scared, as long as you keep going.

Books by Adriana Locke

My Amazon Store

Brewer Family Series
The Proposal | The Arrangement

Carmichael Family Series
Flirt | Fling | Fluke | Flaunt | Flame

Landry Family Series
Sway | Swing | Switch | Swear | Swink | Sweet

Landry Family Security Series
Pulse

Gibson Boys Series
Crank | Craft | Cross | Crave | Crazy

The Mason Family Series
Restraint | The Relationship Pact | Reputation | Reckless |
Relentless | Resolution

The Marshall Family Series
More Than I Could | This Much Is True

The Exception Series
The Exception | The Perception

Dogwood Lane Series

Tumble | Tangle | Trouble

Standalone Novels

**Sacrifice | Wherever It Leads | Written in the Scars | Lucky
Number Eleven | Like You Love Me | The Sweet Spot |
Nothing But It All**

Cherry Falls Novellas

608 Alpha Avenue | 907 For Keeps Way

For a complete reading order and more information, visit
www.adrianalocke.com.

Synopsis

Sweet

Landry Family Series Book #6

Synopsis

USA Today Bestselling author Adriana Locke delivers a "fresh and fun!" romance between a grumpy single dad and his beautiful, spunky employee—the one he can't have.

Chemistry is not love.

That's what my boss, **the grumpy single dad** with brilliant green eyes, says anyway.

I have my V-card. He's ten years older than me. I work for him.

Nate Hughes has a million reasons why a relationship between us would never work. Honestly? It's all a farce.

He can't deny our connection. His soft smiles, brief touches, and protective behaviors come too easily. And when I need a place to stay? He can't stop himself from offering me a room—though I'd prefer his bed. After all, there are sparks—delicious, sizzling sparks—when we're together.

Our **forced proximity** brings things to a head. Our shared experiences and traumas draw us closer. Our undeniable attraction has us toeing the line between **friends and lovers**—whether Nate likes it or not.

He's right—chemistry is not love. But that doesn't mean that I won't fall in love with him ... even if he can't love me back.

Chapter 1

Nate

"**P**ut some clothes on!"

Paige Carmichael looks at me over her shoulder, wearing nothing but a bra and panties. The garments are white and lace—practically fucking see-through—and it takes me longer than I care to admit to rip my eyes away from the curve of her ass cheek.

And even longer to back out of my office.

"Sorry, Nate," she shouts as I pull the door shut.

Dammit.

I rub a hand down my face and blow out an exasperated breath.

I've never yelled at a woman to put her clothes on, least of all one that I've thought about fucking in every position every single day since she walked into my bar eight months ago and asked for a job. But there's a first time for everything, I guess.

"Okay, I'm decent," she calls out. "You can come back in."

I swing open the door and enter the room.

Two bags are piled on the ratty couch that's seen better days. My desk has turned into some kind of cosmetics counter, and there's a curling iron plugged into the power strip by the window.

What the hell?

"I have so many questions that I don't know where to start," I say.

Paige bumps my arm as she walks by.

"Make yourself at home," I say.

"I did."

"*Clearly.*"

She sighs. "Look, I didn't know where else to go."

"Home, maybe?" I toss one of her bags off the couch and sit. "What's going on?"

She glances at me out of the corner of her eye. "Before I say anything, promise me you won't judge me."

"It's a little too late for that."

She rolls her eyes. "Fine. In one of my un-wisest moments, I took my roommate's word that she was paying our rent ..." She grimaces. "And she wasn't. We were evicted today."

This girl is a train wreck.

"I had nowhere to go, Nate," she says, sticking her bottom lip out. "But I knew *my friend* Nate would be more than happy to help me out of my bind. You weren't here, so I came on in. I waved to Shaye as I walked through the front door, so it's not like I was being sneaky."

Like that makes it okay.

"What would you have done if someone else would've walked in here and saw you naked?" I ask, quirking a brow.

She laughs. "Nate, no one else has the balls to walk into your office but you."

"And you, apparently."

"Well, and me." She grins and picks up the curling iron. "I'm glad you're here. I kind of need a favor."

I recline against the couch and prepare myself.

"Now's a little late to be asking for favors, don't ya think?" I ask.

She watches herself in the mirror that she's propped up on my desk. In small sections, she wraps her hair around the iron and then drops the strands into her hand. When she releases them, they're curled into soft waves.

I fight the urge to smile and fail miserably.

Paige is one of those people who you can't be mad at. No matter how hard you try, *and I have*, you can't help but like her. *And it's dangerous to like a girl like Paige.*

The girl is as sweet as she is tough. I've witnessed her threaten to shank a guy who tried to roofie a woman one night in the bar. She's bought Joe, the homeless guy who comes in regularly, soups and sandwiches a hundred times—even paid for a hotel room when it was cold last winter—and she consoled a woman who works here when two men had a showdown over her in the middle of the dining area.

She's also ridiculously hot. That's great for her ability to earn tips, but not so great when you're her boss and she's off-limits.

She grins back at me and then continues curling her hair.

"What are you getting all dolled up for?" I ask.

"I have a date."

A date?

My jaw clenches as I imagine some asshole seeing her in the see-through white panties that I now know she's wearing under those tight, ripped jeans. *He won't give a shit about her modesty.*

"Who with?" I ask as casually as I can.

"A guy."

"Does he have a name?"

The corner of her lips twitches. "He does."

My jaw tenses. "Who is it, Paige?"

She doesn't answer me.

If she thinks this is a game, she's wrong. I've watched her parade a handful of losers through The Gold Room without saying a word.

Why can't I say a word? Because she's not my girl.

And why is she not my girl?

Because the world hates me.

Why the universe dropped Paige into my life at the exact moment that I thought about dating again is simply cruel. I'm not *needing* someone per se, but if I was considering what I'd look for, it would be maturity and responsibility—not just a quick fuck. My life

3

is busy, jam-packed with running my bar, working part-time for Landry Security, and being the best damn single dad that I can be.

Despite the obvious attraction, the last thing I should even consider is a twentysomething who clearly likes her freedom.

She never stays with one man long.

Which is why she's off-limits for me.

But if she's going to meet someone I know, some dude like the last joker she dated, I'll figure out a way to redirect her.

"I'm going to dinner with my brother," she says. A smile tickles her lips. "Do you realize that now that Hollis is back in my life, I have six brothers?"

I didn't realize that, but I also don't really care.

"How's that going?" I ask.

I don't know Hollis Hudson well. I've only met him a couple of times in The Gold Room. He seems like a solid guy, but you never know. I'm curious about how things are going between her and the brother she just became reacquainted with—her only biological sibling.

"With Hollis?" She shrugs. "It's going okay. You know, we're sort of getting to know each other again. We have these big pieces of our lives that neither of us really understand, so we're comparing notes. It's nice to have someone who doesn't flinch when you ask if the guy you vaguely remember coming by the house when you were four was a pimp. You can't just ask that to a general audience."

My brain scrambles around her offhanded remark. *What the hell happened to this girl?* Paige, however, brushes it off like we're talking about the weather.

She unplugs the curling iron. "Remember that I did that when I ask you later."

"Remember you did what?"

"*That.* That I unplugged it."

"You know you did it. Remember yourself."

She makes a face and grabs her phone off my desk. Then she snaps a picture of the cord.

"What are you doing?" I ask.

"I'm remembering that I unplugged it. You have no idea the stress of beauty tools and the whole '*Did I unplug that?*' thing."

"You're right. I don't. Thank God."

She turns her head over, sticking her ass out, and douses hairspray all over her hair. I try to be a gentleman and not watch her hips shake as she moves but fail.

Damn this woman.

"Can I ask you my favor now?" she asks, flipping her head upright again. Her cheeks are flushed in the prettiest shade of pink, and her hair looks like she just got fucked.

My cock hardens.

"What do you want?" I ask, adjusting myself as discreetly as possible.

She faces me with puppy-dog eyes and her bottom lip between her teeth.

She has to be kidding me.

"What do you want?" I ask again even though I know. Given her perpetual train wreck situation and the roommate dilemma ... "Spit it out."

"Are the rooms upstairs occupied?"

I nod. "They all have tenants."

"*Oh.*" She moves around with an intentional sexiness in her actions. "Well, I guess I could stay in here."

"In my office?"

She nods.

I roll my eyes. "You can't live in my office, Paige."

"It's just for a week. Two, max. I just need time to find another place. Please, Nate? I have nowhere else to go."

I sit up and rest my elbows on my knees. It takes a lot of effort, more than I knew that I had, to avoid the itch of my fingers to reach for her.

And that's precisely why her staying in my office has to be the absolute last resort.

"What about that Kinsley girl?" I ask. "She's your friend, isn't she?"

She puts her hands on her hips and looks at me.

I raise my brows as if I've somehow just won the argument, challenging her to post a rebuttal. Half of a battle is making your opponent think you're already victorious. I learned that from my brother, Dominic.

While this tactic may work with men in the boxing ring with biceps the size of cantaloupes, it doesn't seem to work with this little minx.

Paige smiles smugly and reaches for her lip gloss. "Her apartment is the size of a shoebox. But fine. I can always call Atticus."

She did not just say that. I'm on my feet in a second flat, staring at her in a mixture of disbelief and barely bridled anger.

"You call that bastard, and I'll break his fucking neck."

She laughs. "Then I guess you're my only option, huh?"

The thought of her with Atticus Jones makes me want to fight. *Again.* The only reason that I didn't break his neck the first time—because he threatened to do the same to her—is because my friend Troy got to him first.

She knows I'd lose my shit if she called Atticus. *Damn her.*

"You're manipulating me," I say. "I just want you to know that I know it."

"Oh, Nate. Like you haven't manipulated me the whole time we've known each other."

"What are you talking about?"

She lifts both brows. "Off the top of my head, let's see. What about the time that you fired Michelle just so I'd have to work the night I had a date with the guy from the band from Memphis?"

"That wasn't manipulation. But if it makes you feel better to think of it that way, cool."

"Then let's go with the time you gave me a raise so I didn't—"

"*Paige.*"

She squares her shoulders to me. "What, *Nate?*"

I scratch my scalp as if the friction will somehow clear the fog from my brain and make my decision easier. Paige is in my office because she knows that out of all The Gold Room staff, I am the only one she's close enough to, and has the space available, to ask for a place to stay. There's only one solution to this problem. We both know that. But having her stay with me ...

It's a recipe for disaster.

I drop my hands. "I have a seven-year-old son, remember?"

"Yes. Ryder. Pretty sure he loves me."

She puts her hands on her thick hips again like *she's* won.

I should do the reasonable, respectable thing and tell her *no*. The two of us have never been alone, and the thought of that happening— *in the privacy of my house*—would be the greatest gift in the history of the world ... if things were different.

But they aren't, so I should rent her a hotel room for a couple of weeks and call it good.

Just as I'm opening my mouth to say a version of that scenario, the script in my brain changes.

"You can't bring guys around my house," I say. "And you can't be coming and going at all hours of the night."

"Of course and fair."

"And you can't be naked. My kid can't be walking in and seeing you in lace fucking panties."

Her eyes sparkle with mischief as she sashays her way toward me. "What about you? What if you walk in and see me bent over—"

"*Stop.*"

She rolls her eyes but surprisingly listens to me. She turns back to my desk and fills a purse with a few cosmetics. "Why are you like this?"

"Like what?"

"The way you are?"

Because I want what's best for you, and that sure as shit isn't me.

"Because you're too young and too mixed up to know what's good for you," I say. It's time to change the subject. "I lock the doors

7

and go to bed at midnight. Be in by then or find another place to sleep."

"Yes, *Daddy*."

I adjust myself again. "Paige ..." I warn.

She giggles. "I'm sorry. I'll behave. Promise."

You don't know what behave even means, you little minx.

"I'll see you tonight," she says.

"Can't wait."

She opens the door. "Your sarcasm is noted and unappreciated."

Her laughter follows her out the door.

I walk across the room and sit at my desk. My exhale is long and comes from a place deep inside me. I'm about to start tossing her things in her bag when a knock comes through the room.

"Yeah?" I grumble. I reach under my ass as I look up and see Shaye.

"Hey," she says, looking around my office. "What happened in here?"

I pull my hand up, and a red bra is twirling around my fingers. The fabric is smooth and silky and does nothing for the temperature raging inside me.

"Paige," I deadpan.

Shaye laughs. "Well, you work fast."

"Trust me, it's not that. I had no idea she was in my office."

I don't know why Shaye finds this so amusing, but her laughter is loud.

"I love that girl," she says, grinning. "I'm out of here. Need anything before I go?"

"A lobotomy."

Her grin grows wider. "I might enjoy that a little too much."

"Get the hell out of here. Tell Oliver I said hi."

"Will do." She backs out of the room. "Tell Paige I said hi."

"You're pushing it."

She laughs again. "Yeah, I'd hate for you to get mad and fire me. How would I ever survive?"

"Why does everyone do exactly as I say except for you and Paige?"

"I don't think that's true. Case in point—Murray. How many times have you fired him, and how many times has he come back?"

I just stare at her.

She grins. "I do what I want because I can. Paige, though?" Her grin slips into a smirk. "She presses every button she can find until you let her start undoing them instead."

I grip the bra and squeeze.

Paige has made it quite clear that she's interested in me, and for some reason, Shaye seems to think that's a good thing. *It's not.*

I have enough on my plate. Too much sometimes. And Paige? Beautiful, hundred-miles-an-hour Paige?

Not only is she too young for me, but I have Ryder to consider. He needs stability. Consistency. Guidance. I can't take my attention away from him and give it to someone else ... even if it's the sexy bombshell who takes over my office. *Naked.*

I clear my throat. "Well, that's not gonna happen, so I better get used to being pressed, huh?"

"Whatever you say." She giggles as she grabs the door handle. "This is going to be so much fun."

Shaye disappears just as the bra propels out of my hand and smacks the back of the door. I collapse into my chair and sigh.

Paige's stuff is everywhere. Clothes, strands of hair, her perfume —it's like I've walked into her closet and not The Gold Room's business office.

"This is going to be so much fun."

I shake my head at Shaye's words.

"Yeah, it's gonna be something like that."

Chapter 2

Paige

"Excuse me," I say. "I'm sorry."

The man I nearly take out like a linebacker gives me a dirty look. He gives me a wide berth. *Oh, come on. I don't have a disease. I'm just late.*

I dart across the street in front of Picante, a fancy hotel near the ocean, and see the word Paddy's written in bold green letters on the building.

Tucking my purse under my arm, I enter the restaurant.

The interior is stunning in an understated way. Large dark beams crisscross the ceiling, and pale-lavender walls are accented with gold details. The light fixtures create a soft, hazy vibe that makes my shoulders relax as soon as I walk in. It's a nice change from the keyed-up energy I've felt since I left Nate's office.

Nate. I grin.

I look around until I spot my brother at the bar.

Hollis has a glass in his hand. His attention is focused on the large television above the alcohol bottles. It gives me a minute to gather myself.

Looking at my sole biological sibling, the only person I know who shares the same blood as me, is like looking into a mirror. We share the same dark hair—except I bleached mine blond in a hasty moment fueled by vodka and self-pity last week. Hollis's eyes are the exact shade as mine. They're a warm brown with flecks of green that nearly turn gold under the right conditions. He also wears a lopsided smile that I've always owned.

"Hey," I say, sliding onto the barstool beside him.

He twists to me and grins. "Hey."

We hug one another in an only slightly awkward embrace. *Progress.*

"Larissa didn't come?" I ask, setting my purse on the counter.

"No. She's at a jewelry show today with her aunt."

"Fancy."

He shrugs as if he doesn't know what to say. A sheepish smile slides across his face.

"Can I get you a drink?" A woman with a tag bearing the name Gina smiles at me. "A sandwich?"

"Um, yeah." I grab the menu she set in front of me and scan it quickly. "Cherry Coke and a burger for me. No veggies. Just meat, cheese, and the bun. *Please.*"

"I'll take the same," Hollis says.

Gina laughs. "Easy enough. I'll be right back with two Cherry Cokes." She winks at Hollis before scurrying off to put in our order.

I sink back in the leather chair and exhale, releasing more into the world than just carbon dioxide. The stress from the morning *and the eviction* —all dissipate from my body.

The silence between us is comfortable. It hasn't always been so easy since he walked into The Gold Room a month ago—when I thought I was seeing a ghost. But we're working on it slowly.

I've thought about my big brother every day since we were separated by Child Protective Services. Our case workers arranged a very brief visit, and at the time, I had no idea it would be the last time I saw him for nearly ten years. I've carried around his smile and penchant for music my entire life, wondering what happened to him.

11

"How are you?" I ask. "What have you been up to?"

"Same shit, different day. I'm heading to Nashville this weekend with Coy to try to nail down a couple of songs for his new album."

I laugh. "I still can't believe you write music for Kelvin McCoy—the biggest name in country music. That's so cool."

He grins. "It *is* pretty cool." A little laugh escapes him. "I'm really lucky that Larissa's family and I get along so well."

"My mother is determined to make you love her like Larissa's family loves you," I say with a laugh. "You've been warned."

"Really?"

"Yeah. Every time I talk to her, she pesters me about when the two of you will get to meet, and I'm pretty sure I've lost part of my inheritance for making her wait."

Hollis folds his hand on the bar top. "She sounds great."

"She is. They all are. They're just ... a lot. Lots of big personalities and they can swamp you if you don't watch it."

"Was that hard for you? Not getting swamped by them?"

I take a deep breath. *I hate talking about this.* Lying would be an option that would definitely make me come across as a better human. But the act of lying would make me a shitty person, so I don't have much of a choice but to tell the truth and hope it comes out right.

"I can't say it without sounding like a brat."

He lowers his chin and looks into my eyes. *"Try me."*

I feel heat in the apples of my cheeks.

"Look, I understand how lucky I am to have been adopted by the Carmichaels. Okay? I get it. I went from being invisible and ignored in foster care to chaos and candy on the beach. They're absolutely wonderful. All of them."

"But?"

I sigh, taking my drink from Gina and then thanking her.

"It wasn't that it was hard getting swamped. It was more about my ..." I restart. "I had a hard time understanding that I belonged there. It took me a long time. Years. I struggle with it now some days, if I'm being honest. I don't look like them. I don't like the same foods they like. I'm not doing a marathon on Thanksgiving morning, or any other day if we're being honest, and I never met my grandma Carmichael, who was like the patron saint of fucking sunshine, I guess."

He chuckles.

"Clearly, I didn't get that DNA." I grin. "It can be hard. And it makes me feel like a jerk, and then I get sweaty about it, and then I need space because who wants to feel like a sweaty jerk in front of the people who shouldn't make you feel that way to start with?"

Hollis brings his glass to his lips. "Punctuation is your friend."

I snort.

My brother's attention is taken away by the television—or that's what it seems. In reality, I think he's just trying to process what I've said and figure out how to respond. This is something I've learned about Hollis. He's a quiet processor. I appreciate it.

I twirl my straw around my glass and think about my admission too. It's the truth. All of it. But I've never vocalized it to anyone. I don't think I've ever even said it out loud.

I wanted nothing more growing up than to find a family. Then I did, and I just wanted to be one of them. *Desperately.* I wanted to fit in somewhere.

What I didn't want?

I didn't want to be the dark-haired little girl who everyone judged with hefty skepticism as I walked with my fair-haired family down the beach. I resented my curvy build that stuck out in family photos. I also seriously hated that I couldn't answer what my heritage was in school or if my family had any medical conditions like high blood pressure, diabetes, or kidney disease.

I don't know, Doc. The last thing I knew, I was being carted off from school in a white van, and my parents were sent to the pokey for manufacturing methamphetamine in our basement. Could be some issues there, clearly.

Gina sets our plates in front of us and asks if we need anything else. We politely decline.

13

"You know," Hollis says, taking a napkin and folding it onto his lap. "I felt just like you do until I met Larissa."

"So she fixed you?" I pick up a fry. "She have any brothers?"

He grins. "No. She didn't fix me, smart-ass. She just made me look at things differently. Before her, I thought there wasn't a place for me. I had no one, right? And then she came along, and I realized that I belong where I say I belong."

Deep.

I blink twice and avoid discussing how that might apply to me ... or not. "And what about the brothers?"

"No brothers." He laughs, bringing his burger to his mouth. "You're funny."

I bite off the end of my fry. "I guess when God was handing out brothers, he gave them all to me."

Hollis swallows and then takes a sip of his drink. I ignore the impending question by squirting a heavy dose of ketchup onto my plate in the shape of a moon.

"You've always done that, huh?" He motions toward the ketchup design. "I have memories of you doing that."

My heart warms that he remembers. You don't realize you've missed someone *knowing* things about you until someone does.

"Tell me about your brothers," he says. "You've not said a lot about them."

I drag a fry through the ketchup. "They're good guys. They're all older than me, but we're pretty close. We have a siblings text group that gets a little wild."

He smiles.

"I want to throttle Banks sometimes, but what can you do?" I shrug and eat another fry.

"Is he the one you're closest to?"

"Yeah. He's a turd," I say, laughing. "He always said that Mom and Dad bought me because they couldn't have a girl. We'd pass this little shop in town with this big pink-and-yellow sign out front. I think they sell surfboards or something. Anyway, every time we'd pass it growing up, Banks would whisper, '*Look, it's the store where Mom bought you. She still has the receipt.*'"

A shadow passes over Hollis's face. "Sounds like an asshole."

"He was kidding," I say, picking up another fry. "I mean, he *is* kind of an asshole, but he broke a guy's nose for me once, so I can't talk too much shit about him."

Hollis considers this as he takes another bite of his burger.

We eat in comfortable silence, both of us getting used to the energy of the other. It's a bit disarming how easy it is to be around him, and a part of me wonders if that's just our sibling dynamic. Whatever it is, I'm thankful.

"Oh," I say, patting my mouth with a napkin. "I got evicted today."

His head whips to mine. "Really? Do you need a place to stay? Do you need money?"

"No. No, no, no. Nothing like that. I paid my rent to my friend, but she did not pay the landlord. It's a huge mess. All I know is that I had to move out today or ..." I think of the landlord's threats. "I had to move out today."

"Are you sure? Because Larissa and I have two extra bedrooms, and we'd love to have you stay with us. It would give me someone to shoot the shit with when she's out shopping for organic vegetables."

I wink at him. "That sounds fun."

"Harlee—I mean, *Paige*." He winces. "I'm sorry. That's still a hard one for me."

I take a deep breath and look at him. No one has called me *Harlee* in forever—just Hollis when we met a few weeks ago in The Gold Room. That was before he knew that I go by Paige now.

"It's fine," I say. "You can call me whatever you want."

"Can I ask you a question about that?"

"Sure."

"Why did you change it? Or did your parents change it without asking you?" He frowns. "Am I asking too many questions?"

"No, of course not. Mom asked when we were going through the adoption process because I, uh, didn't really like my name. I mean, what kid doesn't want to change their name?"

I laugh like it's no big deal. Hollis sees right through my bullshit but lets it go.

"Right," he says, nodding. "Makes sense."

"Yeah. So I asked if I could change it. Paige was the name of Dad's mom—you know, The Patron Saint of Sunshine."

Hollis laughs.

"And I thought it was a nice name." *And that they might love me more if I was named after someone they love.* "But back to needing a place to stay. I don't. I have it covered. I'm staying with my boss, Nate."

"Nate Hughes? From The Gold Room?"

"Yup." The *p* pops as it falls from my lips. "I'm gonna stay there until I find a place."

Hollis forces a smile. "You think that's a good plan?"

"Yeah. I mean, we flirt around, but it's all fun and games. He's literally one of my best friends, which is probably why I can flirt with him like I do. It's safe."

He narrows his eyes. "So it's all good?"

"I'm doing it, aren't I?"

We sit shoulder to shoulder, yet it's as if a giant crevasse plunges between us.

I've always hated having to justify myself to my brothers as if they didn't believe I was capable of making good decisions on my own. I wonder if Hollis and I would've had the same relationship. Would he be the older brother who speaks, and I, as the younger sibling, listens? I think so.

Well, maybe. My other brothers speak, and I don't really listen to them either.

Hollis finally acquiesces and grins. "Have you always been this headstrong, or is this a new thing?"

"Oh, it's one of my most consistent traits." I laugh. "I used to imagine that it was a biological trait. I really clung to that in a weird way."

"You might be right. Our mom was really hardheaded. That or she was just totally negligent."

My heart clenches. "Well, being that she was cooking meth in our basement, maybe a little of both."

"You're probably right." He taps his fingers against the counter. "Do you remember sleeping with that big dog we had?"

"I do. I have this weird memory of a black dog between us and being cold. I remember lying in bed and watching our breath billow into the air."

"You know, I still can't be cold when I sleep. It drives Larissa nuts. I need it to practically be a sauna, or I just lay there in a pit of anxiety."

My eyes go wide. "Me too!"

He smiles. "Riss grew up very differently than we did. I have a hard time talking to her about some of the wild shit we experienced because she could never get it. I swear she thinks I'm making some of this up." He chuckles. "Some of those stories do sound fabricated."

"*I* get it." I lean back in my chair. "When the Carmichaels adopted me, my new life felt like a fairy tale. I mean, they sat down to dinner. They read books at bedtime. There was food in the fridge."

Hollis nods as if remembering is hard.

"Can I get the two of you anything else?" Gina asks. "More to drink? Dessert?"

I look at my brother. The look on his face says the memories ruined his appetite too.

"I'm good," I say. "You?"

"I think we're finished." He fishes a credit card from his wallet. "Here you go."

Once Gina is out of earshot, I sigh. "You didn't have to pay for my food."

All I get is a look not to push. So *I push.*

"I mean it," I say. "I'm getting yours next time."

17

Gina brings the receipt. Hollis adds a tip, signs it, and then slips his card back into his wallet.

We get up and head outside. The air is warm and smells like the sea.

"You need a ride?" he asks.

"No. My car is in the Picante parking lot, but thanks."

He nods. "Where are you headed now?"

Good question.

I glance down the street at all the little shops and people moseying along the sidewalks. "I think I'm going to run by Kinsley's for a while before I go to Nate's for the night."

He draws me into a quick hug. When he pulls away, there's a hint of concern in his eyes.

"You can call me anytime. For anything. I want you to. Okay?" he asks.

I smile at him. "Okay. Call me when you get back in town, and we'll do something together."

"I'd like that." He walks backward down the sidewalk. "Be safe."

"Always."

After a little wave, I start back to my car.

Stay safe, big brother. I'd hate to lose you again.

Chapter 3

Nate

"**R**yder! Come here, please?" I shout.

I open the closet in the hallway and pull out a fresh set of sheets. They're mustard yellow with some kind of navy geometric design. *Must've been on sale.* As ugly as they are, they're all I have since Ryder puked up hot dogs on the other spare set.

My stomach recoils at the memory of the wretchedness.

"Ry! Where're you at, kid?" I yell, closing the closet door.

My son comes running around the corner, sliding into the wall. He catches himself about a half a second before his face hits the drywall. Then he bursts out laughing.

"You running from something?" I ask, laughing.

He looks up at me, his eyes sparkling. "No."

"Looked like you were. Was there a monster in the living room?"

"If there was, I would've beat it up." He throws a couple of punches into the air that aren't half bad. "See? Boom, boom, *boom.*"

I ruffle his hair as I walk by. "That's it. No more hanging out with Uncle Dominic."

"I'm not supposed to tell you this," he says as we enter the guest room. "But he took me to Percy's Gym with him last week."

"*He what?*"

"Yeah. He said you wouldn't be thrilled."

The word *thrilled* comes out muddled due to his missing front teeth. It would've sounded adorable if I wasn't hung up on the fact that my brother took my kid to the gym.

I toss the sheets on the bed. "Don't ya think you should've told me about this without waiting a week?"

He shrugs as if the idea never occurred to him. *Little shit.*

"Well, I'm going to have a talk with your uncle. And you are gonna help me make this bed," I say.

"It's already made."

I look at him as I grab one of the pillows. And then, quicker than he can process it, I toss one at him. It smacks him in the side of the arm.

Ryder bursts out laughing. He picks it up and throws it back at me.

I catch it midair and then toss it on a chair by the window.

"Come on," I say, handing him the other pillow. "Help me. Put that one on top of the other."

He groans. "Why do we have to do this? I want to finish my show."

"You can. Once we get this done."

I strip the blanket off and drape it over the chair. My brain sorts through all of the ways I've considered explaining this to Ryder today. I want to keep the explanation as simple as possible.

If there's one thing I don't do, that I refuse to do, it's bring women around my son. *I won't do it.* Flat out. The only exception was a woman named Joy a couple of years ago. We had a real relationship for a while. When it ended, Ryder was a mess for a week, and I vowed never to get myself or him into that kind of pickle again.

Paige will be here as a friend. I need to make that clear.

"Do you remember Paige?" I ask. "She works for me."

"Yup. She gives me Sprite, and you get mad."

"That's right," I say, having forgotten all about that. "Well, she needs a place to stay for a little bit, and I told her she could crash here with us. Is that cool?"

"Yeah. That's cool."

I strip the sheets and toss them onto the floor. Then I grab the new set.

"Take this corner and put it over the mattress," I tell Ryder. "Like this. Watch me."

He does as instructed, and we make quick work of the fitted sheet. Then I grab the flat one.

Ryder wrinkles his nose. "Don't use that one."

"Why?"

"Because it just gets all tangled up in your feet, and then it makes a chunk at the bottom. Then when you wake up in the middle of the night, it looks like someone is watching you."

I laugh. "I'll let Paige know if she doesn't like it, she can take it off."

"She can take it off." My brain immediately goes to my office earlier today, where Paige had taken it all off. Or most of it, anyway.

The thought of her peach-shaped ass and how it bounced as she moved makes my cock hard. The lines of that fucking lace stretched over her tanned skin—the fabric almost disappearing between the cheeks—is permanently imprinted in my head. Even the cellulite on the backs of her thighs somehow made her hotter and more real.

Dammit if I don't need a cold shower.

"Dad?" Ryder asks, snapping my thoughts back to the guest room. "Are you okay? Your forehead is all sweaty."

"Yeah, bud. I'm fine."

I toss the flat sheet down and roughly situate it. Then I grab the blanket.

"You're acting weird," he says, curling his lip like Elvis.

"Why are you staring at me?"

"I'm not."

I make quick work of switching out the pillow cases. "Why are you even in here?" I tease.

"You told me to! I want to watch my show!"

I laugh and walk to the door, pulling him into my side along the way. "I'm just kidding ya."

"Were you kidding about Paige too?"

I flip off the light. We stop in the hallway. I look down at my son with a concerned look.

"I wasn't. She really is going to stay here for just a little while. Is that okay with you? If not, you can tell me," I say.

He hops from one foot to the other like standing still might kill him. I have no idea where this kid gets his energy, but I wish I had some.

"It's okay," he says. "She's sleeping in there, right?"

I nod.

"And she's making me breakfast?" he asks.

"What? No," I say, laughing. "Why would you think she'd be making you breakfast?"

He shrugs. "I don't know. I like breakfast, and the girls on the shows I watch are the ones making breakfast."

"You're watching some messed-up cartoons if the guys never make breakfast. What are you watching? I need to block that."

Ryder giggles. "I'm not telling you because I like them. But does this mean you're the one that's still making my breakfast because, if you are, stop burning my toast. It makes me throw up a little all morning."

"Dude, I'm not burning your toast."

"Yes, you are."

I grin at him. "I'm not even toasting your toast. I'm warming up a piece of bread. I can't toast your toast because you complain."

"You toast it too much because it still makes me burp."

I shake my head because I'm not sure what to say. *How do you argue with a seven-year-old over toast making him burp?*

Sighing, I wipe a piece of banana off the side of his face.

"Toast aside," I say, getting serious again. "Paige isn't here to make anyone food or to play games with you or pick up your toys. She's our guest, and we're going to remember that, okay?"

"So don't ask her to play *Minecraft*?"

"No."

"Or check my room—not for monsters," he says, his eyes going wide. "For ... spiders."

I snort. "Right."

"And no to breakfast."

"No to breakfast." I shake my head. "Just manage not to ask her for anything, okay?"

And I'll manage not to slip inside her room and eat her like a dessert.

My balls tighten. *I have to stop thinking like this.*

"Okay." He licks his lips. "You should take some medicine because you're sweating again."

Ugh. "You go ... brush your teeth."

"Dad!"

"And wash your face. You have banana goo all over your mouth."

He stomps his foot. "Can I finish my show first?"

"Nope, but you can finish it after *if* you stop giving me lip and just go do what you're told."

His eyes meet mine like he's going to press his luck. This is a new thing with him. He used to be so sweet and easygoing. Now he's a borderline teenager with a taste for arguing that has me a little worried about the *actual* teenage years.

He stares me down and waits for me to flinch. *Men bigger and meaner than you have tried and failed, kid.*

Finally, he sighs. His shoulders slump in a dramatic performance worthy of an Oscar.

"Fine," he says, stomping toward the bathroom.

"Good decision."

I wait until I hear the water turn on before I head to the kitchen. Sure, he might be screwing with me. I could peek into the bathroom

23

and see him standing in front of the sink while the water runs down the drain. Actually, that's happened before. Lucky for him, I'm too preoccupied to be that solid of a parent tonight.

"*Fuck.*" I groan as I face the sink. I grip the counter and bow my head.

The sun is going down, the day coming to a close. The distractions from work—the late delivery of produce, my failure to order straws *again*, and a water leak in one of the apartments above The Gold Room—kept me busy. It kept my mind occupied.

It kept me from thinking about Paige.

Now that the world has settled and my tasks have either been completed or delayed until tomorrow, I have nothing else to think about. There's nothing else to focus on. Just this one thing—a frustratingly gorgeous vixen who gets under my skin like no other.

Her moxie is magnetic. She has one of the best senses of humor that I've ever known in a woman. Something about her intrigues me because she never gives enough to satisfy my curiosity. She never thoroughly scratches my itch.

Also, there's that ass.

"I have to get a handle on this," I mumble to myself.

I make myself a glass of sweet tea. I take a drink and watch Ryder run past the doorway in a full-speed effort to get back to his show.

"I can do this," I say. "I can handle having her here. I have to. What choice do I have now?"

None.

I take another drink. The cool liquid slides down my throat. It helps me get outside of my head.

Even though it'll be a challenge to keep things chill between us, it was the right choice to let her stay. She's not just an employee; she's a good friend. I couldn't leave her to the streets.

I blow out a breath.

"You did the right thing," I tell myself.

It's interesting that she asked me for a place to stay, though. And the way she keeps playing it? With all of that *Daddy* shit? It's a front.

One of the few things I know about her for certain is that she hides behind her personality.

Paige doesn't really want me.

Which is fine because I can't really want her either.

Ryder's laughter rings through the house. It makes me pause. *And smile.*

If I've done one thing in life right—one thing that I wouldn't change given the chance—it's that little boy in the other room. He's the best fucking thing that ever happened to me. Ryder is the thread that holds my life together. He's my son, my blood, my best friend. I'd do anything for that little boy.

If that means holding myself back from the woman who draws me in like a siren, I will. Because if I ever bring another woman into his life, it has to be for keeps.

"I have to be fair to him above all," I say.

I finish my tea and set the cup in the sink.

This is gonna suck. I know it.

Chapter 4

Paige

I glance at the clock. *I have thirty minutes until midnight.*

Frustration washes through me over the choices I made this evening. *What should I have done?* I should've gone to Nate's after meeting Hollis or, at the very least, while the sun was still up. It would've been the right thing to do. *Which is probably why I didn't do it.*

I sit back in the driver's seat and release a long, tired sigh.

Why do I make bad decisions? Repeatedly.

I bite a fingernail, pulling off some of the red paint from my manicure last week. The jagged edge will drive me crazy. *At this point, what's one more thing to deal with?*

Nate's house sits in front of me, lit by two solar lights shining up at it. The railings need a new coat of black paint, and the front door could use a nice wreath or welcome sign like the one my mom has hanging at her house. But the porch light is on, probably for me, and that helps soothe the acid bubbling in my gut.

This whole idea felt a whole hell of a lot better when we were at The Gold Room. Sure, things between us are always flirty, but they're always flirty *there*. In public. In places where it can't be anything more. In places where my actual attraction for the man has nowhere to go.

But now, when I'm about to walk into his house, it feels a little different.

"It's going to be fine," I say, practicing talking to myself like I would my best friend. It's a tactic my mom has reminded me to use four million times in my life and one I struggle to remember most days. "It's Nate. My friend. What's the worst that can happen?"

I watch the house for movement. *The worst thing would be for him to already be in bed, and I miss seeing him tonight.*

I take a long, deep breath and grab my purse. Then I climb out of the car and lock it behind me.

The night air is chilly, and the sky is dark. Only a spattering of silvery stars peeking out from behind the fast-moving clouds provide any sort of light from above.

I make my way up the wooden steps and then tug on the screen door. It opens with a squeal. Not sure whether to knock or just walk in, I decide to test the handle.

It's openfree.

I wrap my hand around the knob and push the door open.

I've been to Nate's house twice. Both times were to drop off paperwork from The Gold Room since he only closes it himself on the weekends, preferring to be home with his son during the week. *Which I find ridiculously attractive.* And both times I've been here, I didn't make it any farther than the small foyer.

The door shuts as softly as I can manage.

The walls are painted an eggshell white. It could probably use a refresh, but who am I to judge? To my left is a wooden storage unit that goes from the floor to the ceiling. Jackets are hung haphazardly on hooks across the middle of it, and shoes are shoved into the four small compartments at the bottom. To my right are three art pieces that definitely came from a first-grade classroom.

They make me smile.

I tiptoe a little farther into the house, unsure what to do. *This wouldn't have been a problem if you didn't procrastinate coming over here.* I get to the doorway and stop.

A dining area with a circular table is on my right. In the middle sits a basket filled with magazines and crayons. But to the left? That's the showstopper.

My mouth goes dry. My insides do this interesting mix of shriveling up and melting into a heated pool of need.

I don't know what's hotter—the way he sits in the chair. *Reclined back, knees apart, thumb feathering his bottom lip.* Or the fact that he waited up for me.

I know he said he doesn't go to bed until midnight, so there's a distinct possibility that he would be up and sitting here anyway. *But I don't think so.*

He lifts a heavy brow. It's an unspoken question, a prompt for me to speak. And I do.

"You didn't have to wait up." I sit on the sofa—on the opposite end. *I just need a minute.* "Did you happen to grab my bags from The Gold Room? They weren't there when I went back to get them."

He holds my gaze for a long moment before dropping his hand and sighing. "Yeah. I got them."

"Awesome." I grin, finding my footing. "I'd hate to have to sleep in my underwear, considering the whole *don't be naked* rule."

Nate wants to smile. The corners of his lips twitch. But instead of giving in, he sits up and rests his elbows on his knees.

"Where have you been?" he asks, ignoring my comment about sleeping in the buff.

"Running errands."

"What errands can be run at eleven o'clock at night?"

I shift around on the sofa until I'm comfortable. He watches every move I make. Satisfaction slips over my nerves and settles them down.

"You know," I say, toying with him. "There's a Daddy joke here if I wanted to make it."

He takes a deep breath and loses the battle with his smile. A slight, barely-there grin licks at the corner of his lips.

"But I won't," I say, content with his reaction. "You're welcome for that."

"So you're just going to ignore my question?"

"I'm staying with you. I'm not your child." I wink. "See that Daddy workaround? Didn't even touch it."

He chuckles, although begrudgingly.

"But, because I appreciate your hospitality, I'll humor you," I say. "I had an early dinner with Hollis. Then I got a coffee, gas, and then hung out at the bookstore for a couple of hours. I was going to go to my friend Kinsley's house, but she had a date like a boss."

"You hung out at a bookstore? This late?"

"Yes," I say, rolling my eyes for effect. "I fretted between the romance section and self-help but went with the latter figuring it would behoove me to help myself before trying to fall in love. Right?"

He narrows his eyes but doesn't say anything.

"Anyway, I probably shouldn't have waited until the last minute to show up here, but I did, and it's done. Now that the Band-Aid has been ripped off and the awkwardness of, well, *this*, is over, I'll be earlier from here on out. Promise."

"I don't want this to be awkward, Paige."

"I don't want it to be either."

He stands up and stretches overhead. The edge of his white T-shirt pulls away from the waistband of his black joggers, displaying a sliver of muscled abdomen.

Good God.

"Are you hungry? You said you had an early dinner," he says over his shoulder as he walks across the room, into the dining area, and through a doorway.

I jump up and follow him like a puppy. "No. I'm good."

We enter a small, cozy kitchen. There is no discernable theme—no color palette or common element like lemons or beer cans, even. Yet somehow, it all pulls together in a warm and inviting way.

The countertops are black with tiny gold flecks. The floor is the same hardwood as the rest of the house. The appliances are black, and a plethora of various items—from a fake plant to a tequila bottle to an oversized Tonka truck—sit on top of the counters in a show of dramatic bachelorhood.

It's a complete one-eighty from the curated kitchen I grew up in, but I don't hate it. Not even a little bit.

Nate stops at the narrow island and plants his hands on the counter. "There are drinks and your basics in the fridge. Milk, eggs, cheese, sweet tea. Pudding cups."

I smile at him.

"The pantry is behind me. Same thing. Help yourself."

"Thanks." I bite my lip to keep from smiling. "Just wondering—is pudding a staple?"

"Hell, yeah. It's the easiest, most versatile dessert ever." He cocks his head to the side but humors me anyway. "It's the best. All you have to do is eat it."

"Now you're talking my language," I quickly reply.

His cheeks flush. He gives me a warning glance but doesn't indulge me.

"I also like to dip a banana in it," he says, turning toward the pantry. "I—"

"*Kinky.*"

He spins around. When his eyes meet mine, they're so dark, so brooding that I almost gasp.

"You, little girl, have *no fucking idea.*"

I do it. I gasp. I have no idea if he heard me or not because all I can hear are those words, *that tone*—the grit that rumbles from my ears and buries itself deep in my core. And I don't care if he heard me or not because clearly, he was trying to elicit a response.

I'd almost give Nate Hughes anything he wanted.

He paces toward me. His bare feet smack against the hardwood. My breath gets shallower with every step.

He stops in front of me so close that his chest nearly touches mine. I peer up, lifting my chin so I can look into his eyes.

My mind races with what he's going to say, or hopefully, *what he might do.*

"You like fucking with me, don't you?" he asks.

His voice sweeps across the quiet kitchen. It mixes with the hazy lights hanging above us, and all I can think is that this would be the perfect setting for an illicit sexual encounter.

"I do," I say, the words a smidge less confident than I'd like. "You want to know something?"

He hums.

"I think you like it *when I fuck with you.*" I bite my bottom lip. "Don't you, Nate?"

His grin isn't friendly or amused. *It's sinful.*

He shifts his weight, widening his stance. It makes him appear bigger, wider, more imposing.

"Is that supposed to intimidate me?" I ask, lifting a brow. "Because it just makes me want to *fuck with you* more."

His eyes narrow ever so slightly. "You don't know what you're talking about."

"You don't think? Because I think I know exactly what I'm talking about."

The air between us heats. If air that wasn't moving could push two people together, that would be happening now. The room seems to shrink as we stand, *barely touching*, and feel each other out.

I might've gotten myself in a little too far with this. *Do I enjoy messing with him?* Yes.

Do I think he likes it? Also, yes.

Would I love for him to actually act on the undeniable chemistry between us? Absolutely.

But am I a virgin playing ball on a court that might be a little too big for me?

Let's hope not.

Nate's shoulder twitches, and I flinch, thinking he's going to reach for me—that he's finally going to break an invisible seal between us. Instead, he runs a hand through his hair and turns away.

A rush of air leaves my lungs as I slump against the counter.

"You're gonna need to behave," he says gruffly.

What?

"You ... perplex me," I say.

I shove off the counter and regroup. I've never been particularly shy, and if I learned one thing from my brothers, it's to fight for what I want. *Otherwise, you always lose the battle.*

I'm not reading Nate wrong. He wants me as badly as I want him, and that's a huge turn-on. *So here goes.*

"I know you want me," I say matter-of-factly.

He paces to the other side of the kitchen. He doesn't stop until he's the farthest away from me that he can get.

"A part of being an adult is knowing what you can't have," he says.

"Oh. *Okay.* I'm getting philosophical Nate tonight. That's fun."

He shakes his head. "Go to bed. I'm gonna lock the door and go to bed too."

This conversation is over.

"Awesome," I say. "But I don't know where my room is."

He points at the doorway. "Down the hall. First room on your right. I put new sheets on it earlier, and your bags are in there."

Looks like I've been dismissed. "Thanks."

He makes a face that possibly conveys a response but mostly tells me he's as frustrated with the end of the conversation as I am. Then he turns toward the doorway.

"Nate?"

"Yeah?"

He looks at me over his shoulder. In his face—the one I work so hard to get to react to me—is an inherent kindness, a sturdiness, that I appreciate more than I could ever tell him.

"I've given you a lot of shit today, and maybe it wasn't quite fair of me to just show up like I did. And then ... *manipulate* you into letting me stay." I half-smile, half-frown at him. "That was probably a dick move, actually."

"Paige—"

"But I didn't know where else to go, and that doesn't absolve my jerkiness. But I do want you to know that I realize it, and I appreciate you for overlooking all of that and letting me crash. If you want me to go tomorrow, I will."

Nate turns around so his shoulders are squared to mine. He watches me for a few long seconds. Each second that passes by makes me inch closer to jumping out of my skin.

Just say something, dammit.

Finally, he sighs.

"I would've been pissed if you didn't have anywhere to go and didn't ask me," he says, his voice low.

My heart swells in my chest. "Really?"

"Really."

We exchange a smile—one that calms me from the inside out.

"But the rules still exist," he says, broadening his smile. "No guys. Don't be late. And keep your clothes on."

I laugh as I follow him into the hallway. "Don't lie. You liked it. I know you did."

He dips his head, shaking it as he turns toward the foyer.

I could tell him a hundred things, share a thousand things with him that I think he might appreciate. Everything from the fact that I'd like to see him naked too, all the way to the reason I asked him to let me stay.

Because I know it's safe with him.

But I don't say any of it. It's late, and none of it matters, anyway.

I hear the lock click into place. Then I turn and head to my room.

Chapter 5

Nate

"Heard you took my kid to the gym," I say to my brother as I enter the Landry Security conference room. "Imagine my shock when that little nugget just toppled out of my son's mouth last night."

Dominic leans back in his chair. "I never had Ryder pegged to be a snitch."

Ford Landry, the CEO of Landry Security, laughs from the head of the table. Troy Castelli, Ford's right-hand man, laughs along with him.

Troy and I met through Landry Security. It was a little tense at first because we're both used to getting our way and won't back down from a fight. But once we got to know each other, the exact reasons things were tense between us actually brought us closer. He's probably my closest friend, aside from Dominic.

I pull a chair out next to Dominic and sit. I yawn, arching my back as I fight off the sleepiness that I've battled all day.

That's what you get for staying up all night thinking about your housemate.

As hard as I thought it might be to have Paige under the same roof, I was wrong. It was harder.

Just knowing she was there, possibly naked and totally willing, was temptation on a level that I didn't know existed. Staying away from her was a feat in and of itself.

But I did it. I survived one night.

"I promised Percy that I'd come by and help him with a camera he had some quack install," Dominic says. "I don't know why the hell he just didn't call me to start with."

"If I were venturing to guess, I'd say it's because of your stellar personality," Troy says with a grin. "You always make me feel all warm and fuzzy."

Everyone laughs. Everyone but Dominic.

He levels his gaze with Troy. "What are you saying? That I'm an asshole?"

"Yes," the three of us say in unison.

Dominic tries to act like he's pissed but ends up chuckling too.

"How's the bar?" Ford asks me, always the epitome of class. "Business good?"

"Yeah. Yeah, it's going good. We've started opening for lunch and increased our dinner menu. It just keeps growing."

I beam. I know I do, and I probably look like a schmuck. But the fact is that I'm proud of what I've built. I took a seedy joint in a risky part of town and made it into something that even the Landrys come to for a drink now and then.

"That's great," Ford says. "I'm glad to hear it."

"Me too."

He takes an envelope out of a black folder and slides it to me. "That's for the Burgundy event last week. We charged the host a fee for the crowd control mess, and I gave you a cut of that since you were the point man." He rubs his temples. "That was a nightmare."

"You're telling me."

I instantly touch my right shoulder. The pain has gone from getting my arm nearly jerked out of the socket by a crazed protestor.

"Have I mentioned my unwillingness to work any more political events?" I ask, joking but also not really joking.

Ford makes a face. If anyone in this room understands political events it's him. His family's roots in public service go way back and end with his oldest brother as the governor of Georgia.

"You handled it like a pro," Ford says, resting his hands together in front of him. "I really wish you'd just come work with us full time."

"*Yeah,*" Dominic says, teasing me. "Come work with us. What could be better than working with me all day?"

"Oral surgery," I say without thinking. "Swimming in chummed waters with sharks. Petting a cobra. Hiking through the Outback with no water."

Troy laughs. Dominic rolls his eyes.

"I mean it," Ford says. "If you ever get to the point where The Gold Room is operating on its own, or you can hire someone to manage it, I'd hire you full time. No questions asked."

"I'd hope you wouldn't ask any questions since I'm already on the payroll."

Ford grins. "We're working out contract details for a job in Atlanta. Will be a whole weekend the first weekend next month. You interested?"

I lean back in my chair and exhale.

Usually, I grab some of these jobs here and there. The money is nice—*very nice.* I sack it all away for a rainy day because those kinds of days happen more regularly than I care to admit. *Especially with a kid with loads of energy.* So when I can get my day manager to close at night and can talk my neighbor, Mrs. Kim, into watching Ryder for the weekend, I'll sign on to help Ford out.

But now I have something else to contend with—Paige.

"I'm sorry, Ford," I say, sitting back up. "I have a ... situation that precludes me from leaving town for a while."

"How long?" he asks.

I shrug.

Dominic looks at me, confused. "What situation?"

Shit. If anyone can see through me, it's my brother. "Just a situation. Relax."

"I want to know."

"Do I poke around in your life?" I ask, irritated. "Come on, man."

"What do you want to know? Hit me with your questions." Dominic sits up, screwing with me for the sake of screwing with me. "You wanna know how hard Camilla fuc—"

"That's my sister." Ford's voice booms through the conference room, effectively silencing my brother. "For your sake, don't go there."

Troy sits back and cackles.

Dominic looks at Ford. "Sorry. That got a little out of hand."

"You think?" Ford shakes his head. "Just be glad Lincoln didn't hear you say that."

Dominic snorts. "You know I'm not scared of Lincoln."

"Did someone say my name?" Lincoln asks, eyeing each of us.

We all turn toward the door as none other than Lincoln Landry walks in. He removes his sunglasses—*why was he wearing them in the building in the first place?*—and plops down in the chair beside Troy.

Out of all the Landrys, I like Lincoln the least. He's not a *bad* person. Actually, he's pretty funny and one hell of an athlete. *But he knows it.* His cheekiness might work on the women in his life, but it doesn't work on me.

I look at my brother. *Or Dominic.*

Troy smirks. "Nah, I don't think so. Dominic was just talking about getting a new car. Right, Dom?"

Dominic rolls his eyes.

"Oh, what kind?" Lincoln asks. "I love cars."

"A Lincoln," I say, elbowing my brother.

Ford takes a deep breath. "What are you doing here, Linc?"

Lincoln cracks a piece of gum. "You want the truth or bullshit?"

"What kind of question is that?" Ford asks.

"I'm here for the bullshit answer." I look at Ford and shrug. "Hey, the last time he swung by and I was here, he said he was helping Graham with paperwork." I look at Lincoln and grin. "We all know you were full of shit that day. There's no way in hell G would let you help with paperwork."

Lincoln rolls his eyes. "It's all fun and games and '*Graham is so responsible and works so hard*' until he has a heart attack."

"Good point," Dominic mumbles.

"*Anyway*," Lincoln says, "I was here to see if anyone wanted to go golfing with me."

Four various forms of *no* ring out through the room. Even if we had the day to blow off, doing anything remotely athletic with Lincoln is not fun. The guy is a phenom. Although I would absolutely knock him out in a fight. Probably in the first thirty seconds.

Lincoln gets up, his lips twisted in displeasure. "You guys are no fun."

"We have work to do," Ford tells him.

"Heart attacks. All of you," Lincoln says, pointing at each of us as he walks to the door.

"We'll take our chances," Dominic says.

Lincoln puts his hand on the door and starts to push it open. "You still owe me a bottle of tequila, Nate."

"It's been three years. Let it go," Ford says just as Lincoln disappears into the hallway.

Once he's gone, it's as if all the air in the room is momentarily sucked out with it. It takes a few seconds for us to regain our footing. It's no secret that Lincoln and I butt heads from time to time, but it's not easy for me to deal with a grown-ass man who plays golf randomly in the middle of the work week. *Must be nice.*

Ford looks at his watch. "All right, guys, I gotta go. I have a call in fifteen minutes." He gets to his feet and glances at Troy. "Where are we meeting Holt Mason this afternoon?"

"Hilary's House."

"What's going on with them?" I ask.

"A recommitment ceremony," Ford says. "Holt's parents are renewing their vows and are going all out. Coy has some bands coming to town from Nashville, so there'll be celebrities. It's going to be nuts."

Cool.

"See you there," Ford says to Troy. "Talk to you guys later."

"Later," Dominic and I say.

Once the door closes behind Ford, Dominic elbows me in the side.

"What?" I ask.

"What's the situation?"

I sigh.

It's not a big deal. I might as well just tell him. But even though having my friend stay with me as a favor to her isn't a big deal—right now? It feels like it is.

I know exactly what Dominic and Troy will think when I say Paige is at my house. They both know her and have seen us together. They've independently made comments about how much she wants my cock and I should give it to her. Naturally, they'll think there's a fuck fest happening on Galloway Drive.

Do I care if they think I'm banging her? Not necessarily. But I don't really want to talk about it.

"Paige got evicted," I tell them.

Dominic furrows his brow. "The hottie who works for you?"

I nod.

"Dude, make sure she doesn't go back to Atticus out of desperation."

"Oh, she isn't ..." I exhale sharply. "She's staying with me for a little while."

Troy looks pleased. "Okay. Well, I can't say I didn't see that coming."

I chuckle, wishing I had never brought it up to them. "Yeah, well, it's not like you think."

"Why the hell not?" Dominic asks. "She's a ten outta ten. She wants your cock. Hell, she'd probably spin around whatever way you asked her to, and you're telling me she's under your roof and not under your sheets?" He gasps. "What's wrong with you?"

Troy jabs a thumb Dominic's way. "What he said."

I get up and pace around the table.

"Have you ever talked to her?" Troy asks my brother. "She's funny. Great sense of humor."

"I haven't said much to her, but I know her well enough that she seems pretty cool."

I feel both of their gazes land on me. The weight of them makes me stop moving.

"You guys are right," I say, surprising myself. "But just because I can doesn't mean I should."

"She's an adult. Consent is a real thing, and I bet she'd be more than happy to give it to you," Troy says.

"You do know me, right?" I ask, raising a brow. "I don't bring random women back to my house with Ryder there. I'm not gonna confuse him like that."

"But you like her, and she's already at your house ..." Dominic says, raising a brow. "I think you've already stepped in that puddle, brother."

"She's there as a friend. Ryder understands that. I'm not going to let him get attached to her."

"You're the parent." Dominic looks down at the paper in front of him. "You do you."

I will. Tension spans the back of my neck. Coupled with my lack of sleep, I know my patience is thin—even for these two.

"I gotta go," I tell them, picking up the envelope Ford gave me. "See you guys later."

They respond, but I don't know what they say. I walk out, leaving them and their tempting take on my status with Paige behind.

Chapter 6

Paige

"Do you ever sit still?" Kinsley Clayton throws a piece of popcorn at me. "You just roam around like a ... I was going to say a mountain goat, but I don't know if they roam."

I snort. "I don't know either, but that's a bad analogy anyway. They're so ugly."

"True." She pops a handful of the cheesy snack in her mouth. "So did you ever hear from Marcie about the whole eviction thing? Has she called you or anything?"

I sit down on the couch beside Kinsley.

It's been over twenty-four hours since I was forced out of the apartment, and I haven't heard a word from our mutual friend.

"Nope. I've literally heard nothing. No call back, no texts—nothing." I frown. "I called her mom this morning to just ... I don't know. A welfare check, I guess. She said Marcie was in the shower, and she'd tell her that I called."

Kinsley frowns too. "I guess she's okay at least, right?"
"Yeah."

"Are you pissed? I'd be pissed. I'd be so freaking mad that I couldn't see straight."

I think about it. *Am I mad?* Not really. *Should I be?* Maybe.

"Want anything else to drink?" she asks as she climbs off the chair wedged between the sofa and the wall. "I need another water."

"Nope. I'm good."

She walks across the tiny living room and into the even smaller kitchen. Then she pulls a drink from the freakishly small refrigerator that somehow meets her needs.

"What can you keep in there? A water bottle and cheese stick?" I ask.

She laughs and flops back on the chair, her legs dangling over the side. "Basically. But it beats going back to my parents' house and admitting that moving in with Josh was a bad idea. That's a lot of crow to eat."

It is a lot of crow to eat. Kinsley's parents never liked Josh, so when Kinsley said she was moving in with her boyfriend after only two months, they weren't happy at all. Josh the Jerk, as he's now known, was an even worse roommate than Marcie. And a douche for dumping Kinsley about six months after she moved in.

The sun begins to set, casting shadows across the walls of Kinsley's apartment. We spent the day looking for apartments and making appointments to see them. All in all, it was fun.

"You know, I'm not mad," I say, having had a moment to think it through. "I think I'm more worried about Marcie than anything. Like what was she doing with the money I was giving her for rent? Is she in some kind of trouble? Did I miss a sign somewhere?" I pause. "Will I ever know?"

"I get that. It's a good take on it. A very *Paige* take on it." She smiles. "And how can you be mad when you get to stay with Nate?"

She flops her head back as if she's going to replay a dramatic movie scene but bops her head on the wall instead. We both laugh.

"How's that going?" she asks.

"Fine. I mean, do I lie awake at night and listen for him? Yes. Am I waiting to catch him fresh out of the shower with a towel around his waist? Also yes." I giggle. "But, no, things are going fine. I got there super late last night, as you know, and I felt a little bad about that once I got there."

"I kept telling you to leave the bookstore! How many times did I text you that?"

I roll my eyes. "*I know. I know.* I just ... internally, I'm not quite the confident bitch that I lead people to believe I am."

Kinsley eats another handful of popcorn, her eyes crinkled at the corners.

"So you basically thought twice about stripping down in his office and inviting yourself to his house and felt a little embarrassed by that? I mean, that tracks."

"Don't put it like that. Damn." I laugh. "That makes me sound like a hussy."

"You are a hussy."

"I'm a virgin, Kins. I can't be a hussy. It's the exact opposite of the definition."

She furrows her brow. "There's a definition for hussy?"

"There has to be. It's a word."

"Huh. I guess you're right. It's just funny to think that you can look up a word like that and find an actual definition. Like somebody, somewhere had to sit down and type it out."

I stretch out, wiggling my toes, and yawn.

I could curl up and close my eyes and fall asleep. All I'd need is a blanket. But if I do that, I'll be up in a couple of hours because my neck is tweaked from the couch, and then I'd have to roll into Nate's late. Again.

Yeah. No, thanks.

"Did you sign up for classes this semester?" I ask Kinsley.

"Yeah. Get this—I have biology, a bio lab, chemistry, a chem lab, a math class, and a physical therapy class of some sort. I'm going to die."

"You know, I like to be optimistic about most things but yeah. I think you might die."

She whimpers. "Why did I take three years off between high school and college? What a mistake that was."

"Well, I didn't go straight there either. So ..."

She grins. "What classes did you end up getting? I know you were debating how many hours to carry this semester."

I stand, afraid of getting too cozy, and stretch again.

"I ended up with twelve hours, which is just enough," I say. "I promised my parents I'd go full time because they seem to think I'd take half of the classes, screw off the other hours of the day, and then end up thirty with no degree and no job."

"Because they know you."

"Maybe." I smile. "I really think it's because Maddox partied his way through school, and they're worried I'll follow suit. Even though I don't party."

As if summoned by the use of his name, my phone chirps with a text alert. I look at the screen.

Maddox: What's the password to Mom's Amazon account?

I laugh as I type out my response.

Me: Why would I tell you that?
Maddox: Because I need it. Now give it to me.
Me: What are you going to do with it?
Maddox: None of your business.
Me: I have the password, so I'm making it my business.

I don't really care what he's doing with it. I just can't give in too easily. *Gotta make him work for it.*

. . .

Maddox: Fine. I was going to send you a present. You ruined the surprise.

I laugh. "Lies."

Me: Make it new shoes. Black ones.
Maddox: I'll send two pairs.
Me: It's 0310abc
Maddox: Is that 0310 for March 10th? Your birthday?
Me: Maybe.
Maddox: Why is it never my birthday? *pleading face emoji*
Me: Because she loves me more.
Maddox: Bye.

I shove the phone in my pocket. "Sorry about that. Maddox needed Mom's password."

"Did you give it to him?"

"Yeah. He's probably trying to get a movie pulled up for Dad. My parents can't operate their electronics."

I get to my feet and take the five steps to the door. "I need to get going. Want to check out those two apartments with me tomorrow?"

"If I get out of work. I'm supposed to have a half-day, but we'll see how that works out. If it's Polly coming in for me, I'll be there until close. I love that for me."

That sucks. She has to pick up Polly's shifts all the time. "Well, let me know."

Kinsley gets to her feet and pulls me into a quick hug. "Have fun tonight." She wiggles her eyebrows.

I snort.

"That's *exactly* how I meant it."

"I'd be game," I say, slipping on my shoes. "I'd probably die because I don't think he'd ever really take me up on it. I needle him all the time because I know I'm off-limits to him. Man, I talk good smack but don't really have the ass to back it up."

45

"No—your ass is hot. You just need to, you know, tread carefully, or you might get yourself in pretty deep."

"I bet it'd go deep."

We laugh together. But as I laugh at my joke, I start thinking about what I said. I do talk a lot and push a lot of buttons for someone who's never had sex. I always panic at the last moment and stop. The idea of giving my body to someone, especially for the first time, is overwhelming. I've never wanted a guy to have that piece of me, never wanted to let them in that far. It's cost me a lot of relationships.

But the idea of being with Nate doesn't feel as terrifying. Would I freak out when the time came? I don't know. Maybe. But a part of me knows I'd be safe with him ... and a part of me really wants him to be that guy.

"I'll let you know of any status updates," I say.

"Please do. I'll light a candle for your virginity tonight."

"You do that." I laugh. "Talk to you later."

"Bye, Paige."

I slip into the hallway. Then I walk through the lobby that smells vaguely of curry and make my way outside.

I tug my sweatshirt closer against me as I bow my head against the wind. My car is at the end of the parking lot, and by the time I get there, I'm nearly a popsicle.

After starting the engine, I turn the heater on high. Naturally, it bursts cold air into the cab. Just as I yelp from the frigidity, my phone rings.

Mom. I smile.

"Hi," I say, turning the vents down.

"Where are you? It sounds like you're in a tunnel."

"Just my car. Sorry about that," I say, sitting back. "I cranked the heat up, but there's no heat yet. So it was just assaulting me, basically."

She laughs. "Is everything going okay? I haven't heard from you today."

My chest fills with a warmth that I wish I could bottle up and keep forever. But, like it always does, it eventually dissipates.

"I'm fine. Great, actually," I say. "I spent the day with my friend Kinsley and am on my way to Nate's now."

She sighs.

"It's fine, Mom," I say. "I wouldn't be staying there if it wasn't."

"I know. And I trust you, honey. You have wonderful instincts."

But ... I stare off into the distance.

"But it's hard for me not to know any of the people in your life. Are they taking good care of my baby girl? Do they know how precious you are to me? Do they know what I would have your brothers do if they ever hurt you? Because I'd give up my Switzerland status for that."

I laugh. "I love you, too, Mom. And, yes, they are taking good care of me."

Mom hates that she and Dad haven't come to Savannah since the first month I got here. I always try to visit them once a month because I miss my family so much. And, if I'm being honest, I like having my own space and life up here. They'll be here soon. I've probably kept her away as long as I can. *God love her.*

"Also, Maddox has your Amazon password, so be ready for that bill."

She groans.

"He's only had it for fifteen minutes or so. You can minimize the damage by changing the password."

"That boy." She sighs. "Anyway, you are good? Have you talked to Hollis? Did you tell him that I can't wait to meet him?"

Her words do more for me than any hug or *I love you*. Her honesty and genuine excitement over adding Hollis to our family is so apparent, and I love her so much for it.

I know they'll get along great. I just need a little time to get to know Hollis myself, to really build a foundation between the two of us before the Carmichaels roll in with the welcome wagon.

47

"I had dinner with him last night. He can't wait to meet you too. I just need a little more time, Mom. I hope you understand."

"I'm trying to. I promise."

"Thank you. How is everyone? How are the boys?" I ask, using the collective term I started using years ago for all of my brothers.

"Oh, you know your brothers. They're trying to see which one is going to make me gray first."

"Better than being in competition with each other to make you a grandma first."

She laughs. "Oh, heavens, yes. I'd like them to be settled down and happily married—or at least in a serious relationship—before that happens."

"Do you ever think Banks is actually going to be in a serious relationship? He eats cold SpaghettiOs. He's a child—and not a particularly smart one."

"Yes, well, Banks is a special case."

We both laugh.

"Do you need anything?" Mom asks. "I was looking for rentals for you today. I found a couple that look like good leads if you need them."

"Yeah. Will you text them to me?"

"I'd love to."

I grin. "Thanks."

"Of course. Do you need anything else? I can Prime stuff like it's my job."

"Dad thinks that *is* your job," I say, laughing.

"As long as I get something for him too, he can't say a word. That's a little tip for you."

"I think that one will be more helpful than the laundry sorting rules."

She groans. "Don't tell me you're still not sorting your laundry."

"Mom, no one is sorting their laundry anymore. It's whites, lights, and darks. Maybe towels separately."

"I can't take it. This is hurting my heart."

"I'll tell you what—when I ruin my stuff, you can Prime me new towels."

"Deal!"

We chuckle. The heat starts to build in my car, so I crank up the blowers.

"Okay, I better get off here and see what we're having for dinner," she says. "Maddox asked me to make him a pot of chicken noodle soup, and I think I'm out of egg noodles."

"God forbid."

"I'd make a pot for you too if you were here, you little stinker."

"Tell Mad I said hi," I say. "Tell Banks to fuck off."

"Paige!"

I giggle. "I'm kidding, Mom. Relax. Don't tell Banks anything at all. That'll drive him the craziest."

"He does like attention, doesn't he?"

"You think?" I hold my hand over the vent to thaw my fingers. "I'll call you later, okay?"

"If you don't, I'll come up there and find you."

"Love you, Mom."

"I love you, sweetheart."

"Change your password! Bye."

I end the call and then sit back in my seat, relishing in the glow of being my mother's daughter. It took us a while to get here, but we made it. And I'm so happy about it.

Now on to the fun stuff.

I hope.

I back out of the parking spot and head to Nate's.

Chapter 7

Paige

"Hi!" I call out as I shut the front door behind me.

The television is on in the living room. The canned laughter of a cartoon greets me before anything else. Whiffs of spices float through the air as I hang my purse on an empty hook in the foyer next to Ryder's backpack.

I slip off my shoes before walking farther into Nate's house.

"We're in the kitchen," Nate shouts.

I make my way through his home, noting how warm and aromatic it is. I would never imagine that Nate, the burly guy from work who every patron that enters respects out of fear, would have a house that truly feels like a home.

"Hi, Paige!" Ryder stands on a stool and stirs a pot on the stove. Steam rolls from the large orange container. "We're making spaghetti."

"You are? That's fun."

"Yup. We are."

His eyes sparkle with excitement. I follow his gaze to the island. *To his dad.*

Dear sweet heavens. Now my eyes are sparkling with excitement.

Nate stands at the counter with a knife in his hand. A gray T-shirt with Landry Security in bold, black letters emblazoned on the front is stretched over his broad chest. He looks up at me, then at Ryder, and then back to me and grins.

You're lucky your kid is here because damn.

"*I'll behave,*" I mouth to him.

He chuckles.

"Can I help?" I ask, standing tall like a well-behaved woman.

"If you want to eat, you can." Nate winks at me. "Wanna chop the onions? I'd be more than happy to pass this along to you."

"Gotta wash your hands first," Ryder says.

"Of course." I walk to the sink and turn on the water. "How was your day?"

"Mine was great," Ryder says in the precious little kid way like they're the only person in the room. "I got a star for reading, and that puts me ahead of all the other kids in my class. Not in the *entire first grade* because there's a girl Jurnee who has read more than me. But she's in Mrs. Stahl's class, not mine."

I laugh, finishing up washing my hands. "How many more stars does she have than you?"

"Five. I don't know if I can catch her, but I'm trying."

I flip the water off and flick the water off my hands in the sink. Then I turn to the island.

"I want to know what I get out of this since I'm the one reading all the damn books to him," Nate whispers as I get closer.

"You get a kid who loves reading," I whisper back.

He rolls his eyes, but his grin tells me he's joking.

"Here." He hands me his knife and motions to the onions and garlic on the counter with his other hand. "Have at it."

I take the knife. Our hands brush against each other in the transition. A zip of energy races between our bodies at the contact.

We touch each other at work occasionally although I always think Nate tries to avoid it. But here, in his kitchen, it's different. The electricity between us is softer tonight but somehow just as intense.

"How was your day, Nate?" I ask.

"Fine. I had to run by Landry Security for a while. Talked to Dom and Troy and shot the shit for a bit. They both said hello."

I place the knife close to my heart and sigh blissfully. "Troy, my hero."

Nate doesn't turn his head but looks at me all the same. His jaw is tight, and it makes me laugh.

"Sorry," I say, giggling. "You were there too. You can be my co-heroes."

He rolls his eyes.

"When do I get to hang out with Uncle Dom and Camilla Vanilla again?" Ryder asks.

Nate takes the large spoon out of Ryder's hand and sets it on the counter. Then he picks his son up and tickles him. Ryder kicks and giggles before his dad sets him on his feet.

"You're not seeing Uncle Dom until he swears he won't take you back to Percy's," Nate says.

Ryder pouts. "You have to trust him. He's your brother."

"What do you know about brothers? You don't even have one," Nate says, mussing up the little boy's hair.

"That's not my fault! I *want* a brother."

"I have a lot of them. Six, to be exact," I say. "Trust me when I say that it's overrated."

"What's that mean?" Ryder asks.

Nate laughs. "Do you want to watch your show for a little bit until dinner?"

"Can I? We aren't done cooking. You never let me watch TV until we've made dinner, eaten, and cleaned it all up."

"I know. But you can get outta your work tonight. Just this once. Don't get used to it."

Ryder's fist pumps up and down as he runs out of the kitchen toward the living room. Nate watches him with a smile.

"One of his chores is helping me make dinner," he says, turning back to me. "As you can see, he'd rather be doing anything but this."

I grab an onion. "He'll appreciate it someday. Some of my favorite memories are helping my mom in the kitchen. I always loved to help her because it got me away from the boys in the house."

"I bet your house was wild."

"Yeah. That's a fair assessment." I grin as I remember some of their antics over the years. "They were always wrestling and trying to test their new moves out on me or adding me into their shenanigans because our parents gave in easier when I was involved. So if they wanted ice cream, *I* wanted ice cream. If they wanted to go to the water park, I did too. It was a lot of moving parts and personalities, but fun."

Nate laughs. "Sounds about right." He takes a box of spaghetti out of the cabinet. "Do you think you'll have a family like that someday, or are you over that?"

I make a tiny cut in the onion and peel off the layers. *Funny, I feel like he's trying to peel mine back too.*

"You know, I'm not sure," I say, testing out my ability to be honest about personal things. "I haven't really thought about it."

"You've never thought about it?"

"No." I chop the onions slowly. "I don't know ... I'm just not sure. I guess it's a *figure it out when you get there* kind of thing."

The knife slips in my hand. I steady myself and then grab the garlic.

"What about you?" I ask, needing the attention off me.

"Yeah. I'd love to have a sibling for Ryder, but the idea of getting married again ..." He whistles between his teeth. "But then you think about having a baby while purposely not getting married, and that doesn't quite feel right either. So I don't know. I did it once. That's probably enough."

Nate was married?

"Who were you married to?" I ask.

He lowers his voice and glances at the doorway. "Ryder's mom. She overdosed when he was six months old."

"I'm sorry. I had no idea."

53

"How would you?" He shifts his weight from one foot to the other. "It's not like I go around talking about it." He turns back to the stove. "I guess that's why I'm so uncertain about the actual marriage part. I'd love to settle down, though, and give Ryder the family I didn't have."

I look at him and grin. He catches me before I can avert my gaze.

"What?" he asks, the corner of his lip turning toward the ceiling.

"Nothing."

"No, what was that look about?"

"I just ... It was nice knowing that you feel uncertain about some things too."

His smile slips away, and a look of surprise replaces it. "I'm unsure about everything. Most people are."

"Are they? Because it doesn't feel like it."

"Definitely."

I smash a couple of cloves of garlic. "I usually feel like I'm behind on things. Plans. *Life.*" I sigh. "I just can't get it together."

"Who says you should have it together?"

I pause, the knife suspended over the cutting board. *What kind of questionanswer is that?*

He shrugs. "I mean it. Who says you have to have your life together? People like to pretend they have shit figured out, but no one does. That's the secret right there."

I hit the knife with the back of my hand, smashing the clove. But my mind is filled with his words.

"Life is like a boxing match, really," he says, his voice softer. "Every day is a new round. You have to regroup, adjust to what your opponent has thrown at you, and go at it. You have to understand your weaknesses *and* strengths, but lead with the strengths. Over and over."

"I'm sure that was meant to be encouraging, but I walk around with two black eyes." *Or that's how life feels, anyway.*

If it's not getting evicted, it's struggling to pay rent. If the money parts of my life are fine, then I have a hard time at school. It doesn't come easy for me. If that's all going swimmingly, then I have a guy who's messing with my head or breaking my heart. It's always one thing or another.

"You know what's good about that?" he asks.

"No. Please tell me. I'd love to know."

He looks at me over his shoulder. "Black eyes heal."

I wait for more of an explanation—some philosophical reasoning behind his simple sentence—but nothing comes.

"That's it?" I ask. "*Black eyes heal.* That's your big revelation?"

"Maybe it's the only one that matters."

"Yeah," I say, lining up the garlic in front of me into a tidy line. "Most definitely keep your day job."

He chuckles. "What did you do today anyway?"

"I went over to Kinsley's and hung out. We won't get to do that much when school starts back up. Talked to my mom. Looked at apartments. That kind of stuff."

"Really?"

I shrug and head to the sink to wash my hands again. I can't quite make out his tone, so I ignore it.

"I told you I wouldn't wear out my welcome. Or maybe I didn't say that, exactly, but I hope you inferred it through something I did say."

"Absolutely. I think I inferred that as you were shaking your hips in the white panties."

I roll my tongue around my mouth. "*Touché.*"

"What are you going to school for?" he asks, switching topics.

Probably a good choice with Ryder in the next room.

"I've changed my majors twice. I'm one credit away from a bachelor's in communications but changed my mind like the ridiculous person I am and am going for my social work now. I'm really lucky. My parents will be happy to pay for any education I want to do. Books and classes. They'll never say no to that."

"Then I'd milk that for all it's worth. Take all the classes. Read all the books." He glances toward the doorway and then back to me.

55

"Yourself. Read them yourself. Don't expect someone to read them to you every fucking night of the week."

I giggle as I finish washing my hands.

We work quietly around the kitchen while preparing the spaghetti. Nate is very comfortable in the kitchen, and I'm surprised at how quickly the garlic and onions are mixed with the beef, and I love watching him choose the spices to add. Occasionally, we brush arms or bump hips. When that happens, we look at each other and smile.

"Joe came in today," he says. "I was starting to get worried about him."

My heart sinks as I think about the homeless man who comes into The Gold Room. He always sits on the barstool by the door and always orders a coffee—probably because Nate charges him like a quarter to drink all he wants. Especially in the winter. I asked Nate once why he charges him at all, and he said you can't strip a man's dignity. And if he never charged Joe for anything, that's what would happen.

"How long was he gone this time?" I ask. "It feels like forever."

"It was going on five weeks."

We exchange a frown.

"How did he look?" I ask. "Is he okay? No one hurt him or anything, did they?"

Nate sighs. "No, he's fine. I think he's been staying at a shelter downtown."

Relief fills my soul. "That's good."

"Murray made him a sandwich, and I packed him one for the road—and a Snickers."

"His favorite," I say, melting as I look into Nate's eyes.

Nate Hughes is one of the nicest men I know. Sure, he's often surly, rude, and bitches about ridiculous things, but he's genuinely, inherently kind.

To the outsider looking in, it could seem that it puts him out to fix

Shaye's car or make Joe a sandwich on the house. Nate puts on a good show, insisting it's killing him to do good deeds. But it's not.

He cares. Those of us who know Nate know that about him.

Nate might be a work of art on the outside. He might also set my body on fire with a smirk. But it's his kindness, his heart for others that seals my affection for him.

"Hey, do you happen to remember when my next shift is?" I ask, clearing my throat. "I forgot to check the schedule."

"I have no idea. I'll look when I get there in the morning and let you know."

"Thanks."

He carries a pot of boiling water to the sink. "Can you grab the garlic bread out of the oven?"

"Sure."

I find two oven mitts and a hot pad. The kitchen is filled with garlicky goodness as soon as I pull the pan of bread out of the oven and set it on the island.

"You'll love this one. Murray asked not to work with you Friday night again, by the way. He said he can only handle two shifts with you a week."

"Oh, I bet." I roll my eyes. Murray is a spoiled brat, but I can't help liking him. "I'll get him to love me yet. Don't worry about it."

Nate looks at me over his shoulder. "I have no doubt."

Something in his gaze makes me shiver.

He turns on his heel and faces me. His face is damp from the pasta water, and his shirt is splattered with spaghetti sauce. But seeing him like this, all domestic and relaxed, is my favorite Nate so far.

"You apologized last night for your ... *manipulation*," he says, grinning at the word. "I want to apologize to you too."

Apologize? To me?

"For what?" I ask, confused.

"For giving you a hard time about it." He runs a hand over his head. "Like I said last night, I would've been pissed if you didn't reach out to me when you needed help. And I don't think you ask for help much, do you?"

"Not if I can help it."

He drops his hand to his side. "I know we joke around and shit, and that's kind of our jam. But I don't want you to think you're not welcome here or that you have to hurry and go. Because you don't. You can stay as long as you want." *So genuine.* He fights a smile. "As long as you stay dressed." *And dirty.*

My body fills with a warmth that I could get used to. I laugh. "Thanks, Nate. I appreciate that."

"Yeah." He clears his throat. "Okay. So that's done. I'm going to grab Ryder, and then we can eat."

"Sounds good."

He disappears around the corner, and I sag against the kitchen counter. I hear him playing with Ryder and Ryder's laughter.

I take a long, deep breath and blow it out slowly. *Nate would be the perfect family man. It's so easy to see. If only that was something I could be.*

"Are you ready to eat, Paige Stage?" Ryder asks, hanging upside down over Nate's shoulder.

I laugh and look at the boy and his dad.

"I'm ready," I say.

Nate gives me a smile that feels like a whole conversation. I hope he can read what my smile says too because I'm not sure I'll ever be able to say it out loud.

Chapter 8

Nate

his might be the dumbest thing I've ever done.

I watch the shadows from the streetlight move across the ceiling. I never sleep well, but I haven't been up through the night—not even pretending to close my eyes—until three in the morning since Ryder had colic.

I toss to my left side. Again. Then back to my right.

How did I think having Paige in my house would be fine?

At least at work, the flirtation ends at the end of the night. Now I can't get the hell away from it. She's here when I wake up and when we have dinner. I have to hear her in the shower and know she's all wet and naked and all that separates the two of us is the door.

Fuck.

My legs fly off the side of the bed—clad in black joggers because now that she's here, I can't walk around in my boxer briefs... *can I?* ... and groan. There's no point in lying here. I'm not going to fall asleep.

I quietly open my door and step into the living room. The house is dark, quiet enough to hear the leaves rustling outside the window as I walk past. I make my way into the kitchen, turn on the light over the stove, and then rummage around the fridge. A stack of pudding cups is in the back. I take out a butterscotch Snack Pack and close the door.

"Shit," I say, flinching in surprise.

Standing in the doorway is the person of my nightdreams. Because that's a thing now. Paige Carmichael is a mixture of a nightmare and a dream.

She's dressed in a pair of short shorts that barely hide the curve of her ass and a tight black tank top. The fabric looks like it's made out of silk, and all I can think about is how it would feel directly against my skin.

"You're staring," she says, her voice thick with sleep.

"I was trying to figure out ..." *Whether to fuck you or fight you.* "I didn't expect anyone to be standing there."

She yawns. "Got an extra pudding?"

I hand her mine, avoiding any physical contact whatsoever. Then I grab myself a replacement.

"Butterscotch?" She quirks a brow. "Interesting choice."

"They're the best."

"Never had it."

I pull out two spoons from a drawer and hand her one. "It's about to blow your mind." I spot a twinkle in her eye and stay one step ahead of her. "No innuendos after midnight."

She laughs. "You're no fun."

I grin at her as I peel back the lid of my snack. "What keeps you up tonight?"

"I don't know. I never sleep."

"Me either."

We take spoonfuls of the pudding quietly. She nods appreciatively.

"Okay, that's good," she says, licking her lips. "Very good."

"I told you."

"*Mind blown.*" She winks at me before digging in for another scoop. "I might just add dessert to my nighttime routine. It's much more pleasant than what I usually go for."

I lick my spoon. "Which is?"

As soon as I ask, I regret it.

Paige hops up on the counter, her thick thighs pressing against the countertop in a way that makes it hard not to stare. She licks her spoon, running her tongue around it and watching me.

Fuck.

"Forget it," I say and lean back against the opposite counter.

She plunks the spoon in the pudding and sets it beside her. "I was going to say that I lie awake and play the What-If game with myself, pretending I can rewrite history. It's fun. You should try it. You'll feel like a complete loser and will second-guess every life choice you've ever made. Guaranteed to cause anxiety."

"That sounds like a good use of your time."

"It's better than being all curled up in my blankets, drifting off to sleep but just before I get there, my heart starts blasting in my chest like an air horn. I sit up in a panic and imagine a creepy person is standing in the corner jacking off."

She smiles as if it's somehow going to take the edge off her statement.

"What the hell?" I set my pudding down too. "What did you just say?"

"*Yeah.*" She sighs, her smile wobbling until it vanishes altogether. "I stayed with a family when I was really little. It was just after Hollis and I got put into foster care. They separated us, for some reason, and the people I lived with had a son. He was probably fourteen or fifteen, I guess."

She bites the inside of her cheek. I think she might backtrack and stop telling me this story. A part of me hopes she does. My heart is racing so fast that I think I might go find this little punk if the story goes the way I fear it might. But another part of me hopes she opens up to me.

I give her space and don't push. I just stand with her in the kitchen and allow her the choice to tell me more or not.

"He used to sneak into my room once everyone was in bed," she says, her voice softer this time. "I'd wake up when I heard the door. Light would stream in for a split second. Then he'd stand in the corner and just watch me."

"Did he ...?" I ball my hands against my sides.

"No. No, nothing like that. He'd just grunt and then slip back out into the hallway." She shrugs. "Now that I'm older, I figure he was probably jerking himself off, but I had no clue then. I was probably six or seven and scared shitless."

Fuck. That's Ryder's age.

He's scared of monsters that don't exist. She lived with monsters that do.

I run a hand over my forehead. The thought of a little Paige being scared of some psycho in her bedroom makes me want to hurt someone. Bad. But blowing up now isn't going to help, so I just clench my teeth until they hurt. And then blow out a breath.

"Did you ever tell anyone? Your foster parents? Hollis?" I ask.

"No. *Hell, no.* The kid would do these little passive-aggressive things during the day—you know, like remove my Barbie's head. He'd chuckle and then put it back on like it was nothing, but I read between the lines." Her forehead pinches together. "I've never told anyone that."

A ghost of regret or embarrassment, I'm not sure which, streaks across her face. She lowers her eyes to the floor.

I shift against the cold hardwood. "I can see why you can't sleep. But I'll watch your door for you while you're here. Don't worry about that."

"What do you mean?"

"Well, I usually lie in bed and wait for my father to come in and beat the fuck out of me."

Her eyes go wide, but she stays silent.

"He used to just whale on my mom," I say, gripping the counter behind me. "As soon as the sun went down, all hell would break loose."

"Then he'd come after you?"

I shove off the counter and pace around like I have something to do. I really just need to move, to work off some of the energy that this shit brings up in me.

"Actually," I say, "no. My little brother, Dominic, and I used to stick a chair under our door handle at night out of fear. But he never came in after us." I turn to her and grin sadly. "I guess he was satisfied with knocking us around during the day."

She hops off the counter. "Nate, I'm sorry. That's ... awful."

If you only knew the half of it.

"Don't apologize for him," I say.

"I'm not. I'm apologizing for you—meaning that I'm sorry for you. I'm sorry you had to go through that."

Her eyes shine with a genuineness, an understanding that I both appreciate and hate. *Because that means she can identify with my pain.*

My insides twist as I think about someone hurting Paige. It makes me want to pull her into me—makes me want to wrap my arms around her and protect her from the world.

"Everyone goes through shit, right?" I ask. The only alternative to holding her is trying to make her feel better with words. "Some of it is just a little darker than others."

"I guess."

She gives me a small grin and picks up her snack again. "You know, most people avoid talking about the unflattering parts of their lives."

"We live in a social media world. You get everyone's highlight reel, but that doesn't mean the outtakes don't exist."

She nods. "That's really hard for me to manage."

"What is?"

"Remembering that there are outtakes." She licks her spoon and then walks to the sink and places it inside the basin. "I have a habit of looking at other people's lives and thinking it must be perfect. Then I feel terrible about myself because mine isn't. *And I don't have a bad life.* It's a terrible mindfuck."

I walk to the sink and put my spoon on top of hers. The sound clinks through the room.

"I think most people feel that way sometimes," I say. "It looks easy and fun, but if you had to live it, you'd have to deal with their bullshit too that you can't see from afar."

My words bring a lightness back to her eyes. I watch the relief soften her posture and bring a grin back to her face.

"You're not a bad philosopher, Nate Hughes."

I laugh. "I think I'll stick to running a bar and grill, but thanks."

"I didn't say you should quit your day job."

Our laughter flows together so easily that it disarms me, tugging down the guard I keep between us for good measure.

Paige sticks her finger in the pudding cup and rolls it around the rim. "Speaking of your day job, who is closing tonight?"

"Murray," I say, watching her lift her finger from the container.

Her eyes flip to mine as she brings her finger to her lips.

Dammit. Don't you do it.

She does it.

Paige parts her lips, eyes sparkling with mischief.

She knows what she's doing.

"Be careful," I say, warning her not to push me too far. *I can only take so much of this.*

Then she sticks the butterscotch-coated finger between her lips and wraps them around her finger before sliding it back out ever so slowly.

A lump wedges itself in my throat. My cock stretches the fabric of my joggers. The temperature in the kitchen increases twofold as this vixen fucks with me.

Ryder isn't here to save me this time.

I exhale sharply, gathering myself before she causes me to blow.

"Do you want me to pay rent or help with groceries? We really didn't go over any of that," she says, licking her lips.

My gaze settles on her finger approaching the pudding container

64

again. "You're a college student with a part-time job. You don't have any money."

"That's true." She smiles smugly before lifting her eyes to mine. "I'm sure we could come up with something."

She trails her finger around the walls of the plastic before bringing it to her lips again. With her hand poised in front of her face, she smiles at me.

Nope. Not letting that happen.

I clamp her wrist with my hand and suspend it in midair. Her eyes go wide, her breath halting in her throat as she waits for my reaction.

Her skin is warm in my palm. Her wrist is so small, so delicate, that I ease my grip so I don't accidentally hurt her.

I'm not sure why I touched her, but it's either because I'm sleep-deprived and it's late or I want to teach her a lesson. *Or maybe I just want to see her reaction.*

I stare at her as deeply as I can. She holds her breath as she considers—*hopes? fears?*—what I'm going to do.

I twist her wrist and bring her hand to my face. A smirk settles on my lips as her entire body stills.

Then with the most deliberate move I've ever made, I bring her finger to my mouth.

My heart thunders in my chest as my self-restraint shatters into a million pieces.

I suck her finger between my lips. She gasps, her body shaking in response. I run my tongue around the pudding before biting lightly against her skin as I remove her digit from my mouth.

Every muscle in my body tightens. My blood heats to a dangerous degree. My hand trembles as I hold her hand in mine and try desperately not to tug her whole body into me.

Her chest heaves. She forces a swallow as she leans back against the counter. Her breath is loud and quick, breaking the silence of the room.

"*Shit,*" she says, a mixture of a plea and a promise.

I just look at her and smile. "Is that what you wanted?"

She swallows again.

I release her wrist from my palm. Then I lean in until we're only inches apart—until I'm so close that I can smell the sweetness of her breath—and grin.

"That's the only time my mouth will get anywhere near you." I turn toward the doorway, ignoring the protest of every cell in my body. "I'll see you in the morning."

"Nate?" she asks just before I round the corner.

Against my better judgment, I stop and turn around.

"Was that a challenge?" She grins. "Because it sure as hell sounded like one."

The woman looking back at me is the Paige I know. The one full of spunk. The girl who's filled with every damn thing that makes me want to break my resolve.

I grip the doorframe and meet her stare.

"Don't take challenges you can't win," I say.

I give her a wink and retreat to my bedroom. *Alone.*

Chapter 9

Paige

Kinsley and I walk down the steps of the last apartment building on our list for the day. The sun is out, shining happily in the sky but not really warming the air. We huddle into our sweatshirts and start the walk back to our cars.

"I'm glad we're done for the day because it's freaking cold," she says, her breath billowing in the air.

"I would've been happier if we had found something. Those were all trash."

She frowns. "Maybe you'll have better luck tomorrow."

We move down Magnolia Boulevard with much fewer hopes than we did when we walked up it a couple of hours ago. It turns out that a street with such a pretty name can, in fact, have terrible housing.

"Thank you for coming with me today," I say.

"Of course. You're entirely too wishy-washy to be left to your own devices. You'd rent an apartment because it has a cute wall but not bother to consider the size or proximity to laundry or stores. Or parking, for that matter."

"I should've listened to you and just got a place on my own

67

instead of bunking with Marcie. But she had all the furniture and pots and pans and life stuff. It was so much easier to do that." I consider that. "Until now."

She laughs.

"I just need a place before school starts. I need to be settled and ready to roll."

"I'm still surprised at how that went down with Marcie."

You and me both.

I shake my head. "I don't know what to do. Like is our friendship over now? Is she just embarrassed? I have no idea."

"She hasn't called me either, and we always binge-watch a show on Thursdays. I texted her but got nothing back."

We stop at a crosswalk. Kinsley pulls her phone out of her pocket and swipes across the screen.

"You doing okay at Nate's?" she asks. "You didn't text me a *status update* last night, so I assume you're still in possession of your V-card."

"Yeah."

She laughs at the look on my face—one of sadness and despair.

Except that face is for her. Not me.

Every pause in a conversation today, each moment of silence has been filled with Nate.

I shiver at the memory of my finger in his mouth. The softness of his tongue, the warmth that traveled from his mouth all the way to the apex of my thighs.

Remembering the look in his eye—the look that contradicted the words he spoke as he left me in his kitchen in a pool of lust—sends a delicious chill down my spine.

"That's the only time my mouth will get anywhere near you."

I spent all night trying to figure that mess out. *How can he look at me like that, touch me like that, and then come at me with that line?*

When he told me that I had no idea what he was capable of, he might've been right.

"Are you all right?" Kinsley looks at me curiously. "You're over there shivering. It's not *that cold.*"

I haven't told her about last night in the kitchen. I think it'll come out wonky and not nearly as sexy as it was. So I decide to keep it to myself. Just for now. At least until I work out what it means ... and doesn't mean.

"So," Kinsley says after we crossed the street, "are we one-wording answers about Nate? Or was that an anomaly?"

"What are you talking about?"

"I asked how things were going, and you said '*yeah.*' You don't give one-word answers to anything, so I'm trying to decide whether that's because things *are* okay or if they're not."

We stop at the opening of the public parking area central to all the apartments we looked at today. The breeze catches my hair and whirls it around my head. I gather it at the crown and twist an elastic from my wrist around the locks.

Kinsley narrows her eyes. "So ..."

"So ..." I look at my car in the distance. "Things are fine so far. Great, actually." *Confusing, but great.*

"Great, huh?"

"His kid is cute—"

"I didn't know he hads a kid! Ew."

I laugh. "Ryder is adorable and better behaved than that dog you had last year. He takes himself to the toilet, hasn't stolen food out of my hand yet, and doesn't whine."

She cringes. "I'm so glad my dad fell in love with that dog because I couldn't manage him. It was like having a baby, I think. He cried at night. Wanted up and down. Had to pee then didn't. Then peed on the floor." She shakes her head. "Nah, I'm good—with kids *and* dogs."

"I love dogs. Kids? Eh. That's case by case."

"Anyway, you were saying his kid is cute when I cut you off."

"Oh. Right. So yes, his kid is cute. Very well-behaved. Oh! He makes dinner with his kid. Dude, seeing him as a dad?" I place a hand on my heart and bite my lip. "Hot as fuck."

"I'm not into the dad vibe, but I'm glad it's working for you."

"You're not into the dad vibe? *How?*" My eyes bulge out. "What's *not* hot about a big, strong guy being all tender and sweet to their child? That's super hot."

She nods like I've lost my mind. I shrug.

"I guess maybe I just look at the guys I sleep with and think, *I hope you're never my kids' daddy.*" She laughs. "That's not funny, but it's true. Men are great until they have to behave that way."

"Maybe you need to hook up with better guys."

"Oh, definitely, I do. For sure. One thousand percent. Just point me in the direction of where they hang out, and I'll trot my ass down there and gather numbers. Hell, I'll get you numbers too, and you can avoid the upstanding citizens you usually go out with."

I give her a look.

"What? Do you enjoy getting all of your dates from the parole board?" she asks.

"You are not funny."

"You're right. I'm not because it's no laughing matter."

I roll my eyes, but we both know she's onto something.

It's not like I don't know this about myself. I routinely pick guys I would never take home to my parents.

I know I do it, but I don't know why. It's a vicious cycle that I find myself in.

Do I want to pick the asshole that will inevitably treat me like a piece of shit and I'll have to break up with him in some dramatic fashion?

No. No, I don't.

Do I always seem to be in that situation?

Yes.

It's maddening.

"Do you want to know why I think you do that?" she asks.

No. I just look at her.

"I think," she says carefully, "that you intentionally go after men who you can't see a future with. It's as though you don't want to risk giving someone your heart—apart from yours truly, of course—so ... maybe so they can never truly hurt you? I don't know. Just guessing."

I laugh. "That's crazy town. Why would I do that? Wouldn't that be a complete waste of time?"

"Yup. Sure would."

"You do it too. Why do *you* do it?"

She looks at me like I'm stupid. "*Paige.*"

My name as a whole sentence is never good.

"The guys I date aren't anything like the guys you pluck out of the gutters," she says. "No, I don't want Derrick or Tom to be my baby's daddy, but they never threaten to physically harm me."

I point at her. "That was just Atticus, and Troy beat the shit out of him for that."

"Okay, then let's talk about Bobby and how you walked in on him having an orgy with three college girls."

I glare at her.

"Do you see what I'm saying?" she asks. "I self-medicate with men. You self-sabotage. We aren't the same." She wraps her arm around my shoulder. "I'm not saying I'm better than you because Lord knows that you are much less petty and unreasonable than I am. But I do think you do this to yourself on purpose."

I want to be mad at her, but what would I be mad for? For telling the truth?

Her arm slips off my shoulders as we approach our cars. I don't want her parting ways with me and thinking I'm upset. It'll bother her all night.

"I should've just had sex with one of those guys," I say, bracing myself for her reaction.

"What? How can you say that?"

I grin. "Why do I want to wait and let some guy I actually like—who deserves to take my virginity—ruin the experience? I should've ruined it with a loser, so the guy I actually like has a chance to beat that. That would've been nice of me."

"Paige, *good grief.*" Kinsley laughs. "I love how romantic you are."

"I've read enough on Reddit to know that I should go into a sexual encounter, especially my first, with super-low expectations."

Kinsley's laughter gets louder.

"I mean it!" My cheeks flush. "It seems like half of the population has wild, graphic, she's getting choked, and he's ... you get the picture. And the other half is highly unsatisfied."

I cross my arms, proud of my research.

"At least you're informed, I guess," she says with a laugh.

I wink at her, letting her know I'm just kidding. Kind of.

"I have to get home," she says. "Maintenance is sending someone out this evening to check my vents because they're not blowing any air. They keep telling me I have them closed, but I don't. I'm not an idiot."

I smile at her. "Have fun. Call me if you need my help. I don't have a ladder, but I have a right cross." I swing it in the air and laugh. "I learned this from Ryder."

"You are getting so weird."

"Bye. Be safe."

"Love ya."

"Love ya too, Kins."

I climb into my car and lock the doors. But before I start the car and pull away, I grab my phone. There's one unread text.

Mom: Maddox bought a 50 lb bag of birdseed. Why?

I snort.

Me: I have no idea. Did you ask him?
Mom: He gave me a bullshit answer about saving ducks.
Me: There are things in life you're better off not knowing, Mom.
Mom: *grimacing emoji*

Me: Just finished looking for apartments. They all sucked. Trying again tomorrow.

Mom: How many did you look at?

Before I can answer her, another text comes through.

Maddox: You little tattletale.

Me: 50 lb bag of birdseed? Do I want to know?

Maddox: It's probably better that you don't. If Foxx brings this up, DEFLECT AND DENY.

Me: *laughing emoji*

I flip back to my chat with Mom.

Me: Four, I think. But I'm pulling out of the parking lot and no texting and driving."

Mom: Love you. Bye. Don't text back until you're home.

I toss my phone in the cup holder and start the car.

My heart beats more rhythmically than it has in a while. I smile at my reflection in the rearview mirror and take off toward Nate's—the one guy I've ever liked that's not my type.

I wonder what that means.

Maybe that you know if you ever gave him your heart, he could hurt you.

Chapter 10

Paige

"Girls don't know anything about cars." Ryder's voice echoes through the house. "They can't be mechanics."

"Dude. Stop it. Girls know things about cars."

"Have you ever seen a girl mechanic? Because I haven't."

"You're seven," Nate says. "How many mechanics do you know?"

"On YouTube, there's not any."

"How are you watching car stuff on YouTube? Give me your device, and let me check your parental controls."

I stand in the kitchen and listen to them go back and forth in the living room. It makes me smile to hear Nate defending the female gender.

Dinner was nice and fairly comfortable after last night's kitchen scandal. I just kept my cool and tried not to talk too much for fear of appearing nervous. I also tried not to stay too quiet so Nate wouldn't think I was down in the dumps over his declaration that his little show was a one-and-done.

Me: Give me a random car fact.

It takes my brother a minute to answer me.

Banks: What the fuck?
Me: Just give me a car fact. Quick.
Banks: What are you doing?
Me: Trying to impress a seven-year-old.
Banks: Do I need to call Mom?

I roll my eyes.

Me: Do I need to call your best friend and ask him to give me a car fact? Because he's the only other person I know that actually knows shit about cars, and I know he'd answer me. *winking emoji*
Banks: I wouldn't do that unless you want to see me break his face.
Me: Then help me.
Banks: Fine. There are more than 30,000 parts in a car. Is that cool enough to impress a toddler?
Me: He's seven. And, come to think of it, you're more of a toddler than he is.
Banks: Yet you're texting me for help. *thinking emoji*
Me: You're useful for once. Congratulations.
Banks: You're welcome.

I shove my phone in my pocket and make my way into the living room. Nate lounges in a chair by the window with Ryder's iPad in his hand. Ryder sits on the floor playing with cars like my brothers used to play with. I settle beside him and wait for an opportunity to bust out my fun car fact.

"Give me the red one," I say, pointing at a red sports car by a random army man.

Ryder hands it to me. "Do you like to play cars?"

"I mean, I don't love it, but I've played my share of cars. One of my brothers loves them."

75

"I love them too. I want to be a mechanic someday."

Nate looks at him over his device and shakes his head.

"Well," I say, sitting a little taller. "You'll have a lot to learn. There are over 30,000 parts in an average car, you know."

His eyes get big. "There are?"

"Yup."

"Wow. I didn't know that."

I look up at Nate to see him snickering. I laugh.

"Maybe I'll do a different job," Ryder says.

"Weren't you going to be a boxer or something last week?" Nate asks him.

"I forgot about that. But maybe I should be a firefighter. There aren't 30,000 parts to that, are there?"

I shrug. "I don't know, but you can't let that scare you out of being a mechanic. There will be lots of things to learn no matter what you do."

He runs his car up my shin bone. "What are you going to do when you're big?"

"Me?" I laugh. "I'm already big. But I'm in college to be a social worker."

"What's that?"

"Well, they help little kids and families with different things," I say.

He looks up at me and grins. "You'll be good at that."

His compliment warms my heart.

"Thank you, buddy," I say.

Nate leans forward and hands Ryder his device.

"You better get your shower, kiddo," Nate says. "Use soap and wash your nasty feet."

Ryder hops up, turns around in a sort of spiral, then runs to his room while making car sounds.

I lean back with my hands behind me on the rug and look at Nate. I'm not sure if he's going to walk out of the room now that we're alone or if he's going to act like nothing happened ... or if he's going to address it.

"You've been awfully quiet tonight," he says.

"I have?"

He shrugs.

Very perceptive of you, Nate. "Kinsley gave me a lot to think about today."

He rests his elbows on his knees and laces his fingers together. "What about?"

"Honestly? Self-sabotaging." I get up from the floor and sit on the couch. The power was too lopsided with me on the ground. "She made some good points that I've been mulling over."

"She thinks you self-sabotage? In what way?"

I don't know if I want to talk about this with you.

I watch him for a long time. The shower turns on, and Ryder begins to sing a song about getting lucky. *That's a topic for a different day.*

"Kinsley thinks that I purposely pick guys who are bad for me."

"I think she's right."

I flinch. "What? You do?"

He makes a face. "You can't tell me that you really thought Atticus Jones was a good match for you. Hell, Paige. He has a rap sheet as long as my arm."

"I didn't know that."

"Then do better research. I thought that's what women do. They went online and found out everything they wanted to know about a guy."

"That's a misogynistic statement, sir." *True, but still.*

He rolls his eyes. "What do you think about that? Do you think you do that?"

Do I?

I take a long, deep breath and blow it out slowly. My heart beats faster than I'd like it to. It makes me nervous. Or maybe the nerves came first, and the erratic heartbeat is a reaction. I don't know.

"If I do it, it's not a conscious thing," I say honestly. "I can't deny the facts of the situation. It definitely looks like I pick the same type of guy repeatedly, and obviously, that doesn't work out."

"Why do you think you do that?"

"I don't know," I say, the answer almost a whine.

I don't want to have this conversation with Nate. But I know that if I don't give him this—*open up to him*—then he won't open up to me. And if there's one thing I've learned over the last eight months of working with Nate Hughes, it's that I value his opinion. And right now, I need to know what he's thinking.

"I don't know if I believe in forever," I say.

The words flow from my mouth well before I realize I'm going to say it. It's like my guard slipped, and my brain took advantage of the moment.

The problem is that I've been mulling it over and over since Kinsley drove off earlier. *What does forever look like? Is it really even feasible? Is it real?*

Does love actually work that way?

I gulp. *Would anyone ever want me for that long anyway?*

Nate's eyes widen. "Really? You don't believe in forever?"

"Look, my life has been ... a lot of things, okay? My first nine years were either a shit show or in foster care—which also was a shit show sometimes. And I've never seen anything that lasted forever. My parents didn't love me forever. I haven't had Hollis in my life forever. I haven't had the Carmichaels either. I don't even have a baby picture of me. So why should I buy into the idea that anything can last forever?"

I stand, needing to move. Nate watches me like a caged tiger.

"I've never been the little girl to imagine a big wedding or a houseful of kids," I admit. "I just remember lying in a bedroom with blue-and-white checkered curtains and crying myself to sleep because I was alone. I felt detached from myself. I didn't know the family downstairs, and Hollis, my protector, was gone. And I never wanted to feel that again."

Nate's face sobers. He continues to watch me pace the room. I move around until the hollowness in my chest starts to fill, and I can breathe easily again. Then I turn to look at him.

He's so handsome. There's a tenderness in his eyes that could elicit tears if I let it. I just want to hug him—to have him hold me, but I can't do that.

Why would I do that? What would be the point? He's not my type, which means letting him hold me would end in destruction. I know that. I can't and won't let him hurt me like that.

You don't give them your heart ... It's why I pick the men I do.

"So maybe I do self-sabotage to avoid heartbreak." I shrug. "What about you?"

"What about me?"

I wait until his eyes lock with mine.

"Why do you do one thing and then say another?" I ask. "That feels a little like self-sabotage too."

He gets to his feet, running his hands down his thighs. "I'll be really honest with you."

"Please do."

"I know what you're getting at. I've given off mixed signals, and that's not right."

My heart thunders in my chest. I swear he can hear it.

"Paige, look ..." He groans, running a hand through his hair. "My life is work and my kid. And my other part-time job at Landry Security. If I get serious about someone, it's because I want forever with them."

Oh.

"I've run around. I've dated. I've done all of it, and Ryder is seven now and impacted by all of that shit. And, quite frankly, I'm tired. I just want to settle down and maybe have another kid or two and build something together."

"I can understand that," I say, gulping a mouthful of hot saliva.

He steps toward me but stops. "I'm attracted to you. *Clearly.* Some days, it's all I think about."

Really? I shift my weight from one foot to the other.

"But here's my conundrum—if something happens between us, it's for naught. It's only for a fleeting moment because I want forever, and you're running from it," he says, his words ringing with truth.

My spirits sink.

"And we can't be a fleeting moment because if I touch you— really touch you, it would change things permanently." He grins sadly. "I couldn't stand to see someone else have you after that. We'd lose our friendship too. You'd have to get a new job. It would just suck."

"Yeah," I say, nodding like I'm not at all screwed up over what he just said. "Good points."

They *are* good points. And he's right. Not one piece of me wants to even pretend I want to get married or have a kid or raise someone else's kid. That's for other people. Not me.

How can I be mad when he's being honest? How can I be upset when he's actually being thoughtful by being open with me and laying it all out there?

So I know nothing will ever happen between us.

"That moment in the kitchen was impulsive, and I shouldn't have gone there," he says. "It messed with your head, and I'm sorry."

"No. I'm fine," I lie. "I mean, I was unsure what you were thinking or whatever, so I'm glad to know. That helps. A lot."

"Paige, I'm sorry."

"Stop apologizing." My cheeks heat. "Everything is fine. We're on the same wavelength now so that's good. But on that note, in the spirit of being transparent with no manipulation involved ..."

He half-grins.

"Do you want me to move out now? It's not a problem if you do."

He sighs. "I want us to still be friends. I want you to work for me, and I want to be in your life. Like we have been. Okay?"

I take a giant breath and hold it in my chest. I do want to be friends with him. That's been the best part of what we've had. It's the core of who we are—the reason we could flirt so harmlessly and tease one another. I don't want to lose that either.

But I have to get our dynamic back.

"I hate to tell you," I say, shrugging. "We can definitely be friends, but I'm going to have to start flirting with someone else. Maybe Murray."

He stiffens but forces a smile on his face. "Good luck with that."

"I wonder how he'll take seeing me in my panties."

I don't wait for his reaction. I just turn around, grin, and walk to my room.

Chapter 11

Nate

"Are you all right?" Murray asks, standing on the other side of the kitchen with his hands on his hips.

"Yeah. I'm fine. Why wouldn't I be?"

Because I told Paige we should just be friends.

"You're just quiet. That's abnormal for you," he says.

Try introspective.

I don't respond out loud, and instead, I focus on putting away the vegetables fresh from the delivery truck.

"You know, you're always borderline irritable," Murray says. "But I can usually figure out why based on what's happening around here."

Irritable? I'd go with frustrated.

"Yet you've managed to hold your fuse very well. I usually get you to explode by this point when I poke at ya."

It's all this brand-new self-restraint I found.

My mind switches easily—way too easily—to the subject of my irritation. My frustration. *My fucking demise.* A chill ripples slowly down my spine as a series of images, almost like a photograph, plays through my memories.

Paige's cheeky grin. Her big, brown eyes that I now know turn almost golden when she's turned on.

My balls tighten so hard I grimace.

The slight gasp when her finger slid into my mouth and the rush of breath when I released it.

Dammit.

I clench my teeth together and close the cooler door. Then I turn to him.

"Is that what you want?" I ask, looking him in the eye. "Do you want me to blow up on you? Because I can. I can take all this *irritability* you say I have and just spew it across this kitchen. You want to see that?"

Instead of taking the hint and backing down, Murray does the opposite. He flashes me the smile that gets him re-hired at least once a month.

It reminds me of Ryder, in a way. It's the same sort of move he pulls on me when he knows I'm pissed. Apparently, I'm a sucker for it.

Lucky for Murray.

"Do I want you to blow up on me?" He points at himself. "No, man. I was trying to be a gentleman and extract information without actually putting you on the spot. Like prying with a spoon instead of a crowbar."

I stare at him. "First, that's a stupid analogy."

"I thought it was brilliant, especially considering we're in a kitchen."

"Second," I say, undeterred from my opinion. "Prying with a crowbar would be more effective and cause less damage than prying anything with a spoon."

This satisfies him. He grins. "Okay. Crowbar it is. How's it going living with Paige?"

His eyes meet mine with a steadiness that I think I taught him. When he first started here, he was a squirrelly little shit with no backbone and a big mouth. He's still foolish and has a huge mouth, but he's growing a backbone.

Next lesson—when to use it and when to back off.

"You better mind your business," I say.

"You're my boss, and she's my co-worker. You're like family to me, man."

I roll my eyes.

"What kind of dude would I be if I didn't care about Paige's health and safety? Not one my mama would be proud of."

"Murray? Shut up."

I don't know if I just didn't consider everyone would find out it or if I didn't care. *Par for the course because I obviously didn't think the entire premise of Paige staying with me out too much either.*

Either way, I wasn't ready for this to come up in conversation.

Blowing out a breath, I lean against the cooler. Murray faces me on the other side of the kitchen and waits. *Bastard.*

"Is she staying with you permanently? Like, are you guys now a thing—"

"No. It's not like that. We're friends. I'm just helping her out like I would you."

"I hope to God you wouldn't do things to me that I bet you're doing to her late at night."

"Murray," I warn.

He chuckles. "So you're friends. I'm supposed to believe that?"

"I don't give a flying fuck what you believe. It's none of your business."

"True. It's not. But I will say that I'm glad you let her stay with you. I'm not surprised because that's the kind of guy you are. And Paige, well, Paige is probably safer with you than any of the savages she usually entertains."

I shove off the cooler and pick up a box of to-go condiments. "I didn't know you cared so much when it came to Paige. As much hell as you give her, I thought you hated her."

"Sometimes I do." He picks up another box and follows me into the storeroom. "She's just ... I don't know. When she's here, you can't get away from her. She has her hands in everything, and once she gets an idea in her head, you can't tell the girl no."

Don't I know it.

My body aches from fighting that very thing—from fighting her. I've never experienced this before, this inability to satisfy an urge. *Especially when the urge wants to satisfy me too.*

It takes everything I have to remind myself repeatedly, *hourly*, that I made the right call. I can't give in and level up our relationship from a friendship to ... whatever it would be because it would be a disaster in the making. The next person I see will be with the intention of making it forever. That's not Paige's modus operandi. *She told me as much.*

Part of what she said stayed with me throughout another mostly sleepless night.

I've never seen anything that lasted forever. I don't even have a baby picture of me. So why should I buy into the idea that anything can last forever?

And I also know that if I did try something with her, if—*when*— things ended, I'd lose our friendship. Because if I couldn't have her at that point, there's no way in hell I could watch some other dude have her. I'd have to exile her from my life.

That whole scenario pisses me off already.

Murray chuckles. "But you can't really *hate* Paige."

"Yeah."

"I mean, she's hot. She's hilarious. She does a damn good job here even though I'd never tell her that."

I look at him curiously.

"And she's nice. I mean that." He pulls his brows together, forming a bunch of wrinkles in his forehead. "She's super helpful, and she'd give you the shirt off her back. *There's something I'd like to see,*" he says, chuckling and nearly getting himself punched in the face by me. "But she's also solid. Like, old-school she'd go to jail for you if she loved you. You know?"

"Yeah."

He grins. "You're saying *yeah* a lot today."

"Yeah—*shut up.*" I shake my head. "Put that box over there by the rice."

I set the condiments on a shelf next to the cherry syrup.

"Shit. I forgot to make an order of onion rings. Be right back," he says, jetting by me on the way to the kitchen.

What the hell? Murray can blab the hell on about Paige like he's a fucking psychologist, but the man can't remember to order onion rings?

I groan. *I can't keep doing this.*

Why does it have to be so hard?

I take a deep, heavy breath and try to release some of the pressure building in my chest.

"Just hold yourself together," I mutter, running a hand down my jaw. "She'll be out of there before I know it."

The thought creates a pang in the center of my chest. I shrug out of it as fast as I can.

Footsteps refocus my attention and I look up to see Murray stick his head in the doorway.

"Onion rings are done and so am I," he says. "You need anything else from me before I leave?"

"I don't know. Did you do the check-off list after your shift?"

"Yes, boss."

I roll my eyes. "Did you bleach the sink?"

"Yes."

"Did you restock everything?" I ask.

"Yes."

"Did you sweep the kitchen and see if the bar needs anything before you go?"

Murray sighs. "Yes. And Kira is already here to take over, so there's two of us on the clock right now."

"Then I guess you can head home."

He steps into the doorway, stuffing one hand in his jeans. The bastard doesn't even try to wipe the smile off his face. "And you're heading home to Paige?"

"Question—do you want to get fired today or save it for later this week?"

His laughter is loud. I try hard not to find amusement in his reaction but fail.

"Get the hell outta here," I say, walking toward him. I grab his shoulder and give it a good shake. "Thanks for helping me with the delivery."

"No problem. See ya tomorrow, boss."

"Later."

He stops to clock out, and I head for the bar. I round the corner and see Joe sitting in his prized spot at the end. I say hello to a few regular customers as I make my way toward the old man.

His requisite ivy cap is propped on his head, white hair poking out from beneath it. He sees me coming and smiles a wide, toothless smile.

"Look who decided to work today," he says, his voice much louder than necessary.

"Hey, Joe. What's happening, man?" I rest my arms on the bar top across from him. "Did you get some coffee?"

"Yeah, and you're still chargin' me a quarter. Can you believe that? It's a rip-off if I've ever seen one."

He winks at me, the hollows of his cheeks sinking into his mouth.

"We gotta make money somewhere," I tease. "I have a kid to pay for."

"What have you been doing today? I heard you back there," he says, motioning toward the kitchen. "But they said you were busy."

"We had a big delivery come in today. And you know how it goes. If you don't do it yourself—"

"It won't get done right." He shakes his head in disgust. "Don't I know it. Back when I worked on the railroad, I was the only one gettin' anything done around there. People these days are lazy. They don't know how to put in a day's work anymore."

87

"Eh, I have a pretty good crew around here. I can't complain too much."

He shrugs. "They're okay. I miss that dark-headed girl. Where'd she go?"

I close my eyes. *Why is everyone wanting to talk about her today? And why doesn't he realize that he was the one that was gone for over a month?*

"You know, the sassy one. The one like this." Joe outlines an hourglass in the air with his hands. "What happened to her?"

"He knows who you mean," Kira says over my shoulder. She bumps my hip with hers. "Hi, Nate."

"Hi, Kira."

"Paige!" Joe smacks the bar top with his fist. "That's her name. Paige."

"She's still here. She's had a couple of days off. You were the one missing for over a month."

Kira clears her throat. "Speaking of that, I'm supposed to be in the kitchen tonight, and Jaycee just called off for out here. Sick kid or grandparent or something. I don't know. What do you want to do?"

If Paige is here and I'm at home, that would give me a bit of a respite.

"I'll call Paige," I say.

"Well, on that note, I'll have another cup of coffee," Joe says, smiling. "Gotta get my quarter's worth."

I sigh. "See you later, Joe." I start toward my office. Once I get to Kira, I lower my voice. "Get him a sandwich, please."

"Will do."

I get to my office, close the door behind me, and sit at my desk. I swear I can still smell Paige's perfume lingering in the air as I take out my phone.

Me: Any chance you can work the bar tonight?
Paige: Yes, of course. What time?

Me: Kira is by herself now, so whenever you can get here would be great. Should be dead until five thirty or six anyway.

Paige: Let me change, and I'll be there.

I bite my knuckle so hard I almost yelp.

Me: I'm heading to Mrs. Kim's to pick up Ryder then going home. We'll probably cross paths.

Paige: Just remember I might be home after curfew. But don't worry. You won't see me naked.

Fucking hell, Paige.
But before I can respond, she fires off another message.

Paige: Phone is dying. Tell Kira I'll be there soon. *waving emoji*

Damn this girl.

Chapter 12

Paige

A bead of sweat rolls down my spine.

The back of my Illinois Legends T-shirt—the one I modified to a more form-fitting, sexier style for work because ... *tips*—is damp from the chaos of the night. My legs are on fire, and I wish I would've worn my other pair of sneakers. But my tip jar is full, the bar has slowed down, and the handsome stranger in the brown flannel is still sitting at the end.

Waiting on me to have a moment to talk, perhaps.

I consider not chatting with him because I'm feeling kind of cranky, but then think—*why the hell not? It's not like I have a man to consider.*

"What about you?" I ask, tapping my fingernails against the bar as I approach him. "You need anything else?"

He looks me up and down, his lips parting into a smirk. "Dangerous question."

I laugh. "Well, it wasn't intended to be dangerous."

He grins. "What's your name, anyway?"

"Paige. Yours?"

"Griffin."

"Cute."

"Hey, Paige!"

I look up to see Robbie waving at me from under the television. He's one of my favorite regulars—always in a good mood, always friendly, and always hungry. Even now, at close to closing time.

"What's up, Robbie?" I ask.

"Can I get some of those little tacos when you get a chance? And if you tell me that Nate forgot to stock them again ..." He presses a fist into his other hand.

I laugh. "I think we have some." I turn back to Griffin. "If you need anything, just shout."

He lifts his beer and tips it my way. It *almost* hides his smirk.

I give him a lingering smile before turning away.

I'm glad Nate texted me to work because I was considering how to get out of the house so I didn't have to see him. *Maybe he was having the same feelings.* Either way, it works for me.

It took me all day to talk myself into a mode of acceptance. There's nothing to be upset about. I just need to treat Nate like a friend—*and he is a good friend*—and move on. That's all. Easy peasy. Ish.

"Hi," Kira says as I enter the kitchen.

I sigh.

"What's going on?" she asks.

Nate. "Nothing much."

"Who is the hot guy at the end of the bar?" she asks. "I came out there to grab a Coke and spotted him."

"Oh, yes. Griffin is his name. Very cute. Has been quiet and patient, which is a plus."

"And, of course, he wants you, doesn't he?"

She throws a pickle at me. I dodge it easily and then pick it up off the floor.

"I don't know if he wants me or if he's being polite. He hasn't said anything to me," I say. "Chill out."

"You can't have all the guys, Paige. You already have Nate."

My insides shrink. *This isn't going to be fun.*

"Nate and I aren't a thing," I say flatly. "I'm just staying at his house until I find an apartment."

"*Oh.*"

"Yeah. We're just friends. Nothing else. Like, facts on facts on facts."

She nods. "Okay. Sorry. I shouldn't have assumed."

"No worries," I say, heading back to the bar. "Robbie wants mini tacos. Okay? I didn't write it down."

"I got ya."

I grab a clean towel and wipe the bar down—starting at one end and working my way to the other.

I might have to get a new job.

I don't think I can work with Nate or listen to everyone assume we're an item. It's embarrassing, given the circumstances.

Last night's conversation was probably the first *real* conversation that addressed our ... situation. Nate might be attracted *to* me, but he doesn't actually *want* me.

He doesn't want me.

I had no idea that everyone here assumed something was between us. If I had, I wouldn't have begged to stay at his place. Knowing that Kira thought we were a done deal is just ... so uncomfortable.

If Nate doesn't want to see me with other men, then I sure as hell don't want to see him with the one. *The long-term woman he wants to settle down with.*

So new job, new apartment ... new me? Well, I guess that answers that.

"Tacos are coming, Robbie," I say.

He gives me a thumbs-up and resumes watching the sports program on the television.

I can feel Griffin's gaze on me as I get closer. I try to shake all things Nate out of my head. *He's just my friend.*

"Can I buy you a drink?" Griffin asks as I stop in front of him.

"Can't drink on the job."

He leans forward. "Well, I guess that just means I'll have to take you out for a drink then."

Griffin looks at me like he wants to lick every inch of my body. And if my body's reaction is any indication, it's game. That or it's in a perpetual state of want from being in proximity to Nate all the damn time.

I rest my torso against the countertop. The position makes my cleavage peek out through the slit I cut in the front of my shirt. I pop my ass because I need a boost of confidence and lean toward Griffin.

His eyes sparkle. "Damn, you're beautiful."

"Thank you."

"So can I take you out? *Say yes.* Don't ruin my night."

I laugh. "That's an awfully big responsibility you just pinned on me if I could ruin your whole entire night."

"You've given me an awfully *big* problem tonight too." He reaches under the bar and widens his eyes. "So can I take you out sometime?"

"What would we do?" I ask, figuring it doesn't hurt to see what kind of guy he is.

I'm on the market, after all. And after a quick perusal, he doesn't come across as my type. It could work.

"We can do anything you want, baby."

"I—"

I jump, but I don't turn around. I don't have to. Even if Griffin didn't look like he'd seen a ghost—or in this case a six-foot tall bar owner with what I can only imagine is a glare, at best, on his face—I'd know from the scent of Nate's cologne.

And also from the feeling of his hands gripping my waist on either side.

What's Nate doing here?

I try to stand, but his fingers dip deeper into my waist. He holds me just like he found me and watches Griffin over my back.

Griffin, the man who was just seconds ago the hero in this

scenario, has faded quickly into the background. Nate is now the main character.

My insides liquify as he holds me so tight that I can't move, but his grip is not to the point of actual pain. It's a delicious kind of burn, a heat so hot and so intense that I lose my breath for a moment.

"You need anything else?" Nate asks, his voice trembling with what I think is fury.

Oh, shit.

Griffin looks at me and then back at Nate. He stands and takes his wallet out of his back pocket. A few bills are laid on the counter.

He walks out without another word.

Nate's grip releases just enough that I spin around. The freedom lights something inside me.

"What the hell was that?" I ask him, giving his glower back to him.

"I was going to ask you the same damn thing."

Out of the corner of my eye, I see Kira take Robbie his tacos.

Nate and I stand eye to eye for what feels like forever before either one of us gives in. He's the one who breaks.

He takes my elbow and leads me toward his office. I jerk my arm away—getting a glare over the shoulder from him in return—but follow him nonetheless. Kira signals to me that she has things under control as we slip by the kitchen.

As soon as my ass is through the door, Nate slams it behind me.

"You know what?" I say, pointing a finger at him. "Check yourself."

"Excuse me?" He closes the distance between us. "*I* need to check *myself*? Come again?"

"I was hoping to *come again,* but you just scared him off."

His eyes go wide, but he doesn't move. Doesn't recoil. Doesn't hiccup so much as a breath to cut the tension between us.

Damn him.

"What are you doing here anyway?" I ask.

"What were you going to do, Paige? Were you gonna let that little rat bastard take you out and bend you over the hood of his car?"

"Maybe. What's it to you, *friend?*"

"Are you just trying to piss me off?"

"*I didn't even know you were here.*"

His chest rumbles with anger.

"You don't get to do this, Nate. You don't get to friend zone me and then come in here and act like I'm out of line for getting some guy's number."

"You got his number?"

"Yeah. And his condom size, if it matters."

Both are lies. I don't know why I even said that but fuck him for doing this. He deserves to be pissed.

His nostrils flare, and it would be super hot if I wasn't so angry.

"Tread lightly," he warns me.

"Or what? What are you going to do? Because I'll tell you what you're *not* going to do. You're not going to see me bent over the hood of *your car*. Because we're friends, which is fine. It's grand. Thank you for being honest about that and not leading me on." I suck in a hasty breath. "But being friends means that you have no say in what I do or who I date. What do you expect me to do? Live my life chaste because you don't want me? Fuck off."

Admitting that out loud to him kills a small part of my soul, but I march on because I'm no quitter. Especially when I'm mad.

"Oh, I know what you're going to do," I say, lifting my chin in defiance. "You're going to just police my dates, aren't you? Sit on the porch with a baseball bat, right, Daddy—*ooh!*"

Nate's hands cup both sides of my head a split second before his mouth crushes against mine. Our bodies are so close that there's no room for even a feather. He moves his lips against mine so assertively —as if he were afraid that I might miss the moment.

I sag against him, overtaken by the sensations rippling through my body. The heat of his breath. The softness of his tongue. The calluses on his thumbs as he presses them into my cheeks.

The smell of his cologne and the taste of peppermint on his lips. How deliciously solid his chest is and how rock hard his cock is pressed against my stomach.

My knees go weak. My nipples are hard. My legs are so heavy they're almost unable to hold me up.

Finally, Nate pulls back and rests his forehead against mine. We struggle to breathe.

We struggle to make sense of what just happened.

He kissed me.

What. The. Actual. Fuck.

"Why don't you go on back to the house? I'll help Kira close up," he says as he pulls away from me.

What?

"Mrs. Kim took Ryder to see her daughter and her grandkids for dinner," he says. "You can have the house to yourself for a little while."

"I ... Oh. Okay." I shake my head as if the movement will jar my senses back into place. "That's what you want to say right now?"

He shrugs as if there's nothing else to say, but his eyes betray him.

"I don't know what this was tonight," I say, pointing at him. "But it better not happen again."

"Paige ..."

I have no clue what he's about to say, but I know that sticking around here isn't going to end well. Not tonight.

"Bye," I say, walking past him like he didn't just give me the best kiss of my damn life.

I don't turn around. I don't look back at him. I just get my purse, clock out, and head home.

Chapter 13

Paige

"*Don't take challenges you can't win.*"

I stare at the ceiling as the bright morning sunlight streams through the windows. Birds chirp happily on the big branch that almost leads directly to my room. If I close my eyes and ignore my headache from going to bed pissed, I can almost be happy.

But I can't do that. I'm still mad.

I rip the blankets off my body and get to my feet. I don't stretch like I usually do, and I don't try to find something cute to wear because I'll likely run into Nate this morning.

Fuck that and fuck him.

I don't want to be mad at him. Heck, he's giving me a place to stay. But the way he acted last night and then avoided me when he got home? Not cool. Not cool at all.

Me: I'm going to look for apartments today. Wanna come with?

Kinsley's message comes through almost immediately with *yes* in all capital letters.

"Awesome."

I throw my phone on the bed. Then I throw on a white tank top and a pair of pink joggers with a word printed on the ass. And then, because I can't remember what the word says, and I don't have a mirror, I grab a lightweight robe out of my bag and slide it on too.

The sound of cartoons trickling through the house reminds me that it's Saturday—which explains why Kinsley had the day off. *I didn't even think about that.* I head into the kitchen for a glass of juice. Just as I open the fridge, the sound of little feet pattering against the hardwood gets closer and closer.

"Hi." Ryder sticks his head under the refrigerator door, grinning ear to ear. "How are you today?"

"I just got up, so I'm a little slow still."

"Oh." He ducks as I close the door. "You know what helps you not feel slow? Do you know what *speeds you up?*"

Nothing fit for a child.

"No," I say, pouring myself a glass of orange juice. "Do you want some?"

He nods. "Well, I know something that makes you feel speedy."

"What's that?"

His eyes twinkle. He hops onto a barstool and smiles. "Pancakes!"

"Really?"

"Yup. And there's a yellow container in the pantry of pancake mix. You just add water to it and shake it up like this." He pretends to play the maracas in the air. "Just like that."

Despite my shitty mood, I can't help but laugh at the cutie.

"Is this your way of saying you want pancakes?" I ask him.

"Well, you see, I'm not supposed to ask you to make me pancakes."

I sip my juice, curious. "Oh, really?"

"Dad said you're our guest, and I can't ask you to do things for me."

He did, did he?

98

"But I'm not asking you to make one *for me*. I'm just telling you pancakes would make *you* feel better, and if you make an extra one, that's not my fault," he says.

"You know what? Someday, you should go into politics. You're very persuasive."

"I don't know what politics is."

"It's where ..." *Adults get on television and lie to the public.* "It's the people who make the rules. You know, the government."

He curls his little nose. "I don't think so. I want to work on cars or fight people like my uncle Dominic."

"I don't think that's what he does for a living. Doesn't he work in security?"

"Yeah, but if anyone gets out of line, he'll go like this," he says before throwing some decent punches in the air. "See what I mean?"

"I do."

He nods, the gesture a punctuation mark on his point. It makes me smile.

"Now, you still feelin' those pancakes or what?" he asks.

I tip my head back and laugh. The action feels nice. It actually manages to remove some of the irritation left in my shoulders.

Ryder hops off the stool and comes around the counter. He rummages around the cabinets, procuring a skillet. He places it on the stove and then retrieves his pancake mix.

"Here," he says, handing me the yellow container. "I'd just make it myself, but Dad thinks I'm too young to operate the stove without an adult."

I look at the mix and sigh. *Guess we're making pancakes.*

"You can throw a big punch, but I think your dad is right about the stove," I say. "Better leave that to the adults for a while."

"But what could happen? I do a good job at dinner every night."

I grab a bowl from beneath the counter. As I stand, a chill rushes through my body.

My eyes squeeze closed as a flurry of memories flashes through my mind.

A kitchen decorated with orange and yellow mushrooms. A white towel with black lines. Reaching for the handle and—my eyes pop open.

I look at my right forearm. The scar is long gone, but I remember it being there. *From the grease.*

A shiver shimmies down the length of my body, and I wonder if this is a natural reaction to shrug off bad memories.

"You do a good job at dinner," I say before clearing my throat. "But you could accidentally knock something off and hurt yourself." I take a deep breath. "I did that when I was a little kid."

"You did?"

I nod.

A wash of emotions fills me up.

The stale cigarette smoke. Powdered drinks with no sugar and the tartness of it on my tongue. The chipped paint on the windowsills as I stare out the window, waiting for Hollis to come home.

A pang of sadness hits me in the chest, and I place a hand over my heart.

Go away.

"Where was your mom at?" he asks.

Who the hell knows?

I turn toward Ryder to change the subject but stop when I see the look in his eye. It's one I know well, one that few can relate to. And although I don't want to talk about my birth mother at all—I've blocked much of it out—it could help this little boy.

His smile wobbles.

Dammit.

I force a swallow. "Well, actually, my mom was standing right there."

"And you still got hurt?"

I scan the instructions and add the correct amount of mix and water to the bowl. Strangely, the routine of making pancakes is comforting.

"My mom ..." *How do I do this?* My heart starts to pound. *How do I tell him my mother was an addict?* "My mom was sick. And sometimes she didn't take very good care of me."

I look at Ryder over my shoulder. He's watching me with a completely blank face.

"Like my mom?" he asks.

His little voice is softer and sounds so much more like a seven-year-old than he does when he's talking Mustangs or right crosses. It breaks my heart.

"I don't really know what happened to your mom," I say gently, trying to tread carefully with Ryder. Nate told me what happened to her, but I don't know what Ryder knows, and I'm not about to hurt him.

"She was sick. That's what my daddy tells me. She was sick and went to heaven, and I'll see her there."

I blink back the tears that pool in the corners of my eyes. *Oh, you poor, sweet boy.*

"My mom was sick too. But I didn't have a daddy like you do. Mine was ..." *In prison.* "Gone. So I was adopted by a new family. Do you know what that means?"

He nods slowly, his bottom lip trembling. "So if something happens to my daddy someday, I'll have to be adopted by a new family too?"

Shit.

"No," I say, walking to him. I have no idea what to do. *What do you do with a crying kid?* I stick my arm out, and he falls into my side, wrapping his arms around me. "I don't want to be adopted."

I pull him close and hug him tighter than I think I've ever hugged anyone in my life. It's as though if I can hug him tight enough, I can put him back together.

"You have all kinds of people who love you," I say softly. "You have your uncle Dominic, right? And your aunt." *With the baking name.*

"Camilla Vanilla."

"Yes. Camilla Vanilla." I swallow the lump in my throat. "But you don't even need to be thinking about things like this, buddy."

He pulls away and looks up at me. His big brown eyes are watery. "I do worry sometimes that something will happen to my dad. I don't have a mom. I only have a dad."

"But you have a great dad. He loves you *so much,* and I know he's extra safe when he's not here because he wants to come home and see you."

"He does?"

I smile at him. "He does." I ruffle his hair. "And that's the difference between your dad and my dad. My dad wasn't a very nice person. But your dad is a very, *very* good man and wants you to be happy. You just make sure you're always safe and good because your daddy only has one little boy."

Ryder pulls away, the tears dried up. "Maybe I'll get a brother someday."

"Maybe." I turn back to the stove and prepare it for the pancakes. "Or maybe you'll get lucky and get a sister."

"Maybe we could adopt one like you. Can we adopt you?"

My heart swells. "No, I'm too old to be adopted. And I was already adopted once. I have a mom and dad."

"So you had two of them?"

"Yeah. Kind of."

"Well, we'd totally adopt you. Wouldn't we, Dad?"

Huh?

I turn around to see Nate standing in the doorway. He has on a pair of black shorts that hang off his hips *just so* and extend down to his knees.

And that's it. That's all the bastard is wearing to see me for the first time since he kissed me and then ignored me.

I waited up to see if he would come by my room, but he didn't. I didn't even hear him come in. Mrs. Kim came over with Ryder when I got home, and I told her to leave him. I tucked him in, and then I drifted off to sleep at three, and Nate wasn't home yet.

He watches me with an unreadable look on his face. I don't know how to respond to that, so I turn back to the stove and don't give him the satisfaction of a reaction.

"Right, Dad? We'd adopt Paige, huh?" Ryder asks again.

"I thought I told you not to ask her to make you breakfast," Nate says as he tickles his son.

Ryder giggles. "I didn't ask her! I didn't! Stop!"

His squeals make me smile.

"She wanted to make pancakes because she needed speeded up," Ryder explains.

I close my eyes and groan internally.

"Then she said she'd make me one too," he continues. "So there's nothing wrong with that."

Nate stands next to me and leans against the cabinet. He faces Ryder, giving me a full view of his ripped abdomen and broad shoulders.

But I don't look at that. When I do look up at him, he's watching me carefully.

"Do you want one?" I ask.

He holds my gaze for a long moment. I hold my breath the entire time. Finally, he speaks.

"No," he says before shoving off the counter. "Ryder, guess who called me this morning?"

"Who?"

"Camilla. She wants to take you to the Landry Farm today. Do you want to go?"

"Yes! Please? Can I?"

"Yup. I'm going to get a shower, and then I'll run you to Dominic's. Eat your breakfast and then brush your teeth, okay?"

"Yes. Okay!"

I don't have to turn around to know that Nate left the room. *I can breathe again.*

My heart thumps in my chest, and my brain goes into overdrive.

What the hell does that mean? Did he orchestrate that? Does he have to work?

Is it a coincidence?

I stack two pancakes on a plate and place it in front of Ryder.

"Here you go," I say, smiling.

After I've turned off the stove, I pop the pancake mix back into the fridge. No matter how speedy Ryder thinks they make me feel, I cannot even face one right now.

Ryder jumps off the stool and grabs a bottle of syrup out of the pantry. "I've got this. No worries."

"No worries," I repeat as I watch him get situated again. I open the syrup and pour a little star shape onto his pancake. "I'm going to get ready. I have a few things I have to do today, okay?"

He shoves a huge forkful of pancake into his mouth. "'Kay."

I head into the hallway toward my room.

"Thanks for the pancake, Paige Stage!"

I close my bedroom door and then lean against it and sigh.

I have to get out of here.

Chapter 14

Paige

"Ooh, that's cold." I grab the door handle and tug it open. "You first."

Kinsley puts her head down and scoots inside Stretch, the yoga studio we frequent. I follow quickly behind.

The studio is warm and smells like orange and cedarwood—two scents that invigorate and relax me. I take a long, calming breath and smile at Mallory.

"Hey," I say as we take off our shoes.

"Hey! It's good to see you again. It's been a while."

Mallory Landry, the owner of Stretch, is quite possibly the prettiest person I've ever met. She's tall with perfect chestnut-colored hair and has the best smile the world has ever seen. She's also ridiculously kind and funny.

"I know. I ... had *a thing* happen," I say, relieved to know that she won't press. She never does. I don't want to have to go into the eviction with her. "You know how *things* go."

She laughs. "I do. Especially super-vague things that will make me think you really ran off to be a superhero and then came back to play your normal person role."

"That's me. Superhero."

"That's all we need," Kinsley says. "Paige thinking she's Superwoman."

Mallory waves at us and then answers a call.

Kinsley and I get our things situated and then find a spot in the far corner. Thankfully, the session we chose is pretty empty.

I sit on my mat and reach for my toes. My back cracks, releasing the stress from the past couple of days. *Really just the last day.*

"What did you think about that last place we looked at?" Kinsley asks.

I remember the one-bedroom unit we stumbled upon just a few blocks over. It's above a coffee shop near Halcyon, a trendy little boutique that I'm obsessed with. We had wrapped looking at four different places and were going for a quick cup of coffee when we found the available sign in the window.

It felt like kismet. And when we went inside? It felt like an answered prayer.

And a terrific distraction from my anger at Nate.

"It's a great size," Kinsley. "And in a great location."

"And the landlord is super sweet."

The little old lady wearing pearls—Mildred was her name—was a doll. *And I think she liked me.* However, the decision will come from her daughter, who was a little more standoffish.

Fingers crossed.

"I hope they choose me," I say, knowing that they had multiple applications submitted for the space. "I need to get out of Nate's. Stat."

My stomach tightens at the mention of his name. The inside of my body becomes a cacophony of emotions—a harsh discordant mixture of feelings that I can't sift through fast enough to make sense of them.

"Did he ever talk to you?" she asks.

"Ha. Yes, actually. He said exactly one word to me. Wanna guess what it was?"

Her eyes go wide. "I'm afraid to."

"He said *no*." I spread my legs and bend to the side. "There's an irony in that, don't you think?"

"What did he say *no* to you about?"

"Pancakes, of all things. Ryder asked me to make him pancakes," I say, stumbling over the words because he didn't quite ask me, but for all intents and purposes, he did. "Anyway, he stood by me—shirtless, no less—and leaned against the counter. I avoided making eye contact because I had a hot skillet in my hand, and I know my limits."

Kinsley laughs.

"But I asked if he wanted one, and he said *no*. Then went over and talked to Ryder."

"What's his deal?" She moves her legs and bumps my foot in the process. "Sorry. But seriously, Paige, what's going on with him?"

"I have no idea. One minute, he's kind and playful, then the next, he's telling me he'll never touch me again, and the next, he's kissing the hell out of me ..." I squeeze my eyes shut and just let myself relive the kiss for a moment. "And then that shit last night? Hell, no."

My eyes open again, and I look at Kinsley. She's biting her bottom lip, awaiting my rant.

"So which Nate do I believe?" I ask. "Do I believe the guy who wants to be friends? Or the guy who wants to be friends and then orally penetrates me late at night?"

"No. *Never say that again.*"

I laugh. "Or do I believe the guy who just wants to make sure that I never date another man because he and I are friends?"

She holds her temple as if she has a headache too.

I stretch to the other side, irritated that my body is tightening more than it's loosening.

"Maybe Mildred will call you soon, and you can get out of there," Kinsley says. "You know you can always stay with me too."

"Honestly? I might. I'm going to be calm today and look at apartments. Then go back and get a shower, and then I'll find something to do tonight away from the house. I'm going to give him today to talk to me—not that I even really want to hear his excuse if he has one. But if he doesn't even try, then all of it is bullshit, and we aren't friends anyway, and I'll sleep in a cardboard box."

She gasps. "Don't call my place a cardboard box. It's an inch bigger than that."

I laugh and recline back, placing my palms on the mat behind me. The sunshine streaming through the window hits my face. I soak up the rays. *This is all the D I'm going to get, apparently.*

"I'll be right back. Gotta pee," Kinsley says.

I nod but don't move. For the first time since last night, I'm actually comfortable.

"Dad said you're our guest, and I can't ask you to do things for me." Ryder's cute voice echoes through my brain.

Is that why Nate was cold to me this morning? Or was he just a jerk over last night?

I stretch in front of me again and groan. *This is so stupid. I shouldn't have to guess this shit.*

What did I even want from Nate, anyway? I don't know. Besides a safe place to stay, I'm not sure what else I hoped for or expected.

Sure, we flirted. It was fun and definitely a give-and-take sort of scenario. *But did I think anything would come from it?*

Not really. That was part of the fun of it.

But then as we tiptoed to the line of it being a little more than flirting ... I did have hope it could be something else. If I'm being honest with myself, I did kind of have a little spot in the back of my brain that held on to the possibility that the flirting wasn't all for naught.

Being in Nate's orbit is different than any other guy I've been with. He's smart and calm and sensible. He's kind and caring. Not my typical type, which makes my insides wobble.

He's usually all of those things, anyway. Last night he was a giant dick.

Maybe we ruined our friendship, anyway.

My mind goes from Nate to Ryder and the pancakes this morning. I squeeze my eyes shut and replay our exchange. His face is clear in my head. I can visualize the shadow that crept across his eyes as we talked about his mother.

"I did that when I was a little kid."

Why did I say that? I never talk about my life before the Carmichaels with anyone. Well, not with anyone except Hollis, and that's because he understands. I've never shared much about my time with my biological family with anyone. But the words toppled out of my mouth this morning to Ryder like I was talking to a mirror.

I understood him. And I think he connected with me too.

That can't be wrong. Can it?

"This is way too complicated for what it is," I say, getting to my feet.

"What's too complicated?"

I turn around and see Kinsley standing behind me. I make a face, and she grimaces.

"You know what?" I say. "As much as I know you don't have the room and I don't want to sleep on the floor, can I please stay with you until I can find an apartment? Or I can get a hotel room or something."

This isn't good for my sanity.

"You know you can. I've already told you that."

I nod. "I've been thinking about school and how hard it will be to concentrate on that with him walking around. Not to mention how uncomfortable it is in his space." *And how Ryder seems to like me, and I don't want him to be sad when I leave.*

"Can you do me one favor, though?"

"Sure. What?"

"I have a date tonight with Leo. Actually, you can totally come with because we're going to this bar by the beach and it should be a lot of fun. We've been there before. It'll be a reason to get you out of the house."

I frown. "What's the favor?"

"Can you please stay at Nate's one more night? Give me one last hurrah with Leo at my place? It's already planned or else—"

"Speak no more. If I have to, I'll stay in a hotel tonight. I'll call Maddox and get him to pay for it."

She laughs. "I wish I had brothers to help me out."

"It's a trade-off. Trust me."

I look over my shoulder to see the instructor head into the back room for class. "We better get in there."

We pick up our mats and head toward the class.

"So come over tonight around six? Seven, maybe?" Kinsley says. "You can leave your car at my house, and we'll take an Uber. It'll be fun."

"I like the sound of that."

She grins. "Wait until you see Leo's friend, Griffin. He's—"

I stop in my tracks. "Griffin? Like blond hair that spikes up in the front and wears a brown flannel, Griffin?"

"Yeah. Sounds like him. How do you know him?"

I stare at her.

"No." She cocks her head to the side in disbelief. "That's not the guy ... He wasn't the one in The Gold Room, was he?"

"*Yes.*"

"What are the freaking odds of that?" She laughs. "Oh, my gosh."

I cover my face. "He'll probably run. He didn't say a word when Nate came up behind me. I feel so bad."

"This is your chance to explain. It could be a second-chance romance."

"Why does my life just keep getting more complicated? Why can't something just go smoothly?"

She shrugs as I wave to the instructor. Sounds of a rainforest trickle through the speakers. It would be so wonderfully pleasant if I could find anything wonderfully pleasant.

We place our mats on the floor and sit in the center. As the other classmates get situated around us, Kinsley leans in.

"Wear your denim skirt and that white top with the ruffled sleeves. You know which one I mean?" she whispers.

"Yeah."

"And your black booties with the heel."

I shake my head. "Anything else you want me to do?"

"Nope." She leans back and grins. "Just have fun."

Just have fun.

Why does that seem like it's going to be harder than it sounds?

Chapter 15

Nate

I'm such an asshole.

I smack my hand off my steering wheel and growl into the air.

No matter what I do—or what I intend to do—I keep making shit worse. *Why couldn't I have talked to Paige last night when I got home? Why couldn't I have at least been cordial this morning?*

Because you still had fire roaring through your veins at the sight of her talking to that douchebag.

And I was a little embarrassed.

I need to talk to Paige. I need to try to explain myself and, first and foremost, apologize. She's livid, and she has every right to be.

Yet she was still sweet enough to make Ryder pancakes this morning.

My heart squeezes in my chest, and it compounds the guilt riding on my shoulders. Listening to her talk to him while she made him breakfast nearly killed me. She was so gentle with him and handled a tricky topic so well, even sharing a part of her life that she doesn't ever really talk about. *But she opened up to my kid to make him feel better.*

112

Fuck.

I take a left at the stoplight.

What do I say to her? Where do we go from here?

Are we done? Does she see through me and just want to be left alone? Because I wouldn't blame her if she did.

Or is something between us salvageable, and if so, what does that look like?

My stomach churns like it has all night and all day.

I don't know.

I don't see a way of resolving this.

If we stay friends, clearly I won't be able to stand seeing her with another man. Because that kiss? That kiss made every part of me feel alive. The taste of her. Holding her soft cheeks. *Feeling as though she was mine to take.*

It turns out that I don't have to have sex with her to feel territorial. I already feel like she's mine, and no one else deserves her. *Not that I do either.* But at least I know I'd protect her and care for her and not treat her like shit.

Even though that's kind of what I've done lately.

"Fucking hell," I grumble.

But what if we try a relationship together? Would that make any sense?

It really seems like it's that or we never see each other again because I'm not mature enough to handle anything in between.

But there would be no point in trying something with Paige. I want forever, and she's scared of it. *Unless I could get her to see it's possible.*

But could I see forever with her?

All day, I've driven around Savannah and mulled this over. I was going to call Dominic for advice but realized he'd just berate me for being an idiot, and I can do that myself. I've tried to get some space, some fresh air—some perspective. But, if anything, it's made me look at the last eight months and see something quite surreal.

Throughout all the banter and flirting, we've grown close. I've trusted her with things that I rarely give to others. Parts of what makes me, me. I've focused on thinking I want someone mature and stable, but the fact of the matter is—maturity isn't determined by age. Our friendship is ... was solid because we've been real with each other. I allowed her to stay in my house because I trust her with my son, *my world*. And I wouldn't do that with just anybody.

The only time you do that with someone is if you're already in a relationship, right? *Isn't that just perfect.*

And I'm more than pissed because I think I might've blown it.

The fact that she might be gone when I get home has my stomach so tight that I think I might throw up. The very real possibility that she might tell me to fuck off has my palms sweaty. The idea that she might walk out of my life completely feels like a hole has been drilled in my heart, and that's when I know I've already started to see the potential of forever with her.

Do I actually want that? I don't know. Epiphanies can take a while to process, apparently. *And is it even real, considering her take on things?* It's a potential problem.

All I know is I like the idea of my life a whole lot better with her in it than the feel of it without her.

Ryder already loves her, too, so it's not like I'm bringing her into his life for the first time. *I've already pooched that kick.* So maybe if we take it slow, not act like it's a big deal in front of him, it'll be okay.

If she'll even consider it. And if she doesn't ... *Ugh.*

I turn onto my street and then into my driveway. Her car sits in her spot, and seeing it there is a huge relief.

I kill the engine and hop out of my truck, jiggling my keys in my hands as I get to the front door.

Lead with the apology. You have to own what you did last night.

I open the door and step inside. It's quiet. Shutting the door softly behind me, I then measure my steps to find her.

I'm nearly to the living room when I hear a clinking noise behind me. I whirl around just in time to see Paige see me.

Holy. Shit.

All thoughts of apologies and forever go out the window because all I can think about is *right now*.

Her legs are a mile long, the tops of her thighs covered by a piece of denim. A white top hugs her torso with two tiny buttons just under her cleavage. Red lipstick draws attention to her kissable mouth, and it takes me a minute to remember English.

"*Oh*," she says in a way that makes it impossible to distinguish how she feels. She runs a hand through her wavy hair. "I didn't know you were home."

The light catches on her bracelets as she drops her hand.

Remember how to speak. Talk!

I clear my throat.

"Don't worry," she says, heading for the door. "I know you aren't speaking to me."

"Where are you going?"

"*Out*."

Dressed like that? "Where, Paige?"

She pivots on those sexy black boots and tries to rip my soul apart with her glare. It's so cold, so icy that I shiver.

"You know what? Fuck off." She narrows her eyes. "I don't owe you anything while you definitely owe me an apology."

I think she thinks I should apologize for something different than I think I should say I'm sorry for. *And that irritates the hell out of me.*

"What do you want me to apologize for? For not letting you run off with what's-his-face?" I ask, my voice a little louder than I care to admit.

The longer I think about him touching her, the madder I become. Steam rolls out of my ears as I think about that shit's hands touching those tanned legs or worse—what's between them.

He won't care about her. He'll only care about getting a piece of ass and that makes me want to blow. *She's so much more than that.*

Paige laughs angrily. "You didn't *not let me do* anything, bud. You acted like a fool in front of the *whole damn bar* and then thought, *what*? That you could kiss me and dazzle me with your expertise, and

I'd forget the whole damn thing? I don't know who you thought you were dealing with, but you must've forgotten."

She turns toward the door. I leap forward and grab her hand. She flings it off her and faces me, her fingers clenching at her sides.

"I didn't forget who I was dealing with. I know exactly who I was dealing with, and that's why I stepped in," I say.

"Well, I'm on my way to see Griffin tonight. What are you going to do about that?"

"Dressed like that?"

"Hopefully not for long."

She tenses her jaw, staring me down. I scowl back at her.

This is not how I wanted this to go, but I can't figure out how to defuse the situation now.

"We need to talk," I say, the words shaking. "*Now.*"

She steps to me like a fighter in the ring. "*If* we talk, it'll be when *I* say. You don't get to call the shots, Nate. You had a chance— multiple ones. And you blew it." She lifts her chin. "Besides, we're just friends. *Why do you even care?*"

It's a taunt. She's leveled another challenge my way, and all I can think of are the words I told her long ago—*Don't take challenges you can't win.*

Slowly, a smile spreads across my face. *Game on, baby.*

I walk toward her. She walks backward. Her eyes go wide as her back hits the wall, rattling a piece of artwork.

Her breathing is rushed as she breathes in and out quickly. Her pupils dilate as she watches me *watch her.*

My insides burn, my fingers itch to grab her and pull her to me. *To make her mine.*

But first ...

"You want to know why I care?" I ask her. "Because I'm not about to let you run off and fuck some guy because *I* got it all wrong."

Her lips part. "What's that supposed to mean?"

"That means that I—"

"No. You know what? I don't care."

She presses her hands against my chest, but I don't budge.

"Yes, you do," I say, looking down at her. "You care as much as I do. You care so much it scares you."

Her hands drop from my torso, and she stills.

I take a breath in an attempt to settle myself before I just scoop her up and kiss the hell out of her.

"You want to know what I think?" I ask.

"No."

But her tone says differently. It shakes, wobbling just enough to give me an opening.

"I think you've been covering how you really feel about me with your little flirting games and innuendos, thinking if you make light of it, you don't have to face the truth."

She falls back against the wall again.

I step even closer. "I've avoided you. I've turned you down. I've told myself a thousand times, jacked off in the shower more times than I can count just imagining your tight little body wrapped around me, that we were incompatible. That I should leave you alone."

She gasps.

I plant my hands on the wall just above her head, caging her in. Her eyes widen even more, but she doesn't flinch. She doesn't pull away.

"But do you know what I realized today?" I ask her, my voice gravelly.

"What?" she whispers.

"I realized that it doesn't matter what I tell myself. *You're already my girl in my head.*"

Hearing the words out loud scares the shit out of me. Knowing that my admission might make her panic. It might be too much for her.

But if me telling her the truth, the way I truly feel, is too much for her, then I damn well would be too much for her too. If that's the case, she should just go now.

"That means you have two choices," I say, fear creeping up my spine. "The first one is this—if you walk out that door today, you can't come back because I can't take it. I'm gonna get arrested, Paige. I can't take the thought of you being with someone else, especially after I know what your mouth feels like against mine."

"Or?"

"Or you stay here with me, and we address this situation we've found ourselves in."

The silence extends between us. We just stare at each other, inches apart, and breathe in the same air. My inhale is her exhale. If she breathed too deeply, her chest would hit mine. If I move a muscle, flex my forearm just a bit, it would brush against the side of her head.

But neither of us does that.

Instead, I wait for her to react. And with every second that passes, I think she's going to leave.

"What did you mean when you said you got it all wrong?" she asks, her voice strong and clear.

That's my girl.

"I meant that I was wrong. I gave you just enough to hang your-self with," I say. "I told you no, drew lines in the sand, and then crossed them when it was convenient for me."

She didn't expect me to say that. The long breath she releases is proof.

"I did all of that to keep us from getting here because I thought—incorrectly—that getting *here* was avoidable. That somehow, some-way, we could just continue as friends and avoid the chemistry boiling between us."

"Nate ..."

"*I'm sorry.* And I don't know what all this means or how it could work, but I'm telling you this—I'm past the point of no return. Either you're mine or you're not. And if you're not, let me rent you a hotel room, and we'll work separate shifts or something because I'm not strong enough to see you, knowing you're not ... mine. That's totally a *me* problem, and I get that."

I don't know what goes through her mind or what she actually thinks about what I've said. But I know the moment that it happens.

She lifts her chin and raises off the wall. Atoms are the only thing between us now.

My insides pull taut. My heart races. My brain screams at me to kiss her now.

Instead, I keep my gaze glued to hers and wait.

Finally, she ducks under my arm and walks to the table. I hang my head and sigh.

Fuck!

I turn around to see her set her purse on a chair. Then she faces me.

"Now it's my turn," she says, the strength in her voice slipping.

"For what?"

"*You* have two choices."

"Between ...?"

She licks her lips. "Choice one is that we can stand here all night and *address this situation*."

"Or?"

A slow, so-fucking-slow grin slips across her kissable lips. My whole body comes alive, pushing, pulling, all-out boiling for this woman.

God, help me.

"Or you can get over here and *undress me* instead."

Chapter 16

Paige

Nate's eyes widen.

I'm playing with fire.

Then as if it took him a second to believe what I said, he smirks. I feel it in every cell of my body.

I hope I don't get burned.

I drink in the sight of him—all alpha with a slice of vulnerability that makes my knees so weak I nearly melt to the floor—and realize what I've done. *What this means.*

What he's going to do to me if I let him.

"Come here," he says, stalking toward me.

As soon as I'm within reach, he wraps one arm around the small of my back and pulls me into him with such force that I gasp.

His mouth covers mine, his free hand palming the back of my head like there's any chance I'm going to pull away. His fingers lace through my hair, tugging the roots until I turn my head sideways.

He plants kisses across my jaw and down the side of my neck. I moan as the feeling of the barrier between us, the wall we've kept up to protect us from this moment, comes tumbling down, and it's incredible.

I don't realize he's picked me up until my legs wrap around his middle. He whirls me around, never breaking contact with his lips, and presses my back against the wall. I'm flushed, drunk with the intensity of this man's desire.

I can feel his fingers sinking into my bottom as he holds me up. My skirt, now bunched around my waist, allows the drywall to scratch my skin. His erection is hard against my stomach.

I think I might pass out.

My body burns. Heat pools between my legs. My back arches in an attempt to get more contact, any contact, with him.

Nate buries his face in the curve of my neck, nibbling the skin before he works himself back to my mouth. A shiver shifts through my body as the anticipation of what's to come settles over me.

This is it. Am I ready?

The flick of his tongue against my lips is not a request but rather a command to open. I do, giving him what he wants, and he takes advantage. His tongue strokes my mouth, firm and determined as if he wants me to remember this moment.

He adjusts himself so that one forearm is under my ass and my back is flat against the wall. He pulls his body away just enough to get his free hand between my legs.

The lace covering my sex is pushed to the side. My clit pulses in a way I've never felt before. It's swollen and hot, and when he presses his thumb against it—*I cry out.*

He catches the reaction with his mouth, sweeping the exhale away with his tongue. I dig my head into the wall and press myself against his hand.

One finger slides between my folds. He growls at how wet I am. Then he inserts it inside me, making me squeal.

God, that feels so good. I moan, unable to fully separate the sensations barreling through me. It's too much but also not enough. It's also somehow everything I thought it would be.

His kisses are measured, intentional—full of desire as he continues to finger my opening. He pulls back, having had enough to satisfy him for a moment, and smiles. Then he removes his finger and sets me back down on my feet.

A *whoosh* of air is released from my lungs. "*Why did you stop?*"

When I look up into his eyes as we pant for air, I feel something strange in my gut: peace. It's a tranquility that I've never known at this moment. A space without fear or a question of whether this is right or wrong. I answer my own question as I bask in his grin.

I'm ready for whatever he wants to give me.

He pushes the hair off my face with a tenderness that makes me swoon. He peers into my eyes and studies me.

"What are you doing?" I ask him, shifting my body around to ease the fire roaring through my veins.

"Just looking at you." He grins sheepishly. "Give me a moment, will ya?"

I fist his shirt and pull him to me.

"No," I say like I've done this before. "I said *undress me*. Not *caress me*."

He laughs. "I'm sorry. I thought you would like a little foreplay."

"I've had foreplay before. It's great. Now give me something I haven't had."

As soon as the words leave my mouth, I realize what I've done. *I told him I was a virgin.* I release his shirt.

His eyes go wide, filled with a mixture of wariness and disbelief. He leans back and cocks his head to the side.

"What are you saying, Paige?"

"I'm saying I want you to fuck me. *Please.*"

"No. Not that. I heard you there." His eyes narrow. "You've *had foreplay before*. Does that mean ..."

My mouth goes dry. I force a swallow and try to ignore the rush of blood to my cheeks.

"I'm a virgin, okay?" I say, pulling my skirt down.

"Are you kidding?"

"No. Why would I joke about that?" I flush even more. "It's embarrassing."

He runs a hand down his face until it stops at his mouth. With it still covered, he says, "You have nothing to be embarrassed about." He shakes his head. "Fucking hell."

I don't know whether to laugh or cry or just leave. *What does his reaction mean?*

Why did I even say anything?

"Forget it," I say, my nerves getting the better of me. It's hard to think with every hormone in your body swirling around without control. "I'll go."

"The hell you will." He chuckles. "You're a fucking virgin?"

I sigh. "I already told you this. Can we not stand here and repeat it?"

"I'm just ..." He sighs too. "And you want to give that to me?"

I cross my arms over my chest, avoiding my nipples because they're still hard, and look at him.

"Do you give every woman you sleep with this kind of Q and A? Because it's kind of a turn-off. But what do I know? As we've said a hundred times, *I'm a virgin.*"

"Any other woman I've ever slept with hasn't been you."

What's that supposed to mean? I drop my arms.

"Look, I've always stopped things when it got to this point because it's never felt right. Hence, the reason Atticus said he was going to break my neck."

"That's why? That motherfucker."

"But this, with you ... it feels right, Nate. If me being a virgin doesn't make you not want me."

He pulls me into him again, but this time with a tenderness that makes my heart bloom.

"Oh, *I want you.* Whether you're a virgin or not doesn't change anything ... except for the fact that I can't just fuck you," he says, grinning.

"Why—"

He stops me with a kiss. "I'll make you a deal."

"What kind of a deal?"

"Let me take my time with you tonight. I want you to enjoy your first time, okay? And then the next time, we'll do it however you want. If you want to be fucked, then—I'll fuck you."

I squirm at his choice of words. "Deal."

He looks at me like he can't believe what just happened. It would be adorable if I wasn't soaking through my panties.

"Hey, Nate?"

"What?"

"I'm still dressed."

He chuckles and takes my hand. "Let's go fix that."

"Yes. *Please.*"

We exchange a smile as he leads me toward his bedroom.

Chapter 17

Paige

"Stay right here."

Nate presses a kiss to the top of my head and then disappears into what I assume is the master bathroom.

"All right," I mutter to myself. "This isn't awkward at all."

I use the opportunity to check out Nate's bedroom and distract myself from what's about to happen. A simple wooden bed is covered with a navy-blue comforter. There are two small tables on either side of the bed and a rug at the foot.

Across the room is a long, narrow dresser with a television hanging above it. And above the bed is a painting that looks as though someone took a paintbrush, dipped it in various cans of paint, and flicked it against the canvas.

I turn a full circle, and just as I come to the end, Nate fills the doorway.

Wow.

He's lost his shoes, socks, and shirt. The man is standing in front of me in a pair of jeans with a set of abs that you could grate cheese on.

Don't drool.

He watches me for a long moment as if he's not sure what to do with me. This makes me smile.

"Look, I'm just telling you now—you've talked a big game, buddy. If you aren't sure how to do this, we have problems," I say.

A low rumble slips past his lips. "Funny girl."

And just that one comment seems to bring us back to who we've been for so long. Friends. Except ... *I don't know what all this means or how it could work, but I'm telling you this—I'm past the point of no return. Either you're mine or you're not* ... Nate wants more.

And right now, I'm absolutely certain that I want to be his too.

He enters the room and sets a few things on the table by the bed. Then he faces me.

"First, I cannot read your mind," he says.

"That's obvious, or we would've been here days ago."

He laughs. "What I mean is, there's no way for me to know how something feels to you. *I want to know.* I want to know if you like it, if you hate it, or if it hurts. You have to communicate with me."

"Okay. I'll be sure to be vocal."

He rolls his eyes but maintains his smile. "Second, if you decide you don't want to do this or if something makes you uncomfortable, you have to promise you'll stop me. No matter what. Okay?"

I tap my finger on my chin. "But what do I say to start you?"

"I'm being serious, Paige."

"Me too." I take in the frustration in his eyes and feel bad. *I appreciate his attentiveness.* "Okay. I'm sorry. I promise."

"Good girl. Now come here."

Even if he hadn't touched me at all today—even if I wasn't already so wet for him that my thighs are sticking together—the look on his face would get me there. It's a smile so sinful, so delicious, that I whimper.

Nate touches his mouth to mine softly. Slowly, he licks across my bottom lip, then tugs it between his teeth. The sharpness of the act is in stark contrast to the way he holds me in his arms as if I'm a porcelain doll.

I dangle my arms over his shoulders.

He guides me across the room. We stop next to the bed. He grabs the hem of my shirt, and he slips it over my head.

The air is cool against my skin. I can feel the heat rolling off my body as I say a prayer of thanks that I wore pretty underthings.

"You just get better and better," he says.

"I didn't fully express my appreciation of your body. It's ... a work of art."

He grins. "I gathered that by the look on your face."

"Well, I'm glad my face doesn't lie."

He undoes the button on my skirt. His Adam's apple bobs in his throat as he pulls the zipper down with the care of a surgeon. I shimmy myself out of the skirt and kick it to the side.

I stand in front of him in my booties and underwear. Much to my surprise, *I like it*. There's not an ounce of me worried about the stretch marks on my breasts from gaining the freshman fifteen or the pooch of my stomach that hangs slightly over the waistband of my underwear. The cellulite on my thighs doesn't matter because Nate Hughes looks at me like he wants to eat me for dinner.

"The things I could do to you," he says just loud enough to hear.

"Do them. I'm all yours."

"Damn you," he growls as he picks me up and tosses me on the bed.

I squeal as the bedsprings give and a pillow topples onto my face. I grab it, ready to toss it to the side, when I'm distracted.

Ooh.

Nate is on the bed. His knee is between my thighs, and he uses it to spread my legs farther apart. My heart begins to pound as he gets closer to my face with a glimmer in his eyes that makes them look ridiculously green.

He holds my gaze as he kneels beside me. He brings both of my breasts out of the bra, sitting them on top of the underwire. The position makes my erratic breathing more noticeable.

I gasp as he brings his mouth over one breast and palms the other.

"Oh, dammit," I say, moaning the words. I arch my back, lifting off the mattress as he lightly pinches the exposed nipple. *I think I'm going to explode.*

His mouth is wet and hot as his tongue kisses and deliciously tortures me. He takes his time as if we have all night. I grab the back of his head and tug on his hair, needing relief from the tension that's building dangerously high inside me.

He moves his hand down my stomach, around the curve of my hip, and over the front of my leg.

I hiccup a breath and close my eyes.

His fingers drag through the dampness of my inner thighs and to the swollen bud that's screaming for attention. He dips one finger inside my opening.

"Okay," I say, groaning from the sensations riddling me. I close my eyes, unable to keep them open as shots of pleasure come from almost every part of my body. "I'm communicating. I really, really like that. *And that!*" I add as he rolls his thumb over my clit. "*Ah!*"

He chuckles, the sound vibrating against my breast. Then he releases it and pulls his face away from me.

I shiver a full-body, head-to-toe shudder. He adds another finger, and I think I'm going to lose my mind.

"See?" He works them in and out of my opening. "When you tell me things, I know to keep going."

"But not forever, right? We're having sex tonight."

He bursts out laughing. "Will you have some patience?"

"Just because you can hold yourself back doesn't mean we all can." I grit my teeth. "I can't even keep myself from snacking until lunch—*fuck!* Don't stop doing that!"

He presses down on my stomach as he continues to pleasure me. It makes it more intense and drives me closer to the edge.

Then he stops. My eyes fly open as he crawls off the bed.

"What are you doing?" I ask him. "I communicated. You understood."

If the smile he's wearing never left his face again, I wouldn't be mad about it.

"I did understand." He springs on the bed and lands with his face perilously close to my sex. "Now put your legs over my shoulders."

Oh. My. God. My stomach swirls at the thought of seeing Nate's face framed between my legs. Sure, I've had oral sex before, but ...

"Nate, I don't think ..." I fall back against the mattress. *Oh, shit.*

The rush of air from his laughter sweeps against my very wet, very exposed vagina.

He presses a finger onto my clit and leaves it there. "If you don't want me to, just tell me."

"It's not that," I say, trying to block out the buildup in my core.

"Then what is it?" He blows against my opening. "Come on. Where's the girl who usually won't shut up?"

I lift my head high enough to glare at him.

"I can sit here and play in this all night," he says, shoving a finger in me so hard that I yelp.

Dammit, that feels good.

"Do it," I say before I can talk myself out of it.

"Are you sure?"

Now he's just fucking with me.

I lift my head up and cram a pillow under it so I can see his eyes. He's watching me with amusement as if he's enjoying himself.

I'll fuck with you back.

I pick up each leg, one at a time, and lay them over his shoulders. He then grips my waist and lifts me to his mouth but doesn't make contact.

"If you don't put your mouth on my pussy—*ah!*"

The first sweep of his tongue is like striking a match against a matchbook. My whole body goes up in flames.

My knees fall to the side as he licks and sucks. He tortures my clit while his fingers work magic inside my body, building me up so high that I'm not sure I'll ever come back down.

"*I love that*," I say, the words barely understandable through my gritted teeth.

The burn of bliss barrels through me so hard that it brings tears to my eyes. I give up any fight, any reservedness that I might've been holding on to, and succumb to the waves of sensations.

Just as I think I'm almost too high, to the point I can't take it anymore, he slows. His fingers slip out of me. He presses a kiss to my swollen and tender bud. That alone feels so intense that I buckle.

Gently, he brings my legs to the blankets and slides off the bed.

"I think you're ready for me," he says, winking. Then he wipes his face with a towel by the bed.

"Oh, I don't know," I say as he takes off his belt. "You might need lube."

"We're using lube."

I make a face. "Do you not feel how wet I am?"

His hands pause in the air. He grins so cheekily I nearly orgasm.

"Baby, I just had my face buried in your pussy. I'm pretty sure I know how wet you are."

My cheeks flush. "Then why the lube? I was kidding."

He removes his pants and boxers and stands before me naked. His cock stands straight, a bead of precum glistening at the top.

"Lube helps, especially for your first time," he says, rolling on a condom. "I want this to be as comfortable as it can."

Me too. I blow out a breath as he finishes readying himself. *Don't be nervous.*

The mattress dips as he climbs on the bed.

He hovers over me, his biceps flexing as he holds himself up. I run my hands up his arms and over his glorious shoulders.

I kick my legs in the air, needing to get my boots off.

"You okay?" he asks.

"I'm fine." The shoes fall to the ground. "Footwear problem."

He grins. A twinge of concern flashes through his eyes before it's replaced with confidence again.

"Here we go." He bends down and kisses me gently. "Ready?"

I smile up at him. As long as I look into his eyes, my anxiety stays at bay, and the excitement of the moment takes over. "I'm ready."

He places the head of his cock at my opening.

I suck in a breath and try not to squirm.

He holds my gaze with a steadiness that I appreciate. I grip his shoulders as he starts to push.

"Nice and easy," he says.

"Okay."

He pushes a little more, and a bolt of discomfort tears through me.

"Wait," I say, shoving his shoulders. I squeeze my eyes closed and wait for the feeling to subside. "It doesn't hurt, exactly. It's just uncomfortable."

"Take your time. We're in no hurry."

My chest fills with warmth. *Thank God that I chose Nate for my first time.*

Thank God. Thank God. Thank God.

I'm exposed and vulnerable, and both make a swell of nervousness rise inside me. But then I open my eyes and see him, and I'm okay.

"A little more," I say softly.

He dips inside me a touch more. When I don't stop him, he goes a little farther.

I'm full—or at least I feel that way.

"You good?" he asks.

"Yeah. It's ... annoying." I laugh.

"Annoying? What are you talking about?"

"It feels delicious in a way. Like, I feel stretched to a point where it's almost painful, but it's not. I'm right on the edge of not knowing which way it's going to go."

He pulls back a little and slowly pushes forward.

"See? That. That feels good," I say.

"I'm not going in all the way. I don't want to hurt you."

I smile at him. "The annoying part is that I need to have an orgasm, and I can't quite get around to that because I'm not sure where this is going."

"So you have blue balls?"

"Yeah. Whatever the female version of that is."

He lowers his mouth to mine and slips his tongue between my lips. I grip his shoulders as he works himself in and out in a slow, steady rhythm. With every push, every pull—every thrust of both his cock and his tongue, I relax. And the more I relax, the better it feels.

"Feels good," I say out of the side of my mouth.

He chuckles and pulls away from me without slowing his pace. He reaches for a pillow and then pulls out of me to slide it under my ass. When he enters me again, the change in angle is divine.

"Oh, hell, yes," he rasps.

He palms one of my breasts, massaging it as he strokes himself in and out of me. With each movement, he goes a little harder, a little deeper. And with every addition of power and distance, I move higher and higher toward an orgasm.

"Do you like that?" he asks, rolling the beaded nipple with his fingers. "Because I do. I don't know how in the hell I got lucky enough to be here with you, but I'll take it."

I grin. "I feel lucky too, Nate."

He kisses me again and then places both hands next to my head. I lift my hips, giving him more access as I trust him to take care of me.

And he does.

He builds the tempo, finding a pace that makes me moan.

"*There.* Do that. *Oh, my gosh,*" I say as I try to breathe. "Do that! Nate!"

"*Fuck, Paige.*"

He groans, his arms flexing. I grab his biceps and squeeze hard—probably too hard, but I can't be held accountable for my actions. I dig my nails into his skin and try not to scream.

I'm straddling the line of pleasure and pain, and it's the most delicious experience I've ever had.

"Nate!" I yell his name, my voice filling the house as I reach the climax. "I'm coming. Do not stop. *Don't stop.*"

My jaw aches as I bite down and try to keep my body from coming apart at the seams. My legs ache, my stomach is twisted—my head feels like it's on fire.

His arms tremble as he closes his eyes, his jaw flexing as he falls apart too.

Watching him orgasm is almost as good as feeling it myself.

Finally, when we're both spent, he looks down at me. My arms are lying out like a snow angel, and my legs have fallen to the side.

I think he's going to pull out, but he doesn't.

First, he kisses me. It's sweet and simple but filled with something I'm afraid to name.

"Was that okay?" he asks.

"Nine out of ten," I joke.

"A nine?"

"You made me wait too long."

He rolls his eyes, grinning, and slides out of me. "So what kind of girl are you? A cuddler or a snacker or a don't-touch-me-er?"

"I'm a lie here and watch you walk around this room naked kind of girl."

He laughs as he removes the condom and deposits it in the trash. "Well, let's get you cleaned up, and then I'll lie beside you, and we'll get a snack and cuddle."

"You're gonna cuddle with me?"

All he does is laugh.

Chapter 18

Nate

"Do you know what really surprised me?" I chomp down on a chip and look down at Paige. "There's one thing that really, well, it was mind-blowing."

She stretches out beside me. "Well, I don't know the exact thing you're looking for, but it's pretty awesome to know that I was mind-blowing my first time."

This girl.

"Love the confidence, and you're not wrong. But I was thinking more along the lines of the fact that you can actually take instructions. You listened like a champ."

She rolls her eyes.

"Seriously, Paige. That's the first time you've ever actually done something I asked you—oof."

She slams a pillow against my face.

I roll over before she can suspect it, knocking the bag of chips over, and grab her. She squeals and squirms to get away but can't.

The streetlight outside shines into the room, highlighting her beautiful face as she looks up at me. There's a glimmer in her eyes, a look of contentment that I would do nearly anything to keep there.

I place a kiss on her forehead and sit back up. She scrambles around next to me until she's propped up against the pillows. I watch her get situated, dressed in one of my T-shirts, and looking like temptation itself with her freshly fucked hair.

"You're staring," she says.

"Don't be so beautiful then."

Her cheeks flush.

"There's no sense in getting embarrassed at this point," I tease. "I can still taste you on my lips."

She covers her face. "Don't. Stop."

"That only works in the bedroom."

She drops her hands and grins. "We are in the bedroom, genius."

"Touché." I grab the chips and have another one. "We do need to have a conversation."

"About what?"

I take another chip and touch it to my lips. *I'm going to have to be careful here.*

While I told her how I felt while we were fighting earlier, I don't know if she remembers what I said. I also don't know how clear I was. I was too mad, too caught up in the moment.

But the way I feel now, after being allowed inside her and tasting her and feeling her wrapped around me, I know there's no way—*zero chance*—that I'm going to not have her as mine. And what that means for us and how she reacts to that is yet to be determined.

I drag a finger down her arm. "Right now, things are great. We're in an orgasm-induced bubble."

"Yes, we are."

"But we're going to leave this room at some point. Probably when Dom calls and is on his way home with Ryder."

Paige nods.

"And we need to be on the same page when that happens."

She stills, picking up what I'm throwing down.

I take a deep, shaky breath and blow it out. It does nothing to slow my racing heart.

"I'm not asking you to marry me—"

"*Good.*" She says it so quickly that it catches her off guard too. "I didn't mean it like that."

"It's fine. I'm not ready for that either. Obviously." I shift my weight around. "But I am asking you what kind of box you're going to put us in."

She bites her lip. "I don't know, Nate. I honestly didn't expect this to happen. It's not like I've been sitting around thinking about it."

That's what I was afraid of.

I eat the chip I've been holding forever to give myself a second to get my thoughts together. But it doesn't take too long because I still feel the way I felt when we were in the living room—only more.

"We don't have to call it forever," I say, thinking back to what she's told me before. "I'm not asking for a lifetime commitment over here. But I am saying that I want you. All of you. Especially now."

She almost smiles.

"And I can't see some other guy hitting on you or thinking you're seeing someone on the side. I'm gonna worry about you when I'm not with you, and I'm going to need to make sure you're safe. It's just how I operate. I'm hardwired that way."

She touches my hand. "I know that. I see you do that with the people you love every day. It's one of the things I adore about you."

I lean over and kiss her.

"If you don't want that from me, I understand," I say, reiterating what I told her earlier. "I won't like it, but it's your choice, and I respect that. I spent hours today thinking about us. Trying to get my head on straight. And the conclusion I came to was this, Paige. *I adore you.*"

She bites her lip and waits for me to continue.

"I have for a while now. I love our friendship, our flirting, even, it seems, our fighting. As long as it ends like it did today." I smile. "But if you're not feeling it, seeing that there could be something here for us, tell me. I'll get you a room somewhere, and we'll figure a work schedule out so we avoid each other, but I can't be around you if you're not mine. It will drive me insane."

She stills. She doesn't say a word.

My mind races, overanalyzing the situation. *What does her posture mean? What is the look in her eyes telling me? Which way is she leaning?*

"I won't chase you," I say. "I'm not going to be some creep who follows you around, and you can still call me if you're in trouble. I'll always be there for you like that. No matter what."

She scrambles around until she's sitting upright. A small smile touches her lips. It's one I can't read.

My heart thunders, beating so hard and so loud that I'm surprised I can't hear it.

"Before I answer you, I want to have a conversation," she says.

I sigh. "About what?"

"How many times a day can you do ... that?"

What is she talking about? I open my mouth to ask her what she means when a slow smile stretches from ear to ear.

"Do you mean how many times a day can we have sex?" I ask her, my brows lifting to the ceiling.

"Yup."

I chuckle as my ego expands. "As many as you want."

"Really?"

"Really."

She moves across the bed until she's straddling me. The only thing between us is the thin fabric of my boxers. She pushes down against my cock, and my balls tighten immediately.

I grab her hips and hold her in place because if she moves, this conversation will probably be paused. *Which is most likely what she wants.*

Her head falls to the side, bringing all of her wild, unruly hair to her right shoulder. Her neck is exposed, and I want to bury my face in the bend and place kisses across her shoulder blade.

But I don't.

Instead, I peer into her beautiful golden-brown eyes.

I'm done. I'm fucked. I've fallen for this girl. *Am I in love with her?* I don't know. *But do I ever want to lose her?* No.

I can't say that. I don't trust her not to dart away.

"What about Ryder?" she asks.

"He likes you, and you're already here. He knows we're friends. Maybe we keep a lid on things in front of him for a while until we're sure we're a thing."

Until you're sure because I already know we are.

She bites her lip. "I don't see how things have changed any from the other night. You told me yourself—you want forever, and I'm running from it. I mean, it's a step in the right direction for me in that I picked you and not some asshole. But I'm going to be honest. I'm not ready for some kind of long-term commitment. And I have this habit of just kind of imploding things when I get scared, and thinking about forever scares the hell out of me. It feels like a setup for failure. Like, just having this conversation with you has me thinking about what it would feel like for you to never want to see me again, and my heart is racing."

"That's no way to live your life, Paige."

"I know."

She looks down and frowns.

My heart hurts for her. I hate that she feels this way and can't just be happy in the moment.

I drop my hands to her thighs and give them a gentle squeeze. It causes her to look back at me.

"You know what else scares me?" she asks, her voice wavering.

"What's that?"

"Not feeling this way again."

Sweet girl. I squeeze her legs again. "What way, exactly? I want to know."

"Safe. Relaxed. Wanted. Pretty." She sighs. "Right now, I feel like ... like I can rest. This feels like my little spot in the world, and everything will be okay if I can just stay right here."

I take her hand and bring it to my mouth. *That's exactly how I want you to feel.*

"You've made me feel that way since I met you, in a way," she says. "I liked you immediately. I was drawn to you. It was so easy to talk to you and hang out in your office and tease you."

I smile at the memories.

"And you always knew when something was wrong. Like the whole Atticus thing. You went after him without even really knowing what he did to me."

"He's lucky I didn't know the whole story, or Atticus would have met a much different fate that night."

She smiles. "I just ..." She presses her lips together and closes her eyes. "You know what? I understand what you're saying."

"About what part, exactly?"

She opens her eyes. "There's really only one choice here."

"Are your communication skills only good when I'm performing some sort of sexual act on you?"

She giggles.

"Because I need an answer, and if that means I need to roll you over and finger-fuck you to get you to talk, then lie on your back, woman."

She smacks my chest. "You're right. There's only one choice here, and that's to try this. To see what happens. The thought of walking away and not having this again or having to look for someone else to give me this—which would be stupid because here it is, right? So if I know I'm going to want this kind of thing, why don't I just stay here?"

"Wow."

"What?"

"You can really talk yourself in a circle, can't you?" I furrow my brows. "Tell me in simple English. So I know you're not just staying with me for sex."

"No, Nate. It's not just the sex. It's the feeling of ... safety that I don't think I could replicate anywhere else or with anyone else. I'm choosing you."

She lifts the hem of her shirt up one inch. Then another. A sexy smirk graces her lips. "And sex. I'm definitely choosing that too."

I grab her hands just before she brings the shirt over her nipples because as soon as I see those, shit is going to go south. *Fast.*

"I want you," she whispers. "Only you. And let's see what happens."

My spirits soar, and I flip her over onto the chip bag. She giggles as I smile at her.

"You want to see what happens?" I ask. "I'll tell you what happens."

"Honestly? I'm so sore." She laughs, but the sound turns into a whimper. "I have to learn not to dish out more than I can take."

I laugh at this sweet girl—at *my sweet girl.*

Chapter 19

Paige

"Oh, for heaven's sake. Do you always drive like this? Slow the hell down, Nate!"

I grab the door and gawk at him. He grins mischievously back at me but eases off the accelerator.

The morning sun is bright and beautiful. There's not a cloud in the sky. After a night's sleep curled up against Nate, thanks to an impromptu sleepover for Ryder with the Landrys, it's a perfect start to the day.

And seeing Nate making breakfast in nothing but his boxers? That didn't hurt anything either.

He reaches over the middle console and squeezes my leg.

Maddox: We have a problem.

I swipe open my phone and type out a reply.

Me: Um, pretty sure I'm problem-less at the moment. But thanks for sharing.

Maddox: You know Mom's cookie jar—the one shaped like a shoe or boot or whatever?

Me: Yeah. The one that no one is supposed to touch for any reason? The one her grandmother got for her before sliced bread was a thing?

Maddox: Yes. That one.

Me: Mad, I don't like where this is going.

"Everything okay?" Nate asks. "You're making a face."

"Oh, one of my stupid brothers—and when I start a sentence like that for future reference, I always mean Banks—did something to my mom's beloved cookie jar, I think. Maddox is texting me now."

"What do they want you to do about it?"

I shrug. "Maybe bring bail money because Mom is probably gonna kill him."

Nate considers this and, by the look of it, finds that acceptable.

Maddox: Your dumb-as-shit brother was doing God knows what and broke it.

Me: Dude, that's YOUR brother. You share his DNA. Not me.

Maddox: You know what? I resent you using your adoption status to your advantage in times like these.

Me: How bad is it broken? Does Mom know? What was he doing with it?

Maddox: The lid is in two pieces. No, she does not. I didn't ask. We're better off having the least information possible. It helps with cross-examinations.

I laugh. "Oh, Banks is dead."

Nate grins. "How many brothers did you say you had? Five?"

"Six."

He whistles through his teeth.

Me: Get some kind of adhesive. Try the craft store by the

Mexican restaurant—the one where you sit on the roof. You know where I mean?

Maddox: Yeah. Thanks. I'm too old for this shit.

Me: Then let Banks deal with it.

Maddox: He's blackmailing me. Long story. Thanks. Love you.

Me: Love you.

I look up as we slow down in front of a tall gate. Nate waves at a man in a security building, and the gate swings open.

"Ryder is hanging out with the right crowd. Wow," I say as a huge farmhouse comes into view.

"This is Camilla's family's place. No one actually lives here, I don't think. They just have meetings and get-togethers here."

"Are they nice?"

"The Landrys? Yeah. Some of the best people I know, really. They treat Dominic really well—me too. Ryder and I have come out here for Christmas the past couple of years, and he's invited to all the birthday parties and shit with the kids."

"That's so nice."

He shrugs like it's not a big deal, but he likes it. I can tell.

My phone buzzes again as we pull to a stop in front of the house. I glance down.

"This is Hollis. Hang on."

Hollis: Hey, how are you? I just got home from Nashville. Want to hang out soon?

Me: Yes. I'd love to. I'm busy today, though, and tomorrow, I have to go get my books and stuff for school. How about Tuesday or Wednesday?

Hollis: Wednesday works for me.

Me: Cool. I'll text you then, and we'll nail down a time.

Hollis: Great. See you then.

Me: *smiling emoji*

"You and your brothers," Nate says as he kills the engine.

I take in his handsome profile. The sharpness of his jaw, the slight crookedness of his nose. His high cheekbones and plump lips.

"I really want to kiss you right now, but I'm afraid Ryder will see," I say.

He turns toward me. "We're going to have to figure out how to navigate this, and to be honest, I don't have all the answers."

I hold my pointer finger up in the air. He makes a face but then touches his lips to it.

"There. That'll have to do until I can get you alone," I say.

"Yeah. That totally makes up for kissing you." He rolls his eyes. "If that's all it takes to satisfy you, I'm working too hard."

I look at the house. A man wearing a pair of khaki pants and a blue-and-white button-up comes out onto the porch. He looks so dapper, so debonaire, that I instantly feel underdressed in my casual jeans and black cotton shirt.

"That's Graham Landry," he says. "Wickedly intelligent. Not really a social guy, but he's a great person to know if you know what I mean."

"Is he like in the mafia or something?"

Nate laughs as he opens his door. "No, but the thought of that is hilarious."

"Okay ..."

I get out of the truck and meet Nate at the front. He places his hand at the small of my back and guides me onto the porch.

"Hey, Nate. How are you?" Graham extends a hand. "I'm Graham Landry."

"I'm Paige Carmichael. It's nice to meet you."

"Same." He nods and then looks at Nate. "They're wild in there. I'm warning you."

"Sounds fun," I say.

Graham grimaces and takes a sip of a dark brown liquid. *Tea, maybe? Or bourbon.*

Nate opens the door for me, and I walk inside. Instantly, the noise level is intense. Kids are everywhere.

"Hi!" A heavily pregnant woman comes over to us. "How are you, Nate?"

"Good. Dani, this is Paige Carmichael. Paige, this is Dani Landry."

"It's nice to meet you," I say.

"It's nice to meet you too. I think Ryder had a good time with us—or Mallory and Ellie, rather. I get too tired too fast with the baby on the way."

"Congratulations," I say. "What are you having?"

"A little girl." She beams. "That little guy in the Arrows baseball hat is my little one, Ryan. He never stops moving."

"Like his dad," Nate says.

Dani laughs. "Absolutely."

I take in the chaos unfolding in front of us. "Who do all these kids belong to?"

Dani takes a deep breath. "Okay, the teenager over there reading a book to the little girl? The boy is Huxley. He belongs to Barrett and Alison. They also have a little boy, Harrison, playing trucks with Ryder." She points at a blond toddler with gorgeous eyes. "And the little girl Huxley is reading to is Caroline. She belongs to Ford and Ellie. She's their only child."

"I love that he's reading to her," I say.

"I feel sorry for him." Nate grins at Dani. "Long story. Go on."

"Umm, let's see. Where are the twins?" She looks around. "Okay. Vivian is in the kitchen with her grandma. And her brother, Julian, is over there at the table with the paper and crayons. He's probably trying to figure out how to make his first million like his dad." She turns to me. "His parents are Graham and Mallory."

My eyes go wide. "Mallory Landry? The one who owns Stretch?" She laughs. "That's her."

"Oh, my gosh. I go there. I know her. How weird is that?"

"It's a small world. She married into the family like me."

I give myself a minute to make the connections.

It's fascinating how these people have come together and filled this house with so many people. It's such a nice feeling to be surrounded by so much love.

"This will be what my parents' house looks like one day," I say, laughing. "I'll have to warn them."

"I was an only child," Dani says. "My childhood was pretty cold. It wasn't until I met Lincoln that I realized what a family could look like. And I wanted that for myself and my children someday."

I get that.

"Dani! Can you help Vivi wash her hands? I have cookie dough all over my fingers!" a voice shouts from what must be the kitchen.

I start to put my hand in Nate's back pocket but realize Ryder is watching.

"Hey, buddy. You ready?" Nate asks him.

"Yeah. I guess."

"Go thank Mrs. Landry for letting you stay."

"He already did! I'd come out and say hello, Nate, but I have a mess in here!"

I laugh.

"Thanks, Mrs. Landry," Nate calls out.

"Oh, my gosh. Will you stop calling me that, Nate? There are too many Mrs. Landrys in here."

He grins. "Let's go, kid."

Ryder says goodbye to Harrison and races over to us. He wraps one arm around his dad and the other around me.

My eyes meet Nate's over the boy's head.

"Did you have fun?" Nate asks as we head for the door.

Ryder rambles on about pizza and a movie they watched about cats and dogs all the way to the truck. Nate gets him buckled up in the back, and then we take off back to the road.

"What did you do while I was gone, Paige Stage?" he asks.

Nate smirks.

How do I answer this?

"Well," I say, thinking fast. "I met my friend Kinsley, and we did some yoga. And then I came back home and worked out a little more."

I grin triumphantly at Nate. He tries not to laugh.

"You know what I think we should do?" Ryder asks.

"What?" Nate replies.

"Do you have to go to work today?" he asks. "I need to know that first."

"Not today. Maybe later, but not before bedtime. Why? What's up?"

"Well, I think we should get hamburger buns and pizza sauce and cheese and pepperonis and the green strip things that I love and make those for lunch. Okay?"

I look at Nate. "Green strip things?"

"Green bell peppers. He likes them on his pizza burgers."

"I love them!" Ryder says from the back seat.

I look at him over my shoulder. "I've never had a pizza on a hamburger bun before. Is that a real thing?"

"It is when you're poor." Nate chuckles. "We love them. It used to be our Sunday dinner every week before things started working out better for us, huh, Ryder?"

"It was so fun. I miss them. Can we do it today? Please?"

I can't help but play along with him. "Yeah. Can we do it today? Please?"

It's not until I've already said the words that I catch the innuendo. *Man, I didn't even try for that one.*

Nate looks at me, his eyes darkening. "All you have to do is ask."

"That means we can? Yay!" Ryder yells from the back.

Nate flips on the turn signal and pulls onto a side street. "Guess we need to stop at the grocery store then."

"Turn it up. I love this song," Ryder says.

I reach over and turn the volume up. But before I pull my hand back, Nate's fingertip touches mine.

A flood of warmth cascades through my body as I look up at him.

I don't know what's happening here, but it feels nice.

Chapter 20

Paige

"No one tells you when you go to college that your books are going to cost as much as your tuition," I lament as Kinsley and I walk out of the campus bookstore. "Let's drop these off in our cars and then grab a sandwich. I'm starving."

"Deal."

We cross the street and separate. I find my car, unload my books into the back seat, and lock it. Then I head up the sidewalk toward Kinsley's car.

A gentle breeze brings scents of bread and spices from the nearby restaurants swirling around me. My stomach growls so loud that I don't realize my phone has buzzed in my hand until I look down.

Marcie: Hey, I know I've been avoiding you, and I'm sorry. I completely screwed you over, and I'm sorry for that too. Like, more than you realize.

I stop walking.

Me: Thank you for the apology. Are you okay? I'm worried about you.

Marcie: Only you would worry about me after I got you kicked out of your house.

Me: I'm not happy about that, but I found a place to stay. It worked out. Your mom indicated that you were with her?

Marcie: Yeah. I got myself into some trouble. I should've asked for help from my parents or someone, but I didn't. And I got in too deep to climb back out on my own.

What does that mean? My curiosity is piqued but asking her what she means feels wrong. *If she wanted me to know, she'd tell me.*

Me: So you're safe now? It's all okay?

Marcie: It will be okay. Yes, I'm safe. I just wanted to apologize to you. I feel awful. Truly.

Me: Reach out anytime and when you feel like it, let's meet up for burritos. I think it's my turn to pay. *winking emoji*

Marcie: You're the best, Paige. Xo

"I feel like I weigh one hundred pounds less without all those damn books," Kinsley says. "You'd think we'd have online course material at this point. I'm going to file a complaint with ... someone."

We start walking toward our favorite burger joint on campus.

"You do that." I slide my phone back in my pocket and sigh. "I just heard from Marcie."

Kinsley's head whips to mine. "You did? What did she say?"

"She apologized."

"As she should've."

I frown. Kinsley, Marcie, and I were the three musketeers. It would feel natural to talk to Kinsley about our friends, but the nature of what Marcie shared with me was so personal.

"She just said she was safe," I say, avoiding the rest of it. "And that she'd find me soon for burritos."

"So she didn't mention what the heck happened?"

"No. Not really."

"Weird."

We go inside the restaurant and seat ourselves by the window. The view overlooks the Greens, my favorite part of campus. It's an expansive lawn with tall, towering trees. I love to sit under them and study on sunny days.

The server arrives. We wave off the menus and order our regular go-to lunches. Once she's gone, Kinsley's arms rest on the table. Her look is pointed.

"Okay," she said. "Time to talk. You no-showed on me the other night and then completely avoided my calls and texts yesterday."

"No," I say, waggling a finger in her direction. "I texted you back."

"And said, *'can't talk but can't wait to see you tomorrow'* and a winking emoji. The winking emoji was the only reason I didn't do a welfare check."

I shift around in my seat as my cheeks begin to warm.

Kinsley's mouth drops. "Oh, my .... *Paige*." She narrows her eyes. "Paige."

I don't even try to hide the smile that stretches from ear to ear. "Yes."

She squeals. "Okay. Tell me all of it."

"Kins ..."

"No, dammit. I want to know. Was it good? Did it hurt? What was he like? *What does this mean?*" She squeals again. "Is he as hot without clothes as I bet he is?"

So many things race through my mind that I don't know where to start. I try to grab one of them to begin, but my friend is impatient.

"Paige!"

"Okay. Just calm down." I laugh and relax back into the booth. "Was it good? No. It was ... I mean, I don't know what it's like for most people, but I can't imagine it being better than it was."

Kinsley grins.

I shiver, just remembering the way he touched me, spoke to me—
the way he took care of me.

"It was perfect, Kins."

"I am so happy for you."

"He was so gentle and went so slow. His level of attentiveness was just *wow*." I lean back as the server sets our drinks in front of us. "Those Reddit people don't know shit."

"I had a feeling he would be like that. He walks around like a man who knows what he's doing."

"That he does."

She sips her water. "So what now? What about the apartment?"

I take a drink—a long one—to buy myself some time. *Honestly?* I don't know what happens now. Yes, Nate and I are a thing. A couple. *I need to get used to saying that.*

When I woke up this morning to Nate's arm draped over my stomach and his head buried in the crook of my neck, I panicked. It was a shock to my system when I remembered that *I am in a relationship.*

All it took to calm me was Nate kissing my shoulder. I'm still a little scared about what this all means, but at the same time—it feels exactly right.

But does that mean I stay with him? He hasn't implied that I'm welcome there for the next who knows how long. And what about Ryder? It's only going to get more complicated to navigate our way around him and his needs.

"First, I haven't heard anything about the apartment," I say slowly, still working through the question. "So there's that."

"Will you move there if they call?"

I sigh. "I don't know, Kinsley. Probably. I mean ... *yes*." I grab my water with both hands. "Of course, I will. Nate and I are a couple
—"

"Officially?" Her eyes sparkle. "That's freaking awesome."

It is. I smile at her, my heart swelling in my chest. Because I have never, ever seen this face—such ... *joy*—directed at me about one of my boyfriends. It's as though I've finally chosen right, and my best friend is backing me completely. *That* feels good.

"But we aren't at the point where I'm moving in with him. That would be crazy."

She leans back in the booth. "But would it, though?"

"Yeah, Kins. It would."

"It's obviously working out for you. And I'm sure he loves having you there, being the big, strong, alpha male that I bet he is." She grins wickedly. "It would be much more convenient to walk across the house to *see him* rather than driving across town."

She's right, but the idea of staying there indefinitely makes me itchy. My skin feels too tight when I think about taking things another step in that direction. It's too much, too soon.

"We'll cross that bridge when we get there," I say, happy to move the conversation along. "How was the date with Leo?"

She pauses long enough for the server to deliver our sandwiches. We thank her before she moves on to another table.

Kinsley picks up a fry. "It was fun. We drank and danced and went back to my place for a little nightcap, if you will." She laughs. "It was an all-night cap and then a morning cap. He's quite good in bed."

"I'm glad to hear it." I squirt ketchup on my plate to form the letter *n*. "Not sorry I missed it but glad you had fun all the same."

"I bet you're not. You were in bed with Nate. Well, I assume it was a bed."

I nod.

"And that choice was a solid one because Griffin ... that would've been self-sabotage at its finest," she says with a laugh.

"Oh, crap. Why?"

"Let's just say that I think he's married and has a kid on the way by another woman whose last name he doesn't know that he met on an airplane coming back from a bachelor party in Vegas." She watches my reaction. "*Yeah.*"

I dip a fry into the ketchup. "Wow. Okay. That's a lot to unpack."

She laughs. "Just be glad you're not the one trying to dig into those suitcases because they're probably filled with bedbugs. And lice. And venereal diseases."

"That's such a shame. He was so cute."

"Apparently, half the nation has thought that."

I bite the end off my fry and contemplate Griffin. *Why am I always drawn to guys like him?*

Always, except for Nate.

For as long as I've known him, he's felt like a shelter from the world. He's protected me and supported me and put up with my shit.

Why does that scare me, while the troubled guys don't?

I take another fry.

Because Nate will fight for me in more ways than one.

My stomach twists, and I set the fry down.

"You okay?" she asks.

"Yeah. It was the talk of venereal diseases. It grossed me out." I take a drink. "Leo wasn't at that bachelor party, was he?"

She laughs. "No. Thank God. I'm all for a good bachelor party, but this one sounds like it went off the rails. And not in a funny way like in *The Hangover*. In a *he woke up and didn't know where he was without his wallet and a fresh new tattoo* kind of way."

"How do you know this? Griffin just told you?"

"It's funny what tequila will do to a man."

"Trust me. I've seen a lot working at The Gold Room."

She smirks. "How is that going to go—you bartending and getting hit on while Nate lurks in the back? I can't see him taking that well."

"We've been together now for like a day. I don't have all the answers. I haven't thought about it."

"It could be super hot."

Or super annoying. I think of the way he grabbed my hips from behind the last time I was at the bar. *Okay, or super hot.*

"We'll see how it goes," I say, wiping my hands with a napkin. "But speaking of work, I have to run by there and get my check. If I don't get it in the bank today, I just might overdraw."

"Now you're speaking a language I can understand. I'm always right on the line. Every morning when I check my balance—it could go either way. It's like bank roulette."

I laugh. "I sometimes wonder what it would be like to be a trust fund baby. Oh! Speaking of wealth in buckets, did you know Mallory from Stretch is married to one of the Landrys?"

"Yeah."

I just look at her, eyes bulging. "In a case of the small-world phenomenon, Nate's brother is dating or married to a Landry, and they hang out at their farm—which is not a farm by any stretch of the imagination—sometimes. I went out there yesterday with Nate, and *holy shit*."

"Mallory's husband bought Stretch for her. She told me the story once. It was disgustingly romantic."

I laugh as my phone buzzes in my purse. I grab it and look down.

Nate: Been thinking about you all day.

My body tingles as I read his text. I can hear his voice whispering those words in my ear. And, if I'm being honest with myself, I can feel them being written on my heart.

But I'm not going to be that honest with myself. Yet.

Chapter 21

Nate

"Hey, Murray," I say as I walk through the kitchen. I entered The Gold Room through the back door to check inventory on my way to my office. "Hey, Kira."

Murray turns off the tap. Then he turns around and looks at Kira with a confused look on his face. Kira, on the other hand, stops walking toward the bar.

I stop too. "What?"

"That's it?" Murray asks.

"Huh?" I ask.

Murray looks at Kira. "Are you worried?"

Kira grins. "Yeah. A little bit." She looks at me. "There's nothing else?"

I sigh, putting my hands on my hips. "What's going on, you two?"

"I'm waiting for it," Murray says out of the side of his mouth to Kira. "I think it's going to be bad."

"It has to be. There's always calm before the storm."

"Have you two lost your minds, or are we talking in code today? And if we're talking in code, leave me the hell out of it. I'll just stay in my office until it's over."

Murray and Kira watch one another, their grins lifting higher and higher. Finally, they start laughing.

I have no clue what's going on with them and start to wonder if we don't have a carbon monoxide leak or something.

"Did you guys mix bleach with something?" I ask. "Just tell me. Do I need to open the vents?"

They laugh harder.

I hold my hands out to my sides.

"Nate, my man, there has not been one day in all the days, *months*, I've worked here that you've just walked in with a *hey*," Murray says. "It's always—*why didn't you restock yesterday?* or *the storeroom looks like two gorillas fucked out there.*"

"I've never said that."

"Okay, raccoons then. The point is the same. Right, Kira?"

I level her a look.

She grins. "You do seem to come in with more than a *hey*."

Well, I'm a task-oriented person.

"Fine. Some kind of sauce is smeared all down the wall leading to the back door like someone was taking the trash to the dumpster and just let the bag drag against the drywall. Get it cleaned up." I look at Kira. "There are new pour spouts in a box in my office. Get them all washed and put in the liquor bottles before the rush hits tonight."

"There's our Nate." Murray laughs. "Glad to have you back, brother."

Kira laughs too. "I don't know what it says about me, but I missed this Nate for the whole five seconds you weren't him."

I roll my eyes.

If I didn't like these two so much, I'd fire them.

I grin. *No, I wouldn't. It's not time to fire Murray yet this month.*

"To what do we owe this pleasure?" Murray says cheekily. "Should we assume something has changed in your life and potentially drained you of the testosterone that makes you an asshole."

"I—"

"Wait." Kira turns to Murray. "First of all, are you admitting that testosterone is what makes men assholes?"

Murray shrugs. "I don't know. I was just talking. Don't corner me like this."

"Second of all, if you're inferring that he's had sex with Paige—which clearly he has—sex *increases* testosterone."

"Can we not—"

"It does not." Murray looks at Kira like she's lost her mind. "I'm a man. I know."

"Clearly not. Low testosterone can cause a low sexual desire, but having sex can increase it." She smiles smugly. "Look it up."

Murray pouts. "No."

I wave a hand in the hair. "Okay. Let's stop biology class here and circle back to the topic of me having sex with Paige."

"So you did?" Murray asks. "Atta boy!"

Fuck. "No. It's none of your business," I say, trying to get a grip. "But if I even catch wind of you saying anything to her about this ... I mean it, Murray."

"Yeah. He'll fire you and won't let you come back for three weeks instead of two!" Kira giggles. "Sorry. Couldn't help myself. Continue with your threats. I like hearing him get roasted."

Murray glares at her.

I rub my forehead and wish I hadn't come here. It had to be done, though. I had to let them know that things are fine because I'm sure word has spread about the show I put on the other night. And I haven't been back in since.

My stomach clenches as I consider how Paige may take the ribbing from Murray. The last thing I want, *the last thing I need,* is for him to say something stupid and strike fear in her.

I drop my hand and exhale.

"I'm going to ask you as your friend instead of telling you like your boss to please not say shit to Paige," I say, nearly pleading with Murray. "I know it's funny and whatever, but when she's here, she's at work. Keep it to workish topics, okay?"

157

"We never talk about work."

"Murray ..." I warn.

"I get it. I'm just screwing around with you, Nate. While I do find it funny and the opportunity to tease her is just ..." He touches his fingertips to his lips like a chef's kiss. "I won't do it, mostly because I really like you, and I don't hate her."

His wide smile does nothing to ease my anxiety.

"Now go wash your hands after they've touched your filthy mouth," Kira says.

Murray sighs and turns toward the sink.

"Hey, Paige," Kira says, her voice bright.

I look over my shoulder as Paige walks in. She's adorable in a pair of black joggers and a tight white shirt. I love how her body dips and curves—especially now that I know my hands fit in those bends perfectly.

Paige smiles in a way I didn't expect. I hold my breath, letting her take the lead. *What is she going to do?*

She comes up behind me and wraps her arms around my waist. I grab her hands at my stomach and hold them there. She presses a kiss against my spine, nestling her face in my back.

I hold my breath, shocked at her public display of affection. *Not that I'm against it.* I'd fuck her in the middle of the bar if I wouldn't be pissed that others saw her naked. But I hadn't thought about what it might be like for us in front of other people without Ryder around. And I wasn't sure how she'd take to the whole relationship thing.

Guess she took it well.

I smile.

"This isn't fair," Murray says, drying his hands off.

"What's not fair?" Paige presses another kiss on my back and then slides around to my side. "What are we talking about?"

Murray looks at me with the blankest face I've ever seen. I struggle not to laugh.

"Well ..." Paige says, looking up at me. "What's going on here?"

I wrap my arm around her waist and grin. "I was just dancing around the topic of you and me."

"Are you embarrassed by me?" she asks, grinning back at me.

There's no way in hell, baby.

"Apparently, I'm not allowed to say a word to you about this whole thing, but you can do that," Murray says, pointing at us, "and I have to, what, be blind?"

"No. You have to be polite and not an asshole. Big difference," Kira says.

"Murray not be an asshole? Is that even possible?" Paige asks.

He points at her again. "She's teasing me, and I can't tease her. That's favoritism."

I start to pull away from Paige and escort Murray outside to lay down the law when Paige laughs.

"What's there to tease about?" she asks, stepping to the side and out from under my arm. "I'm going to tell you right now that I'm going to kiss him every time I see him. Do you want to tease me about that? Cool."

Well, all right then.

Shocked, I watch her silently.

Murray looks at me with big, pleading eyes.

"I mean, I'm not going to use my leverage here to make sure I get to work with you on Friday nights or anything," Paige says, trying not to smile. "That would be unfair."

"You told her?" Murray's jaw drops. "*Come on*, man."

Paige puts her hand on her hips. "I'm just teasing you."

"And I can't tease you."

"Yes, you can. Because sooner or later, you're gonna like me too."

He slumps against the sink. "Eh."

"Why don't you like me? Huh? Tell me."

She gives him the look she gives me that makes me squirm. It seems to have the same effect on him.

He shifts his weight back and forth, unable to stand still. Finally, he sighs.

159

"You're so loud. And bossy. And you get your hands in every-thing, and you won't listen to anyone else's opinions."

She grins. "Okay."

He flinches. "Okay? That's it?"

"I'm just listening to you. Do you want to say anything else?"

He drops his jaw, realizing she's one step ahead of him.

That's my girl.

"Murray, I want to be friends. I'll be quieter, and I'll attempt to listen, but I'll probably not be as bossy. Sound like a plan?"

"What just happened here?" Murray looks at Paige, then Kira, then at me. "What did you do to her?"

"You don't want to know," I say, smiling.

Paige laughs, returning to my side. *Where she belongs.* Then she looks at Kira.

"How are you? I'm sorry for running out of here the other night like that."

Kira smirks. "It's fine. He stayed and helped me close, and it all seems to have worked out. I'm a little jealous about that, but I'm happy for you."

"Why are you jealous?" Paige asks.

"Boyfriend problems. It's fine. We'll talk later. I have to get back out to the bar."

Kira gives us a little wave and returns to work.

"You good, Murray?" I ask.

He nods. "I'm confused but good."

"Hey, Murray," I call out.

When he looks up, I wink. "Get that sauce off the wall before I get back out here."

He rolls his eyes and flips me the bird.

Is it time to fire him yet?

Paige laughs as we walk to my office. I shut the door behind us.

"I—*ooh,*" she says as I capture her words with my mouth.

I hold her face in my hands and show her how much I missed her today. *This will never get old.*

She pulls away, grinning, and catches her breath. "That's one way to say hello."

"That's not my preferred way, but it'll have to do for now."

I take her hand and lead her to my chair. I sit and pull her on top of me, wrapping my arms around her.

Hopefully, if she's having any second thoughts about being so open in front of her co-workers, this moment will reassure her that everything will be fine.

And it will. I'll make sure of it.

She rests her head on my chest. "I needed this."

"So did I." I kiss the top of her head. "Did you have a good day?"

"I got a lot of stuff done. So that's good."

"That is good."

"What about you?" she asks.

I sigh. "I had a meeting this morning with Landry Security. I took Lincoln a bottle of tequila so he'll quit hounding me about it."

She grins against me.

"I told them I'd work a job coming up," I say.

"Do you like that job better than this one?"

I consider that. "Well, I like that I built this myself. It's mine. I can be sure it won't fail because I wouldn't let it fail. But I enjoy working with the security company more. It's a bit of an adrenaline shot sometimes, and the pay is great. And it's not all on my shoulders. I can show up, do my job, and come home."

Paige toys with the button on my shirt. "Makes sense."

"I could sit here and hold you all night. But if I make you get up and get my stuff done, I can come home, and we can do this there. Privately."

She hops up. "I like the sound of that."

I lean on my knees. "You do, do you?"

She nods eagerly.

"Get your sweet ass out of here and let me get payroll situated and the order in for wine. If it's not busy, I'll be home around seven or so," I say.

She plants a soft, chaste kiss against my lips. I try to deepen it, but she draws away.

"Nope. I want you to need more so you'll come home," she says, heading to the door. She winks and walks out, closing the door behind her.

If she only understood that needing more will never be a problem.

Chapter 22

Paige

"I feel like a spy," I say, slipping under Nate's blankets.

He wraps his arms around me and pulls me against his bare chest before I even think about where I might get comfortable. I don't mind, though. Not at all.

Nate buries his face in my hair and hums. The peacefulness of the sound swirls around me. *If this isn't how life is supposed to be, I don't want it.*

Moonlight streams into the room, creating a cast of shadows on the walls and ceiling. I watch them move, interrupted by the tree limbs that brush the window softly as I'm nestled in Nate's arms.

"It's cold in here," I say, pushing closer to him.

"Want me to get another blanket?"

"No. Just don't move, and our body heat will warm us up. Two people can get much warmer together than one." *Add a dog, even better.*

He snorts sleepily. "Okay. Do I want to know how you know that?"

I still.

It's an innocent question. But it's a question that stirs something deep inside my soul.

My life has always been delineated from pre-Carmichaels and post-Carmichaels, and the two sides didn't mix. Talking to them about my past felt like I was dirtying up my new life. Not talking about it made me feel like I had shame, and that hurt too.

But could anyone understand the things I had to share? Would I be judged for it? Would they look at me differently?

Hollis didn't. And the more I think about it, the more confident I am that Nate wouldn't either.

The idea of opening up to him about the darker parts of my life terrifies me. I've said things before—just sort of thrown things out there and then changed the subject. But intentionally talking to him about these things, giving him details, and maybe allowing him to respond? To hold space for me?

Bile creeps up my throat, and I have to talk myself out of throwing up. But on the heels of the fear comes a rush of something else—the comfort of knowing Nate will be here anyway.

My throat tightens. My mouth goes dry. I wrap my hands around Nate's forearm for support.

"Do you really want to know?" I ask, my voice timid.

He lifts his head slightly as if he picks up on my hesitation.

"Of course," he says.

I rewrap my fingers around him. "I only have vague memories about most of this. Hollis has helped me fill in some blanks." I clear my throat. "We lived in a three-bedroom house in Indiana. We all had a bedroom, but Mom would often ask me to sleep in Hollis's room. It was fine with me because Hollis was the coolest person I knew."

Nate smiles against my head and presses a kiss at the crown. I don't think about it too much. I might flip out and stop talking. And I need to tell him. *I want to.*

"We'd lay there in his bed and wait. Sometimes, we'd hear a scream or a voice muffled down the hall. Hollis would tell me these knock-knock jokes to distract me. I have flashes of memories about this."

Nate blows out a breath. I wonder if he's nervous about where this is going, but I trek on.

"Hollis apparently went back to our mother for a while in his teenage years. I had already been adopted or was getting adopted—I don't quite know how all of that played out. She ended up losing custody of him again, but he was with her long enough to figure out that Dad was pimping her out."

"Holy shit." He squeezes me tighter.

I close my eyes and remember huddling with Hollis in his bed.

"It seemed like we never had heat—or when we did, it was random, I think. But I have these memories of being cold. And in the winters, *if* I was in my bed, Hollis would come and get me so we could sleep together."

I pause and take a deep breath. *God, I'm so thankful to have had him look after me.* I wonder if it was good preparation for the new big brothers I ended up with.

"Anyway, it was always warmer when we were together. Everything was just ... safer."

Tears fill my eyes, and I blink hard so they go away. But they don't.

"We had a dog for a while, and we'd bring him in and put him on the bed too. He'd keep our feet warm," I say, my voice cracking.

Nate hugs me so tight that I can't breathe. But it's perfect. It's exactly what I need him to do. He doesn't say anything, just holds me, and whispers something against my hair that isn't for me.

I take the deepest breath that I can and blow it out, releasing a load off my heart that I've been carrying my whole life. I can feel it lifting off my shoulders and dissipating into the night.

"It's why I want to be a social worker," I say, wiping my cheeks. "I want to help little Paiges and little Hollises—kids who don't deserve to grow up like we did."

He exhales. It's sharp and heavy.

"I'm so fucking sorry that happened to you, Paige. Like ... I can't even process that."

"It's over, and I made it. I found a wonderful family to love me. I had it so much easier than my brother, and I feel a little guilty about that."

Nate rolls me over to face him. He dries my face with the pad of his thumb. It comforts me to know he cares.

"Listen to me," he says, staring into my eyes. "You can't feel guilt or shame for anything that was done to you. But you can be proud of the woman you've become because *you* did the work to be her. No one else."

He kisses the tip of my nose.

"That's easier said than done," I tell him. "You're really the first person besides Hollis who I've even talked to about all of this. I've always been afraid of opening this wound. Afraid people would think I'm tainted or something."

He drags his finger down the side of my face. "You have no idea what it means to me that you opened up to me. Thank you for trusting me with that."

"Thank you for making me feel safe enough to share that with you."

"It makes sense why you want to do social work now. I get it."

"I can't think of anything else that I ever wanted to do," I say. "What about you? What did little Nate Hughes want to be?"

He chuckles, grinning. "Oh, everything. I wanted to be the guy in Bloodsport. I wanted to be a drummer in a band."

"Really?"

"I have no musical talent, so that didn't last long. What else? I wanted to be a physical therapist for a while. Mom had to see one, and I thought it was interesting."

"Why didn't you do that?"

His jaw sets, and he looks at something over my shoulder. I give him the space I think he needs while ignoring the churn of my stomach.

What did I say?

"My life took a turn," he says, flexing his forearms. "I ..." He sighs.

I kiss him on the nose. The gesture makes him release his jaw.

"I was nineteen," he says. "Dominic was sixteen. It was summer. Super humid out. I remember that. I was in my room just getting ready to go to sleep, and I heard this boom upstairs. And then I heard my mother screaming."

My chest tightens so hard it pinches. I take Nate's hand in mine and lace our fingers together.

"Dom met me at the bottom of the stairs, and we went up to their room, right? I opened the door, and Dad had Mom on her back with a gun pointed at her head."

"*Nate*," I whisper, unable to formulate a sentence.

My heart breaks for the man who's holding it together in front of me. He keeps his gaze steady on the point above my shoulder, and I wish so much that he'd look at me.

"Mom put her hand out like she was telling Dom and me to stay back while Dad held her in place by the neck, pinning her to the bed. Dad looked at us and yelled for us to stay back. And we did. We didn't know what to fucking do."

Tears pool in the corners of my eyes again as I watch him relive the horror.

"Dad started screaming all this bullshit—that doesn't matter. Then he pointed the gun at Dom."

I gasp, a chill running down my spine as I imagine the terror of the moment.

Nate swallows. "The gun went off. The sound was *so loud*. Mom screamed again." He closes his eyes and swallows again. "Like I hate movies with gunshots because of this. It just echoed through the house." He looks down at me. His eyes are glassy. "It was supposed to have hit Dominic. But it hit the wall instead."

"Oh, Nate," I say, tears flowing down my cheeks.

"I lunged for Dad because I knew if I didn't, he was going to kill all of us. I held him down while Dom tried to work the gun out of his

167

grip. Dad just stared at me with this cold cruelness as he overpowered my brother." He closes his eyes. "The second shot would've hit me if Dom hadn't moved the gun at the last fucking half of a second."

The tears are impossible to stop as I watch the man I adore, the man I just might love, struggle through his pain. I bury myself as close to him as I can get without crawling inside his body and hold him as tightly as I can manage.

"I have absolutely no idea how this happened—by the grace of God, maybe—how Dom moved my dad's arm the direction he did, but the shot hit my father ... and not me." His chest shakes. "Dad died. Right there. In a pool of blood in his own bed next to his wife and in front of his sons." His voice wavers. "It was the worst night of my life."

Oh. My. God.

He saw his father ... *his brutal father* ... nearly kill his mother. And then kill himself.

How? How does someone bounce back from that? How do they overcome that and become the great father he is now?

I have so many questions and wonder so many things. But all that really matters is that he shared his pain with me.

He pries me away from him and looks at me. He smiles.

"Don't cry for me," he says, drying my face again. "I'm tough."

"I can't help it."

"Well, help it because seeing you cry makes me feel worse."

I grin, sniffling. "We're a pair, aren't we? I have childhood trauma, and you have teenage trauma. Maybe we can do the next decade of trauma together."

"That would work, but I'm in my thirties." He laces our fingers together. "And if you have any more trauma at any age, I've fucked up somewhere."

I bow my head against him. I don't want him to see this smile. This one is silly, maybe even happy.

And if you have any more traumas at any age, I've fucked up somewhere.

He really wants us to be together. To protect me. To make sure I'm happy.

For the first time, I believe in the idea of ... maybe not forever but a long damn time. And that's progress.

My mind creates ideas of what Nate would've looked like as a child. Was he gangly as a teenager or built as solid as he is now? Did he always keep his hair short, or did he do the middle part that some boys did? Was he energetic and funny like Ryder, or more methodical like he is now?

Maybe someday I'll know.

What?

I still against him, holding my breath as I rethink that through. *Maybe someday I'll know.*

The idea doesn't terrify me like I thought it would. Actually, I sort of like it. *A little Nate to protect from the world. To break the chains of generational trauma.*

"What?" he asks, lifting my chin. "I just felt your whole body tighten."

Do I tell him what I was thinking about? I stare in his eyes and feel a warmth cover me.

"I hope you take this the right way," I say, biting my lip.

"Tell me."

"I was just thinking about how if you and I had a baby someday, like eighty-six years from now, how special that might be. Like a victory for humanity in a very dramatic way."

His eyes widen, the greens turning to gold. A slow smile graces his lips before he flips me on my back.

He doesn't answer me. Just slowly kisses me until I forget what we were talking about.

Chapter 23

Paige

"And he lost the car, Paige. Your father couldn't remember where he parked it. I swear, if he would've parked it in the same row we always park in, we would've been home an hour earlier."

I laugh. "You two are eventually going to just start driving separately to your date nights."

"We can't do that. He'd forget where he told me to meet him."

I shake my head and pull onto Hollis's road.

"Where are you going? You didn't tell me," Mom says.

"I'm going to hang out with Hollis and Larissa for a while. He just got home from Nashville, so we thought we'd catch up."

"I love that you have him there, Paige. I can't wait to meet him."

The last sentence hangs between us, a thinly veiled suggestion to ask her to come to Savannah. And, for the first time since Hollis came back into my life, I don't hate the idea.

"Let me ask him today when he'll be in town, and maybe we can arrange something."

"Yes. Please, baby girl. You have no idea how much that would mean to Daddy and me."

170

"But no brothers," I say, flipping my visor down to block out the early afternoon sun. "We're going to slowly introduce him to everyone. You all can be overwhelming."

I decelerate to give a bird time to fly off the road. I've always wondered if it's their way of playing chicken—getting an adrenaline boost.

"What else is happening?" Mom asks. "You seem happy today. Not that you don't always seem happy, but there's a lightness to you today. That and you eased up on the visit thing."

I think I beam.

Telling my mother about Nate could very well backfire. She can't keep a secret to save her soul, and if she goes telling my father or my brothers that I have a serious man in my life, I wouldn't be surprised if they all showed up with bats. But the idea of keeping the information away from her doesn't feel right either. Nate, and Ryder, feel like a part of my life.

"Well," I say, choosing my words carefully. "I have a boyfriend."

"Okay. Tell me about him."

I hear the caution in her voice, the edge of concern as any mother would have, I suspect. There was a time in my life when that would've annoyed me, but I appreciate it now. Even though there's no need for it.

"Actually, I've been seeing my boss, Nate."

"Your boss? From The Gold Room?"

"Yup."

She pauses. "Well, you've mentioned him many times. It's always been positive." She pauses again. "That's where you're staying. With Nate."

It's a question more than a statement, a way of her working through the thoughts in her head.

"Yeah. I've been staying with him and his little boy, Ryder. He's seven and the cutest little boy ever."

"I have five rather cute boys myself, so I'm going to have to disagree with you there."

I laugh.

"Tell me about him," she says.

I go into a long monologue about Nate and how he makes me laugh, makes me feel good—*makes me happy*. She listens patiently, not interrupting me once, while I word vomit my happiness onto her.

"Well, it sounds like you're smitten," she says.

Smitten. "I think I might be."

"Will he be there when we come to meet Hollis?"

"I don't see why he wouldn't."

"You know we'd love to meet him."

And there's the second thinly veiled suggestion from my mother today.

"I bet you would," I say, pulling into Hollis's house. "And I will take that under advisement."

"Paige!"

I laugh. "I'm kidding. Of course, you can meet him."

The words echo through my brain as I pull the car to a stop. I just said that so easily. *Of course, you can meet him.*

Well, that's new.

"I just got to Hollis's, Mom, so can we continue this lovely conversation where you put your nose into every aspect of my life later?"

"This is my job, and I'm damn good at it."

I smile. I have to agree. "Well, go shove it in Banks's life. He needs a good sorting out."

"Go spend time with your brother," she says. "Love you, Paige."

"Love you, Mom."

I end the call and climb out of the car.

Hollis's house is *nice*. I've been here a few times before to hang out with him and Larissa. It's a three-bedroom Art Deco-style home with smooth stucco walls and rounded corners.

I follow the curving walkway to the front door and ring the bell.

Hollis pulls the door open. "Hey, Paige."

"Hi."

I step inside. He pulls me into a hug, which is the most comfortable exchange we've ever had. *Progress.* I slip my shoes off by the door.

"What's been happening?" he asks as he leads me into the living room.

This room is small but warm with a cream-colored sofa and muted-colored pillows. A television hangs on the fireplace. The curtains are pulled back, filling the room with bright sunlight and a view of a green backyard.

I sit on the sofa. "Not a lot. Working. Getting ready to go back to school. The usual. You?"

"I'm taking a couple of days off," he says, dropping into a brown leather chair. "I was in Nashville longer than I thought I would be, and I've been catching up on shit since I got back. Riss asked me to spend a couple of days with her, so here we are. I can't tell her no."

"Where is she?"

"Upstairs. She jumped in the shower before you came. She'll be down soon."

"Cool." I glance around the room. "My parents are coming to town. I finally caved." I grin at him. "You'd be game to meet them, right?"

"For sure. Do you have any dates?"

I shake my head.

"Let me check my calendar and text you. Coy added a few things —or he was supposed to. I don't want to be out of town while they're here."

"Mom would literally kill me."

He laughs. "Don't let her do that before September."

"Why? What's in September?"

He takes a deep breath. "Well, I wanted to ask you something."

"Okay ..."

My stomach forms a tight knot.

"Riss and I were thinking about taking a vacation in September. It's the first time our schedules align, and we can get away, and we were thinking about heading to Mexico. Booking a resort and just hanging out for a few days. We thought maybe you'd want to bring someone and come with us. It might be fun."

This shouldn't make me want to cry, but it does. *I'm turning into a baby.* I try to smile, but my lips tremble and that only assists the tears. So I just look at him blank-faced.

"I mean, if you want to," he says, thrown by the stupid look on my face.

"Of course I want to. I'm trying not to cry."

"Cry?"

I laugh and pat my eyes with my fingertips. "I've been really ... I don't know who I am anymore, Hollis. I'm a crybaby. I feel things. What the hell is this?"

He snorts.

"Don't laugh at me. I'm being serious. I'm worried about myself," I say, only half-joking.

"I'm not laughing at you. I'm just ... entertained by your spot in life. I've been there."

"You have? So I'm not just a weirdo who suddenly has emotions when it comes to things other than my parents and sad animal commercials?"

He leans forward and rests his elbows on his knees. Then he sighs.

"When I met Riss, I'd sort of trained myself not to get in too deep with things. I don't know if I didn't think I was good enough for her or what. It was coming off a terrible football season, and I was just not in a good place. I didn't know what to do with my life or where to go. I was just wandering around trying to find a path."

"Dude, that's me. You just described me."

He shrugs.

"I've started wondering lately if I don't do it on purpose," I say. "I

174

don't have an excuse not to have my life together. I work in a bar—one I freaking love, by the way. But still. I didn't start college for three years after high school graduation. I've been dating losers with no hope of it actually working out."

Hollis pulls his brows together.

"Do you think I might've been doing it on purpose?" I ask.

"Why would you do that?"

The tightness in my chest makes me gasp for air. I press a hand on my heart.

The more I talk about this, the more it makes sense. *Self-sabotage.*

"I almost wonder if I don't figure life out on purpose because the timer starts for it to end. And ending shit hurts so much that I avoid it by never starting it to begin with."

He nods slowly. "That's really interesting. I might've been that way too."

"Really?"

"Yeah. In college, I was a public figure around campus because of my football career. But I only had two friends I was actually close to. I sort of kept everyone else at arm's length." He strokes his lip with his finger. "I'm going to think about what you said. That's wild."

"Did that change for you, though? Were you ever able to stop thinking like that?"

He drops his finger and smiles. It's pure and raw and genuine, and it makes my heart sing. *I love seeing him happy. He deserves it.*

"It changed when I met Riss."

It's a simple sentence, beautiful and clear. I sit back on the sofa as the tightness in my chest eases.

"How did you fall in love with her?"

"What do you mean?"

I force a swallow down my throat. "How did you know it was okay to be that vulnerable? What made you decide that you could open up and let Riss in? Do you still feel like it could just all end at the drop of a hat?"

He looks at me with understanding. I don't have to explain my feelings to Hollis because he just gets it. And that's another reason I love this man and am so thankful for him.

"When you fall in love with someone, you don't get to choose. You just wake up one morning and realize that this is it. This is your life. It can never go back to the way it was before."

"But what if it all just ends?"

He smiles softly. "Honestly? I don't know. I'd like to think that will never happen. I don't think that anyone can ever guarantee to have anything or anyone forever. That's not true to the cycle of life. But I do know this. No amount of heartbreak could ever erase the happiness she's brought to my life. She's made me a better person. She's given me hope and a life, and ..." He laughs quietly and looks over his shoulder. Then he leans forward. "I told her I'd wait until she came down to tell you, but we're having a baby."

"What?" My jaw drops before I hold my hand over my mouth. "Hollis. Are you serious?"

He nods with the biggest smile I've ever seen—not just on him. On anyone.

I leap to my feet and rush across the room. I pull him into a hug as tears fill my eyes.

He stands, hugging me back. *He lets me love on him.*

My big brother, my protector, the boy who had all the odds stacked against him in life will now be a father. And he's going to be the best father ever. I know because he loved me like one all those years ago.

"I am so happy for you," I whisper in his ear.

He holds me tight, joy rippling off him in waves. "Thank you."

I pull back and wipe a tear from under an eye.

He chuckles. "You have to act surprised when we tell you later."

"I'll be the most surprised I've ever been."

We stand in the middle of his living room, in the house with his name on it—two kids who didn't have a chance.

"I think we did all right in life. Don't you think?" he asks.

I look around the room and think about my life. Someday, I want this too.

All of it.

I look at Hollis again. "Yeah. I think we did."

Chapter 24

Nate

"No! Ryder! No!" *Boom.* "Shit."

My son screws up his face as if my use of profanity somehow outweighs the fact that sugar now covers nearly every kitchen surface.

"Bad word, Dad."

"Thanks. I wasn't aware."

I pick him up off the chair and crunch through four pounds of granulated sugar. I plunk Ryder on a barstool.

"Stay put," I tell him. "Seriously."

He licks his fingers. "That was a tasty accident."

Great.

"What happened in here?" Paige stands in the doorway, making a face like someone's probably in trouble. "Yikes."

"I was trying to make Kool-Aid, the black cherry kind. It's my fave," Ryder says.

"It's your fave? What? Are you sixteen now?" I ask. *Who is this kid hanging out with?*

He licks his fingers. "Jurnee says that."

"The book girl?" Paige asks.

He nods. "Yup. She says *Freckle Juice* is her *fave* book." He giggles. "Isn't that funny?"

I look down at the mess at my feet. "Hilarious."

Paige comes into the kitchen. She removes the towel from her hair as she approaches Ryder.

"Here. Let's clean your hands off," she says.

"No!" He jerks them away from her. "I like it."

She laughs. "I'm sure you do, but Mrs. Kim isn't going to want you bouncing off the walls tonight. Remember? You're supposed to stay over there and play with—"

"Oh! Yeah! I'm supposed to have a sleepover with Mrs. Kim and Jon tonight." He holds his hands out for Paige. "Mrs. Kim bought us games. Have you heard of Sorry?"

"This kid has a better social life than I do," I mutter, grabbing the broom and dustpan.

"I have," Paige says, cleaning the sugar crystals from between Ryder's fingers. "It's a lot of fun. I always like to be yellow. It's the luckiest."

"Okay. I'll try to remember that."

"Ryder, kiddo, let's leave the Kool-Aid making to me," I say, propping the broom against the refrigerator. "Like I told you before you grabbed the sugar off the counter."

"Ugh. It was an accident, Dad."

Paige stands at the edge of the mess and grins. "Yeah, Dad."

I smirk. "Doesn't have the same effect as Daddy."

"I will never call you that seriously," she says, laughing.

Ryder plants his hands on the island. "Why would Paige Stage call you Dad? Are we adopting her?"

Paige giggles as a burst of laughter falls from my mouth. *Oops.*

"Didn't I already explain that I can't be adopted again?" she asks him. "I have a mom and a dad."

"Oh." Ryder tilts his head to the side and watches me brush the sugar from the counters onto the floor. "Well, that's good, I guess."

Paige pulls her phone out of her pocket. "Hey, speaking of my mom, this is her. I'll be right back." She disappears around the corner.

I sweep the sugar into a pile and then onto the dustpan. It takes a solid four loads to get it into the trash can. *There will be sugar crystals lurking for a week.*

Ryder climbs across the counter and grabs two spoons. He entertains himself by using them as drumsticks against the island.

I think back to the text I got from Troy earlier today, asking me if I wanted to hang out with him and his brother Travis to watch a game tonight. I happily told him no.

There's nowhere else I want to be other than here with Paige and Ryder. It's wild. Will I ever want to hang out with them again? Sure. But right now, all I want is in these four walls.

Dinnertime has gone from being my least favorite hour of the day to my favorite one. It used to be a chore. We were both tired from the day, hungry, and thinking about doing other things. But now it's fun. Paige and Ryder have dance contests. They look up random facts about whatever we're making or plan out the next night's menu together.

It's fun. It's easy. It's natural.

Maybe we're a family in the making.

I grin.

"Sorry about that," Paige says, coming back into the kitchen. "Wow. You work fast."

"Or you talked long to avoid having to help me," I tease.

She gasps. "I wouldn't do that."

"I would," Ryder deadpans.

Paige snorts. "So what do you want me to do?"

Ride my cock. She must read my thoughts because she waggles her eyebrows. I have to turn away before things start to spiral.

"Get the chicken out of the fridge for me," I say as I pull out the spices. "Was your mom good?"

"Yeah. She's coming to town next weekend. She wants to meet

Hollis." She opens the fridge and takes out the chicken. "Would, um, would you want to meet her?"

I set the paprika down. *Wow. Okay.* I exhale.

I look at her over my shoulder. She's nibbling her bottom lip and looking at me like she might either take off running or burst into tears.

"Do you want me to?" I ask her.

She pauses, holding my gaze for so long that I'm not sure what she's going to say. The silence causes my stomach to twist into a painful knot.

Finally, she frees her lip. "Yes. I would. If you want to, that is."

I reach for her, then stop. *Ryder.*

She nods as if she understands.

We're going to have to readdress the Ryder situation. This not touching her stuff isn't going to work much longer.

My spirits soar at her admission that she would like me to meet her mother. For Paige, I think that's huge. And I'm certain this is a good sign.

"I would love to meet as many people in your life as you'd let me," I tell her.

She heaves a breath, looking relieved. *Did she consider that I might say no? Silly girl.*

Paige sets the chicken on the counter, lingering next to it.

"So," she says, "I had another call while I was talking to Mom."

I raise a brow. "From who?"

She taps the counter before walking around the island next to Ryder. I turn as she moves, following her with my eyes. *What's she getting at?*

"I looked at an apartment the other day with Kinsley," she says carefully, playing with Ryder's hair. "The lady called me back to offer me a lease."

She fucking what?

If the paprika was still in my hand, I would've dropped it.

"A lease?" I ask. "For what?"

She swallows. "Well, to live there. I don't know what other kind of leases there are besides a car lease, and I don't need one of those."

I don't say anything to her. *She can't be serious.*

"It's pretty cheap," she says, not meeting my eyes. "And in a super-safe neighborhood, which is great. It's a one-bedroom, so no more roommate crap to deal with, and it's above a little coffee shop that has the best—"

"*Paige.*"

When she finally looks into my eyes, I see what's going on.

She's scared.

She doesn't know what I'm going to say or what I expect her to do. We've never specifically addressed this issue—which is stupid in retrospect. It never occurred to me because, in my head, she'll never leave. But in *her* head, the person who doesn't live here, of course she'd be right to worry. I never offered her a permanent place here.

And I hate that I didn't think about that. I should've.

Ryder sets his spoons down. "Who is living there? I don't understand."

I also hate that we're having this conversation in front of him. But maybe it's easier this way. Maybe now is the time.

Paige's eyes don't leave mine. "Maybe me."

"What?" Ryder scrambles to turn around.

The barstool wobbles, and Paige plucks him off the seat before it falls over. He holds on to her neck, hanging off her like a sloth. It would be funny if my heart wasn't in my throat.

"But you live here," he says, squishing her cheeks with his sticky hands. "You live with us."

Her lips are pressed together like a fish. Her eyes get cloudy.

"Yeah," I say, my voice raw. "You live here with us."

"Do you not like us anymore?" Ryder asks her, holding her face in front of him like his life depends on it. "I like you, Paige Stage. I don't want you to leave us. You make the best pancakes—even better than my dad's. And you play cars with me. And you read me books and do all the voices. *Please don't find another house.*"

182

I walk over to them and pry my son off her. "Come on, buddy. You're probably hurting her face."

"I didn't mean to," he says, his voice two octaves higher than normal. Panic rips through his eyes. "You aren't really leaving, are you?"

Paige looks at me, batting her eyelashes to hold back her tears. I can't help it. I reach for her and pull her into my side.

"Why don't you just stay here?" Ryder says, talking faster. "Stay here and just move your stuff into Dad's room because you go there every night anyway, and that way, you don't have to go back and forth, and you'll sleep better. Probably. But Dad snores."

I chuckle. *Guess we weren't so sneaky after all.*

Paige touches Ryder's face but leaves her gaze on me.

"I want to be the guy who tells you to follow your heart," I say carefully. "But I can't do that because if your heart tells you to do anything but stay here with us, then that's the wrong answer."

She buries her face into my chest.

I close my eyes and hold the two people I love most in the world. Because I do. *I love her.*

She came into our life like a train wreck, imposing herself into our lives. But somewhere along the way, we became a unit. The three of us blended together and carved out something fucking perfect.

A family.

This is what I want for my son. To hell with maturity and stability although Paige isn't immature or unstable. I want someone fun, someone strong, someone who will play cars with him and read him books.

Someone who will make him feel loved.

If anyone knows the importance of that, it's Paige. After everything she's been through in her life, she understands how the love of an adult can change a child's life. She understands how *not* receiving love from an adult can impact a life.

And I think she might not just be falling for me, but my child too.

That's a total slam dunk.

I kiss the top of her head. "Will you stay with us? It doesn't have to be forever—"

"Yes, it does." Ryder climbs off me and hangs off her neck. He puts his nose right against hers, making her laugh. "You have to stay here forever because I love you, Paige Stage. All right? More than I love the Camaro, and that's a lot."

Paige and I laugh. It makes Ryder smile too.

He slides down her and then climbs back up on his stool. "Can we get back to dinner now? I'm hungry."

I twist my girl in my arms and look down at her. Her eyes are bright and clear. *They're happy.*

"For what it's worth," I say softly. "I love you too."

Her eyes go wide. "You do?"

"Paige, how could I not? I would've told you before, but I was afraid you'd freak out. But my man Ryder here gave me an opening."

She moves us so that my back is to Ryder. Her hand cups my cock through my jeans and squeezes.

"I'll give you another opening if you need one," she whispers.

I growl, making her smile.

She moves her arms back around my waist, letting her hair dangle on my forearms. For the first time—the first *real* time—she truly relaxes in my arms.

"Guess what?" she says, pressing her lips together.

"What's that?"

"I love you too."

I lean down and kiss her, using everything I have in me not to deepen it.

"You love me too, right?" Ryder asks.

We break the kiss and laugh. And somehow, that's exactly how it should've ended.

Chapter 25

Paige

"That was a long night," I say, wiping down the bar.

Nate pulls the shades over the windows and double-checks that the door is locked. It's our usual closing routine. But tonight, things are different.

He disappears into the kitchen, side-eyeing me the whole time. A smirk graces his lips.

A zip of excitement races down my spine as anticipation sets in. Anticipation for what, exactly, I don't know. But something is about to happen. I feel it.

I toss the rag I was using on the bar top into the bin on the floor. *What do I do now?* Usually, I'd shout at Nate that I'm leaving, and then I'd walk out the back door. But I'm going home with him now. *How does this work?*

We haven't closed the bar down together since I moved in with him. Either one of us has been here or he's had Murray do it.

I walk around the end of the counter and mosey around the room. Chairs are on top of the tables so we could mop. The lights are off except for the light bar over the mirror on the back wall.

I come to a stop next to the pool tables just as Nate walks back into the room. There's a confidence in his movement that could be construed as arrogance if you didn't know him. But I do know him, and I know what's about to happen.

My breathing stalls as he gets closer.

Instantly, my body tightens, ready for the experience he promised me days ago. It's never happened. Ryder has been home. And on the one afternoon, he wasn't, what started as a bath ended up in a deliciously slow oral exchange that I still think about.

"Have you ever played pool?" He walks by me, brushing against my side. His finger hooks the side of my shorts as he goes.

Pool? I don't want to play pool, Nate. Come on.

"Not really," I say, trying not to be frustrated with him. "Once or twice in here just messing around. Why? Do you want to teach me?"

He takes two sticks off the rack. "Get us a couple of drinks, and we'll see what you're made of."

I was joking. I don't want him to teach me how to play pool.

I want him to bend me over a chair. Pull my hair. Slap my ass and make me scream. I want to know what he's capable of. I'm desperate to see the other side of him.

"Okay," I say as cheerfully as I can and head to the bar. It takes everything I have not to flip him the bird as he chuckles softly.

I make two rum and Cokes, although I want a shot of tequila. Nate watches me the whole time.

His gaze is heavy—intentional. The entire room is heated from his stare. The unknown eats at my restraint. *What is he going to do? Is he going to do it now? Here? Is he going to torture me with freaking pool?*

He smiles. *He's doing this on purpose.*

Two can play that game. One probably better than the other, but I'm still tapping in.

I squat down and remove my bra. My nipples press against the white tank top. *I couldn't have planned it better if I had tried.* I stand with my back to him and gather a few cherries into a bowl.

I take a deep breath and gather myself, ignoring the way my stomach tightens at the thought of what I'm about to do.

Breathe, Paige.

Grabbing the drinks, I walk around the end of the bar.

Losing the bra was worth it. Nate's eyes widen, *darken*, as he watches me near him. He licks his lips slowly.

Dammit.

I set the drinks on a table but keep the bowl of cherries in my hand. Nate leans against the pool table and smirks. *We'll see about that.*

My heart pounds as I wonder vaguely if I've let my head, in this case, overload my ass.

Let's hope not.

I saunter his way and stand inside the *v* of his spread feet. "Want one?"

He opens his mouth. I press a cherry between his lips and pull the stem away. He sucks it into his mouth, never taking his eyes off me.

I pop one of the bright red fruits between my lips and make a show out of closing them over it. His eyes darken even more.

His hands grip my hips, digging into the skin just above my waistband. Fingers flexing, he holds me in place as he watches me.

I grab the back of his head, lacing my fingers into his hair, and guide him toward me. It takes little effort to bring his lips to mine. His mouth opens, giving me the access I'm looking for. We kiss slowly—tongues lazily gliding across one another. When I pull away, it's obvious it's too soon for his liking.

He raises a brow and then takes the perfectly tied cherry stem from his mouth.

My body tightens, begging for him to touch me like I know he can. *But he doesn't.*

"That's impressive." His words are controlled. Precise. His tone is low and gravelly, the vibrations lick at my core. "What do you want, Paige?"

My mouth goes dry. A flurry of goose bumps scatters across my skin as I look up into his eyes.

"I want you to fuck me." *Is that not fucking obvious?* "You promised me that you would. I want it. *Now.*"

"Who am I to tell you no?" He grins mischievously. "Unbuckle my pants."

I set the cherries on the table and then reach for him. His cock is already strained against the denim. *Breathe.* I make quick work of his belt and the button, then carefully tug his zipper all the way down.

Slipping my hand into his boxer briefs, I free his cock. He pushes his pants over his hips as I stroke him.

"Now what?" I ask, batting my lashes.

"Get on your knees."

I drop onto one knee and then the other. Running one hand up and down his shaft, I lightly stroke his balls with the other.

He widens his stance.

"What do you want now?" I ask.

"Suck it."

I place a kiss next to his cock. He shivers as I drag my tongue over and up his length. I swirl my tongue over the tip, wiping away the precum gathered at the tip. Instead of doing what he expects, I flick my tongue gently across the underside of his length. He flexes, moving his hips as he groans.

The sound causes my stomach to clench, begging for attention. But not yet. I'm going to finish what I started.

"Does that feel good?" I ask, swiping over the spot that makes him shudder.

He hums. "Don't get used to being in control."

Never letting my eyes lose connection with his, I take him into my mouth. A rush of air escapes his lips as I roll my tongue around the head of his cock. Once I'm sure it's nice and wet, I pull back and blow across it.

"Damn you," he growls.

I laugh. "Following orders."

Pressing kisses down his cock, I lick the underside on the way back up.

"Are you going to come in my mouth?" I ask him, dragging my tongue over the tip again.

He runs his fingers through my hair, pulling the roots hard enough to get my attention. "You are driving me crazy."

"I love it when a plan comes together."

I grin and then give him what he wants. I wrap my hand around his shaft and take him in as far as I can without gagging. After finding a rhythm, I cup his balls and massage them gently.

He bends, reaching his hand down my shirt, and cups one of my breasts.

I swirl the head, spit dripping down him, and smile. Then I plunge his cock down my throat again.

A shock bursts through me, only pooling my desire even more.

"Fuck, Paige," he says.

I sit up a little more so I can take him farther. With both hands in my hair again, he guides me up and down.

I'm so wet it's painful.

"This is so good, baby," he says, struggling to get the words out. "Too fucking good."

I hum against him. The rumble causes him to groan.

He thrusts into my mouth, his thighs tensing and his breathing quickening. The head of his cock swells as my eyes start to water.

"If you don't want come in your mouth, pull back," he grits through clenched teeth.

I pump him again as the first shot of hot liquid hits the roof of my mouth. He gasps, his hands tightening in my hair, pushing my mouth down on him. Another shot pours down my throat.

The veins in his cock pulse with every shot of semen. He moans something unintelligible, his neck stretched and Adam's apple bobbing.

It is, by far, the hottest thing I've ever seen.

I ease my grip and slow the motion as he releases my hair. After a final swipe of the head with my tongue, I sit back.

"That's the quietest you've ever been," he says, catching his breath.

"I'm also the wettest I've ever been." I lick a streak of orgasm off my lips. "So can you please do something about that?"

My sex quivers, aching so badly that I'm not sure I can even be touched. But as Nate shoves the pool balls out of the way and the sound ricochets through the empty bar, I know there's no other way.

He has to touch me.

With rough yet gentle hands, he picks me up and sets me on the edge of the pool table. He guides me so that I'm lying back with my ass at the rim. He bundles my skirt at my waist ... and then sees I'm not wearing panties.

He raises his eyes to mine. "You've been here all fucking night with no panties?"

I grin. "I wanted to be ready in case you wanted me."

He slides a finger inside me. "If I hadn't just come harder than I ever have, I'd be coming again right now."

"Well, in lieu of that, I'd like to come." I smile. "Please."

He licks the inside of my thigh that's coated with my need for him. Then he presses a kiss almost but not quite close enough to my clit.

"Nate," I groan. "Come on, dude."

He laughs. "Dude? Really?"

Reaching behind him, he picks up a cherry. He grins, holding it by the stem and dragging it through the folds of my sex.

I can feel the sticky juices drip from the berry to mingle with my own.

"Are you trying to drive me crazy? Like, is that the point? Because if it is, you win. Winner, winner chicken dinner. Now eat me like one, dammit."

He laughs, tracing a path with the cherry up my slit and back down. "You are so impatient."

"Well, this doesn't feel good. I'm communicating with you about my needs. I am not happy. I want you so bad it hurts."

He grins. I do not.

My body screams for a release. I'm fevered. Tense. Desperate for him to put his mouth on me.

I reach for my clit, but he snatches my wrist well before I get anywhere near my destination. With my hand in his, his eyes glued to mine, he holds the cherry up in the air.

Holy shit.

He drops the fruit into his mouth and smiles.

"If you don't do something soon, I'm going to do it myself," I say.

"Not sure how you're going to do that since I'm in control here. Also, as much as I would love watching you get yourself off, that's my job."

Just as I'm about to protest, he spreads my thighs wider. Once I'm completely open to him, he buries his face between my legs.

I yell, my head hitting the table as I fall back, succumbing to the intensity of his face against my throbbing clit.

He licks and sucks, flicking my pulsing nub like I did his cock earlier.

"Nate!" I almost scream. "Damn!"

I need a release. I need it so bad that I'm desperate.

His tongue flattens against me, allowing me to grind against his mouth.

"This feels so fucking good," I say through clenched teeth. "I'm going to come on your face."

He chuckles, shoving two thick fingers inside me.

"Fuck!" I scream.

The pressure is my undoing.

He twists and pulls his fingers from my body, continuing to thrust over and over as my orgasm crashes over me.

I grab his head and hold it in place as he licks, kisses, and brings me back to earth.

I sag as he removes his fingers and pulls his face back. His mouth and cheeks glisten, coated with my wetness. If he's bothered by it, I wouldn't know. The grin on his lips says otherwise.

"That was a good cherry too." He winks at me. "Was that good for you?"

"Yes," I mutter, too depleted to say anything else.

He chuckles, wiping his face with a napkin. "You're not done yet."

I lift my head and look at him like he's crazy. "No. I am."

He takes my hand and pulls me to my feet. My legs are weak, my knees wobbling as I find the balance that I lost somewhere between the cherry and his tongue.

"You wanted to be fucked. I'm fucking you now."

I jam my thumb over my shoulder. "But ..."

His grin is wicked and devilish. "That was foreplay."

"Nate ..."

He guides me to a bench by the dartboard. "Bend over, ass up."

He can't be serious. But when I look at him, he is. *Very.*

His cock in hand, already hard, he's rolling a condom over his length. *Where did that come from?*

He grips my waist and positions me over the bench. The leather is cold against my stomach. My eyes are so heavy I close them.

I feel Nate come up behind me. I feel him spread my legs with his foot. I feel his hand on my ass, caressing the cheek.

Then I feel him.

The head of his cock parts me open. His hand comes down hard on my behind just as he thrusts deep inside me.

"Shit!" I yelp, fully awake.

He pulls back and then presses in long and hard.

The sensation is intense. It's hard and hot and burns in a way that I know I'll now crave.

There is no ease, no gentleness—no getting me used to him. He takes me in an animalistic way. Dominant.

He grips my hip so hard that his fingers bite into my skin, and I wonder if his prints will be there in the morning.

"I like it!" I shout. "*Oh, fuck.*"

I squeal as he takes me even harder, winding his hand through my hair and tugging backward. My throat is flexed, totally exposed, and for some reason, that makes me feel even more vulnerable.

His balls hit my clit as he finds the tempo that works for him.

It hurts to swallow. It hurts to yell. His balls smacking against my clit burns like hell.

"*Fuck,*" he moans, thrusting as far as I've ever taken him. His body shakes behind mine as his cock pulses another orgasm. I squeeze him as I find mine.

Finally, his grip eases, and he relaxes. Then he pulls out.

I fall forward into the bench, gasping for air. *There's no way I can stand.*

Sweat dots my brow as I struggle for a breath and will my vision to return.

Nate bends down and scoops me up, my legs over one arm and my back supported by the other. When I look up, sweet Nate is back.

I lay my head against his shoulder. It shakes as he chuckles.

"Was it all you hoped it would be?" he asks.

I try to nod and answer him verbally, but neither really comes across.

He presses a kiss on my forehead. "I'm going to take you into my office and clean you up before I take you home, okay?"

"I can't move."

He kisses me softly again. "I'll take care of you."

As he turns toward his office, I grin against his skin. Because I believe him. And that feels better than anything in the world.

Chapter 26

Paige

I groan as I slide into a booth at Paddy's.

"Are you okay?" Kinsley asks me.

If you only knew.

Memories of Nate from last night flood through my mind. The way he was so alpha, so in control, but ultimately so him.

Damn. It hurts so good.

"I'm great," I say, needing to focus on the task at hand and not Nate's actual hands. "What do you think Marcie is going to say?"

Our friend texted our group chat this morning—the one she'd abandoned since the eviction—and asked us to meet her for lunch. We chose Paddy's as the location. Kinsley and I showed up with curiosity and low expectations.

"I have no idea," Kinsley says. "She's radio silent for weeks, and then she comes back with a lunch invite? I'm not sure how to take that."

I place my napkin on my lap and shrug. "Maybe she just wants to come clean about whatever happened, and she only wants to do it once."

"That's a solid suggestion."

194

Kinsley looks over my shoulder. I can tell that Marcie is coming our way by the look on Kinsley's face. For a split second, I wish Kinsley had sat beside me.

Marcie approaches us hesitantly, her bright red curls bouncing. She stops at the table and gives us a tight grin. "Hi, guys."

"Hey," we say in unison.

She takes a deep breath and scoots in the booth beside Kinsley.

"Thanks for coming," she says, setting her purse between her and Kinsley. "I didn't know how else to try to bandage our friendship, so I figured doing it like this was the fastest and best solution."

Kinsley looks at me with a *well done* grin.

"So what's going on?" I ask. "What in the world happened?"

Before she can answer, the server appears. She takes our drink orders and then retreats.

Marcie fiddles with the edge of her napkin. "This is going to sound so stupid. And I'm humiliated about it and even saying it out loud to you ..." She gives us a tight laugh. "I've put this off for days."

"You can tell us anything," Kinsley says. "We're your friends, you know."

Marcie looks at me with tears in her eyes. "And I screwed you over. I could've at least given you a heads-up that we had to leave, but I thought I could scramble and get the money, and it wouldn't be a big deal. Except that's what I had been doing for weeks."

"Did you need the money?" I ask. "Because if you needed it, you could've just asked us."

"You should've," Kinsley cuts in. "I mean, we would've helped you all we could."

"But that's the thing. There's nothing you could do except make things worse."

Kinsley and I look at each other.

"Do you remember that girl who I started hanging out with?" Marcie looks at me. "Lorrie. She had long black hair. I brought her to the apartment a couple of times."

"Yeah. Kind of skeezy. Had that look that made me want to lock up all my valuables? I remember her."

Marcie sighs. "Well, I met her at a gas station one night. We were both buying lottery tickets—the scratch-off kind. It was late, and we were the only ones in there, and we just struck up a conversation."

The server sets our drinks in front of us. "Do you know what you want to order?"

We all look at each other. *It depends on how this goes.*

"Can we get a couple of appetizers?" I ask. "Maybe some cheese sticks and chips with queso? Then we'll figure out our entrees."

She grins at me. "Sure. Thanks. I'll be back with your apps shortly."

Once she's gone, Marcie starts again.

"To make a very long and embarrassing story shorter and less anxiety-ridden," she says, "she introduced me to a world that I didn't know existed."

"Like a sex dungeon or something?" I ask.

She laughs. "No. That would've been preferred." Her smile fades, and she cringes instead. "It was gambling."

"Gambling like my dad does?" Kinsley asks. "He goes to the horse races and stuff. Expensive hobby, as my mother says, but that's the first thing that came to my mind."

"I mean, it's the same theory," Marcie says. "But it started on a basketball game. I was super lucky and hit it big—like I tripled my money on one game. That somehow hooked me. I thought it was easy. I was betting every game every week. I'd lose and then bet more because I had to make that up, and it was only going to take one big one to get me even again. Eventually, I was in so deep that there was no getting even."

Kinsley puts a hand on her shoulder. "I had no idea."

"How could you? It's not like I was physically any different. It was just ... bank account different. And that's why it's so dangerous. You can't look at someone and know they're pissing their money away on a basketball game. It just becomes this addiction, really. You wait for the high that comes with winning. All your problems will go away if you can only hit one more time." She frowns. "Except you don't."

My heart hurts for her. Marcie used to be so confident and walked around like she owned the place. So to see her sitting meekly next to us and having the courage to admit her problems out loud—that means a lot.

"You're okay now? You don't have any bookies coming after you or anything, right?" I ask.

She shakes her head, grinning. "No. I'm okay. I mean, I lost everything I had, but thankfully, my parents have been super helpful and understanding. They're helping me get back on my feet, getting me some help with this gambling beast that I now battle."

"You're going to be fine," I say. "You're strong, and admitting the problem is half the battle, right?"

"Well, it's hard not to admit you have a problem when you come home and you've been locked out."

"That's true." I smile at her. "Things will be okay."

She looks at me, then Kinsley.

"So you guys aren't writing me off then?" Marcie asks.

"Only if you eat all of that queso," Kinsley jokes as the server sets the appetizers in front of us.

Marcie sits a little taller. "Thanks. You guys are so good to me."

There really isn't a choice but to forgive. That's something that's been modeled to me for years. *Well, since I've lived with the Carmichaels.* Those brothers of mine have needed constant forgiving over the years. *Constant.* Marcie and Kinsley are like sisters to me. I've treasured their friendship for the past almost year, and I have leaned on them time and time again. That means—second chances. And if I'm very honest, life has taken the best turn because of her situation.

I reach for a cheese stick. "Well, I can't be mad at you. I don't know if I ever would've landed where I did without a push. Or an eviction. Either way."

Kinsley laughs. "Oh, do we have a story for you, Marcie."

My insides tighten as I prepare to say Nate's name. It feels different now that we're a couple, now that Ryder knows what happened.

Now that he's eaten a cherry soaked in my juices.

He's not just *Nate* anymore. He's *my Nate*. The guy who I go home to. The guy I can call if I have a flat tire—and he will come. The guy who will get me a pudding cup in the middle of the night and not be irritated when I eat it in bed.

There's something really meaningful in that.

"So" I say, shifting in my seat. "Do you know Nate Hughes?"

"Your boss?"

I nod.

"I stayed with him after the eviction," I say, setting my cheese stick down on a plate. "And now we're a couple."

Marcie looks like I just told her the Earth is flat.

"What do you mean?" she asks.

"She means she's living there, sleeping in his bed, making dinner with his kid. That's what she means," Kinsley says.

"Paige. Are you serious?" Marcie asks.

"Yeah. Why? Why are you looking at me like that?"

She lifts a brow and takes a chip out of the basket. "No reason besides the fact that it's *you*."

"What's that supposed to mean?" I ask, borderline offended.

Kinsley sits back in the booth, her eyes wide.

"I'm sorry, Paige. I didn't mean it like that," Marcie says. "I'm just saying ... I've known you for, what, a year? Close to it? And you've always been so anti-*this*."

My hackles raise even though I know she's not being mean. I lean against the table.

"Maybe because I didn't know that it could be like this," I say. "I've never had a nice guy before—someone who takes care of me. That loves me."

"Loves you?" Kinsley says. "Okay. That's progress I didn't know."

I fire her a look to hush and then focus back on Marcie.

"We're taking it slow," I say, defensive. "He understands what I've been through and how I feel about long-term commitment."

"Does he, though? Because you're living there, making dinner with his kid, and he loves you. That doesn't sound slow or like a fling that might end tomorrow." She dips her chip in the queso. "I'm happy for you. You know I am. I'm just shocked. That's all."

Marcie and I have stayed up countless nights talking about things like this. About our lives, our past, our hopes and dreams. And while I've never really told her about what happened to me, I'm sure she can piece together enough to get a decent picture.

To hear her tell me she's shocked that I've made this move with Nate hurts my heart. I want her to be happy for me. And I'm sure she is, in a way, but *why is she acting like this is a bad decision?*

Kinsley sits up and eyes me carefully. "Paige is really happy. I think this is a good call."

Marcie takes a bite of the chip. "I'm not saying it's not. I'm just saying that it's hard to see her go from a girl who maybe dates a guy for six weeks tops to playing stepmom to a little boy. Maybe if I was here to see it all go down, I'd feel differently. But just stepping in now at the end ... I just want to make sure she's not living in la-la land before it's too late."

"This isn't la-la land," I fire back.

She leans forward until her chest is pressed against the table. "I love you, Paige. But I know what it feels like to be in a honeymoon phase in a relationship ... or a gambling addiction." She rolls her eyes. "It's fun at first. The world is your oyster. You can forget all the consequences that are coming because it feels so good at the moment. All the boundaries you've set up, your ability to reason and use logic —it all goes out the door. And then one day you wake up, and the honeymoon is over ... and you owe someone a lot of money. Proverbially, of course."

I level my gaze with Marcie. "You know what? You're coming across really shitty right now, and I don't appreciate it. Our situations are vastly different."

"I didn't mean to be shitty, Paige. I'm sorry."

"I would hope not, considering how kind I've been to you."

"So where are you staying now?" Kinsley asks Marcie, not wanting to see fireworks.

I tune out their back and forth, not caring at the moment where Marcie is staying. Her words ring through my mind.

I'm still using logic. I'm able to reason. Nate and I have communicated, and he understands my need to take things slow, just like I understood his need to protect Ryder.

"You have to stay here forever because I love you, Paige Stage."

My heart swells in my chest, and I look at Marcie.

She might've gotten in too deep with the wrong people, but I did not. I might be falling hard for a man and a little boy who already mean so much to me, but that's exactly where I'm supposed to be.

I know it. I feel it in my soul.

My phone dings, and I look down. "Hey, I need to take this, okay?"

Marcie and Kinsley continue their conversation as I scooch off my seat and walk outside.

The air is warm and filled with the scent of cinnamon from Judy's bakery a few doors down. *I should really get a donut.*

Instead of comforting myself with a pastry, I open my text app.

Banks: Heard you have a boyfriend.

I grin. *Just the distraction I needed.*

Me: Mom has a big mouth.

Banks: I think she wants me to get the scoop—the real one. The one you won't tell her.

Me: Oh, you mean that he's a felon for murdering two women in the Pacific Northwest with a machete and that he kept their heads in a freezer?

Banks: Oddly specific.

Me: We're great at communicating.

Banks: You know, first impressions are a real thing. And this is his first impression. Text wisely.

I can't help but laugh.

Me: Fine. He's great. Very handsome. Owns his own business and works part-time for a security company. He chased a guy off from the bar the other night that was flirting with me and he went after Atticus a couple of months ago.

Banks: For what?

Me: Let's leave it there.

Banks: Let's not.

Me: You're losing sight of the conversation.

My fingers tap against the side of the phone. Bringing up Atticus could go either way, but Banks didn't like the sound of him from the start ... mostly because Atticus answered my phone and that conversation didn't go well.

Banks: Is he nice to you?

Me: Very.

Banks: Is he willing to meet Mom and Dad?

Me: He's looking forward to it. He'll probably cook them dinner.

Note to self: inform Nate of his need to possibly cook my parents dinner.

Banks: What's his last name?

Me: Hughes. Why?

Banks: No reason. Let him know your brother is one bad mother-fucker, and I will kill him and drink his blood from his skull if he missteps. And I don't give second chances.

Me: I'll tell him that verbatim. *winking emoji*

Banks: Love you, little sister.
Me: Love you, pain in my ass.
Banks: *flexed bicep emoji*
Me: *eye roll emoji*

I breathe in a long, slow lungful of air.

It's interesting how different perspectives make you feel.

Banks's comments come from a true place of love because he's family. He wants his little sister to be happy. Mom was absolutely delighted to know that I'd found someone who treated me right. But I haven't ever talked about my past, certainly not my need for safety against the cold things in life.

Marcie's one of my best friends, but she's drawing her thoughts from actual conversations we've had. Was I that jaded that I've never said anything positive about being in a relationship? I'm sure she wants me to be happy too, but do I listen to her voice over the others who are happy for me?

Don't let Marcie get in your head. You know your relationship with Nate and everything is fine.

"For what it's worth, I love you too."

A smile stretches across my face, and I go back inside.

Chapter 27

Nate

I press enter.

The confirmation screen appears on the screen, listing the supply items I just ordered for next week. I screenshot the number and then exhale.

Life is good.

I sit back in my chair and stretch my arms overhead. Paige's perfume still lingers somehow. It crosses my mind that it might be on me and not still embedded into a piece of fabric in the room—and that makes me smile.

Knock! Knock!

"Yeah?" I call out.

The door opens, and Shaye and Kira walk in. They're both grinning suspiciously.

"What?" I ask. "What happened?"

"Nothing," Shaye says. "We need a favor."

"*I kind of need a favor.*" The last time someone asked me for a favor, it changed my entire life.

"What do you want?" I ask.

Kira sighs. "You'll tell us this is stupid and to use our phone, and we did. But the screens aren't big enough."

What?

"You're just going to have to understand that we're women, and this is important to us," Shaye says. "*Okay?*"

"I'm not okaying anything until I know what you want."

"We need to borrow your computer," Kira says.

I look at her like she's crazy. "No."

"Come on," Kira says. "Please?"

"No." I roll my chair back so I can square up to them. "The last time someone used my computer, they looked at porn. I got a virus—the computer got a virus—and I had to get a new one. Then I had to reload all my shit, and that took forever, and I didn't know any of my passwords. So the answer is no."

Shaye scoffs. "You should always use your pet's name followed by your birthday. If you need a special character, use the one above the six and nine."

"That's complicated," I say.

"How is that complicated? It's all the things you should know already. It's the simplest formula in the world," she says.

I lean forward, resting my arms on my knees. "What if I don't have a dog?"

"You've never had a dog? Ever?"

"No. Never had a dog. I went from having a fighting problem to a son. Skipped the whole dog thing."

Kira sticks out her bottom lip. "Well, that's sad."

"What's sad is that the bar is now apparently a free-for-all because my employees are back here wanting to use my computer for some ridiculous thing." I raise a brow. "Am I right?"

"No," Kira says, mocking me. "Murray is taking care of it for a second. There's no one out there. It's dead."

I sigh. "The next employee that I hire, I'm gonna be a dick so they don't bother me."

Shaye laughs. "You're already a dick. You'll need to level up."

I roll my eyes.

I'm not going to get out of this. And, really, I don't even care. I just have to give them a hard time so they don't think I've lost it.

Can't have them think they can steamroll me now that I'm getting soft.

"Fine," I say, motioning to the computer. "But be quick about it."

They waste no time waking the screen out of sleep mode. Then surprisingly, Shaye unlocks it with my passcode.

"Hey," I say, rolling my chair closer. "How did you do that?"

She rolls her eyes. "Everyone knows your passcode is Ryder with a six and a nine."

They do? I better change that.

I watch as they pull up a page full of girly shit.

"Just search it by the item number," Kira says before rattling off a long series of numbers.

Shaye's fingers fly across the keyboard and hit enter with a flourish.

"That's it," Kira says, pointing at the screen.

I lean closer to see what they're talking about. But it's not necessary. Shaye hits some keys, and then visibility is not an issue.

A ring with a purple stone takes up the entire screen.

"What's that?" I ask.

Kira looks at me over her shoulder and beams. "My boyfriend told me last night that he wants to propose to me and asked me to find a ring."

"I don't know a lot about this, but doesn't that take the fun out of it?" I ask. "Aren't you supposed to be surprised and cry and all that gooey shit?"

"Nate, I can play the hell out of acting surprised." She steps away from the computer and then jumps up in the air with her hands on her face. "Oh, my gosh! You didn't! This is the best day of my life!" Then she drops her hands and smoothens her features. "See? Easy."

"You know, it's scary how well you just did that," I say.

But I don't think she hears me. She's focused on Shaye.

"Okay, I love this," Shaye says. Amethyst with rose gold is so gorgeous. But if you want something different ..."

Another set of rings pops up on the screen. Shaye clicks around again and brings up a diamond with a blue and white band.

"Oh, I love that too," Kira gushes. "What is it?"

"A sapphire and diamond band with white gold. But the ring head under the diamond stone is rose gold." Shaye points at the screen. "It just has so much dimension."

I bury my head in my hands.

"You could go with a ruby," Shaye says.

"I don't like rubies. I think they look weird on my hand. My grandmother had a ruby ring that my aunt ended up with—long story, and I remember trying it on once, and it makes me look too yellow or something," Kira says.

I lift my head. "I love all the girl talk, but can you do it somewhere else?"

"What do you think?" Shaye asks me. "Amethyst, sapphire, or ruby?"

"I think I don't care."

"Pick."

"She should get whatever makes her happy or," I say, looking at Kira, "whatever your boyfriend gets you."

She puts a hand on her hip. "Think about it. He's going to spend thousands of dollars on a ring that I'm going to wear for the rest of my life. I'm going to give this ring to my daughter someday, hopefully. Isn't it smarter to make sure I like it before buying it?"

"I don't know. What are you going to say—I hate it?"

"He wants me to be happy, Nate."

"Cool. Be happy. Go to the kitchen, pick a ring, text it to him, and then finish washing the bar glasses for tonight. *Please*."

"Fine. But we're here when you want to talk rings." Shaye winks at me. "You can call me anytime, and I'll help. I'll even go shopping with you."

My stomach flip-flops. "Off you go."

Shaye makes a mean face—or what I think she wants to be a mean face—and they walk out.

I wave as they shut the door.

The room seems quiet without the racket of the two of them. I turn back to my desk and see the rings on the screen.

I sit back in my chair and look at the sapphire. *I wonder what kind of ring Paige would want?*

I make a fist and then cover it with my other hand. Then I bring them to my lips.

I'm aware of how I feel—*I'd marry her tomorrow.* There isn't a scenario in my life that I can imagine without her. *That I want to imagine without her.*

Greeting her when I come home from work.

Grocery shopping for dinner.

Parent-teacher conferences.

Buying a house to fit a growing family.

Having a child.

Sitting in matching recliners with the television up entirely too loud and yelling at each other over top of it.

Everything from the mundane to the exciting is better with Paige Carmichael. *Paige Hughes, if I have my way.*

I stand and mosey around my office, looking for a distraction.

We have to go slow. Tap the brakes just a bit and let her get acclimated to coupling and living together before I push any farther.

"*I don't know if I believe in forever.*" Her words from before sweep through my brain.

"I really think that you don't know if you deserve forever," I say to the empty room. "But I will show you that you do. No matter how long it takes."

Chapter 28

Paige

"Hey!" I wave at Murray as I walk into The Gold Room. "Is Nate still here?"

"Not sure. Just got here."

Great. "Thanks, Murray."

I pace across the floor, wishing I had driven around back to see if his truck is parked next to the dumpster.

I don't know why, but I need to see him. I need his arms around me and to breathe in the scent of his cologne.

Marcie's stupid words come back to me, pummeling my brain over and over without pause. I ducked out of lunch early, needing a reprieve, and came straight for The Gold Room.

Her words might be true to her, but they don't apply to me. *They're not.* I feel it in my heart. All the sweatiness and anxiety since she went on her ridiculous monologue is simply from the salt on the chips.

That I didn't eat.

I knock on his door and then push it open, not waiting on him to answer. The office is empty. I turn to leave when something catches my eye.

208

My stomach drops. I slip inside and shut the door softly behind me.

What the hell am I doing?

I struggle to breathe as I see—rings. *Why are there rings on Nate's computer?*

The website is a popular jeweler in Georgia. I've seen their commercials a million times. And the ring on the screen? Stunning.

"What the hell?" I sit in the chair and stare at the screen. An ad banner flashes at the bottom of the screen.

The key to a happy marriage is buying her beautiful jewelry!

I lean in as if I can't actually see what's on the screen. *Like I can't read what's happening.* The ring on display is billed as *an investment in your happily ever after.*

"No," I say, not believing what I'm seeing. "That's not ... No."

I hit the back button. And again. More rings pop up.

"He was sitting here looking at rings?"

It's as if everything inside me pauses—like it takes one giant breath and stills.

Nate's looking at engagement rings?

It doesn't make sense. I've been super clear about my intentions.

Take it slow. Forever scares me. I have issues I need to work out. I've said it all to him, multiple times, in various forms. *And he's looking at rings?*

A part of me is happy that Nate would want to marry me. But the rest of me ...

Things have been good. *Very good.* It's been the best part of my life, bar none. But the thought of that kind of commitment paralyzes me.

My head spins, feeling the impending conversation that we'll have to have. *How do I pretend I didn't see this?*

What do I do if he has the ring? Is that why he's not here? Did he go buy it?

Oh, God ...

I can't be a wife to someone. I can't create a life with Nate. Hell,

I'm just figuring out what I want to do with mine. *Maybe.* How can I be expected, *be trusted,* to hold up half of a marriage?

The more I think about it, the faster the room spins.

What happens if forever isn't real? What does it look like if things don't work out?

My heart pounds.

Ryder.

"*You have to stay here forever because I love you, Paige Stage. All right? More than I love the Camaro, and that's a lot.*"

Tears pool in my eyes as my insides twist so hard I struggle to breathe. *What am I doing by staying at Nate's house?*

My hands go to my head, sliding down to cover my face. *This can't be happening right now. Not when things were going so well.*

But that's the way of the world. When things are going well, there's only one way it can go. *Bad.*

I stand, needing to move. *Maybe if I move enough, this won't be real.*

Ryder's sweet face pops up in my head. His sticky hands and goofy smile. The freckles scattered across his nose.

The way he holds his hands up when he's pretending to box like Uncle Dom and how his eyes light up when someone mentions Camilla Vanilla.

The tears that have been threatening to fall break free. They cascade down my cheeks and onto my shirt.

Nate has worked so hard to create a great life for him and his son. The only thing I can do is upset the balance ... eventually.

How can I be a mother to Ryder when I work part-time at a bar, and I'm still going to college? Hell, I'm not much better than a teenager.

"*I've run around. I've dated. I've done all of it, and Ryder is seven now and impacted by all of that shit. And, quite frankly, I'm tired. I just want to settle down and maybe have another kid or two and build something together.*"

Nate was right. He's always right. Ryder is impacted by his dad's decisions.

I squeeze my eyes closed and see Marcie.

"A honeymoon phase in a relationship ... It's fun at first ..."

I look over my shoulder at the ring.

"You can forget all the consequences that are coming because it feels so good at the moment. All the boundaries you've set up, your ability to reason and use logic—it all goes out the door. And then one day you wake up, and the honeymoon is over ... and you owe someone a lot of money."

A shiver rolls down my spine as my heart cracks into two jagged, chest-slicing pieces.

"I have to get out of here."

There are too many voices competing inside my head. I can't ... *Why did Marcie have to show me the truth of what I'm capable of?* Or rather ... *what I'm not capable of.*

Because it was the truth. And the absolute truth sucks.

I close the door behind me.

Chapter 29

Paige

I knock on the door.

The sun is hidden behind thick, gray clouds, and the irony is not lost on me.

I knock again.

Finally, when I turn to leave, the door opens.

"Paige?"

I was holding it together pretty well—I'd stopped crying on my way over. But as soon as I see Hollis, I break down in tears.

"What's wrong?" he asks, wrapping one arm around me and pulling me inside. "Paige?"

"I need a second."

"Yeah. Sure. Take your time." He guides me into the living room —the one that I felt so happy in before. "Do you want me to get Riss? Like, is this a girl thing, or can I handle it?"

I sit on the sofa. Using the backs of my hands, I dry my eyes.

"I don't know, Hollis. I'm just so ..." *Scared.*

He sits in the chair that I've pegged as his favorite and studies me. "Are you okay? Physically?"

"Yes." I blow out a breath. "I'm sorry."

The realization of what I've done—driven to my brother's house mid-heartbreak slash panic attack and tossed him into the middle of it —isn't fair.

I start to stand. "I shouldn't have come here."

"*Sit.*"

Okay. I lower myself back on the sofa.

"Something is wrong enough that you came here. Now talk to me. What's going on?"

I open my mouth to speak, to tell him all the things, but it turns out that talking while you're mid-spiral isn't easy.

He sits with his hands folded together, watching me carefully.

What do I say? That I just scared myself shitless? That I have the best damn boyfriend in the world with the cutest kid that I've ever seen, and he apparently wants me to be his wife, and I'm terrified?

Yeah. That doesn't sound ridiculous or anything.

"Have you ever just run?" I ask him. "I don't mean a mile or whatever. I mean, like just ran to get away from everything that terrifies you?"

"More times than I can count."

"Really?"

He sits back and blows out a breath. "The only thing that ever terrified me was people. And I ran like hell from them. I didn't want anyone getting too close to me. Even my two closest friends—I kept my distance from them too in a lot of ways."

"What terrified you about it?"

"The connection," he says, shrugging. "If I had a connection with someone, they could break it. If I just kind of floated around, then whatever. It didn't hurt so bad if something happened, you know?"

Yeah. I know.

"I lived a long time just trying to get to the next day," he says. "The next sunrise. The next meal. The next football game. It was all I had—the hope for the next thing because I couldn't hope for anything beyond that." *Because to believe in anything beyond that meant believing ... hoping in forever.*

213

My tears dry. I sniffle. "I'm sorry you felt like that."

"It sucked. After I graduated, I didn't know where to start with my life. I'd played football, and my life had centered around that. And then all of a sudden, I was on my own with no one to help me, and I ... I almost messed up the best thing that ever happened to me."

He looks at me knowingly, as if he already knows what has happened.

"Paige, I've run from people my whole life. I even left Larissa at a New Year's Eve party because I heard a song that ... just brought up bad memories."

"How did you get her back?"

He chuckles. "She came and got me. Brought the whole family with her." His grin is true. "They showed up for me when I had no one and claimed me as their own. I owe this family my life for saving me from myself."

Thank you for taking care of him.

"Now, what's going on with you? Who are you running from?" he asks.

My spirits fall again. "I'm not running. Not exactly. I just need a moment to breathe."

The voices—Marcie, Nate, Ryder—clutter my head again.

My phone buzzes, and I look down.

Nate: Hey, where are you?

Tension pulls on every fiber of my body as I read his text.

"I think Nate was going to propose to me," I say.

"Whoa. Okay."

"And I ... panicked." I look up at Hollis. "I *am* panicking. This is mid-panic, even if I don't look like it."

He grins. "What are you panicking about? What bullshit did our parents embed into you without your consent?"

My lip trembles.

"Look, Paige—if anyone gets the fucked-up part of your brain, it's me. I've been there. Lived there. Almost died there a couple of times. So talk to me."

I look at my brother and smile. *I'm so glad we found each other.*

"I'm just really scared," I admit, saying the words out loud.

"Of what?"

I shrug. "Of everything. I'm afraid of losing him. I'm afraid of staying and fucking it all up. I'm afraid of getting engaged, and then something happening ..."

"*A honeymoon phase in a relationship ... It's fun at first ...*"

"And then owing people money," I say.

Hollis makes a face. "Huh?"

"Never mind." I sigh. "If thinking about losing him now hurts this bad, then what will it feel like if it ends six months, a year, six years down the line?"

"You can't do that, Paige. You can't live your life expecting the worst. Trust me. I tried it."

"But things don't last. Nothing does. The honeymoon phase is over, and then reality kicks in, and it's just a bigger mess."

I think of Ryder again and how I can't risk ruining his life like mine was.

I force a swallow down my throat. "I don't remember the day we were removed from our home very well. I have random flashbacks about chocolate chip cookies and milk. But that's about it."

"That's the snack they gave us at CPS."

Oh. "But you know what I do remember? I remember the first night lying in bed and feeling so scared and so alone." Tears fill my eyes again. "And Nate's little boy—he loves me. We have the kind of relationship that will have us growing close. Bonding. And what if something happens someday and I need to leave? Or Nate leaves me? What does that do to Ryder?" I stand. "It keeps the cycle of pain going, Hollis. It transfers the shit that happened to us onto Ryder."

"No, it doesn't."

"*Yes, it does.*" My heart beats so hard that I grip the sofa for support in case I pass out. "It takes my abandonment issues, my fears, my stupid shit, and puts them on a little boy who has his own mess with his mother. That will come creeping back to him at some point and I'll be damned if I'm going to add any load onto that poor boy."

Tears stream down my face in hot rivers.

"We can't just live our lives without thinking about what could happen to other people. And I'm too much of a risk."

Hollis gets to his feet and pulls me into a hug again.

"What do you need me to do?" he asks.

I pull away as my phone buzzes again.

Nate: Are you okay? I'm getting worried.

I look at my brother. "Can I stay here tonight? Maybe a couple of days?"

"Of course."

He glances at my phone as it goes off again.

Nate: Hey, call me.

"What are you going to do about him?" he asks.

"I don't know."

Hollis takes a step back. "I think you owe him a conversation. If he was going to propose to you, he loves you. He wants to be with you forever. And I know you love him."

"You do?"

He chuckles. "Yes. So go talk to him. I'll come if you want me to. But at least let him know you're okay and that you're safe. It'll mean a lot to him, and he hasn't done anything wrong. Just loved you too hard, maybe."

That's true. Nate's only offense was loving me too hard, too fast. And I can't punish him for that.

"I'll go talk to him," I say.

"Want me to come?"

I shake my head. "I'll be fine. He's not going to hurt me." *He'd never hurt me.*

"Call me if you need me," he says.

"Thanks, Hollis."

I carry my phone to the door and step outside. Then I look at the sky.

How am I going to do this?

Me: I'll be home in a minute.

As I read that back—*home*—I cry again.

Chapter 30

Nate

"Hey, where have you been?"

My heart drops to the floor.

"Hi," Paige says, tucking a strand of hair behind her ear. Her eyes are dark, her lips swollen, as she stands in the doorway to the kitchen.

"Have you been crying?" I ask her. "Paige, what's wrong?"

"I'm fine. Honestly. I'm fine."

She's not fine. That much is obvious. *But what happened?*

I reach for her to pull her into me, to comfort her—but she pulls away.

My blood runs cold.

I set my Snack Pack down and try to stay calm.

"Where is Ryder?" she asks. "He's with Camilla today, right?"

I force a swallow. "Yeah. They're riding horses or something."

"Nate, we need to talk."

My shoulders fall. She could very well say a million things—there are all kinds of reasons to talk. *But I know what it is.*

I grip the edge of the counter and look at her. "Why?"

It's the simplest word yet the hardest to say.

Tears pool in her eyes as she looks down. "I just need some space."

"What did I do?"

"Nothing."

"Then why? Why are you leaving because that's what you're doing, isn't it?"

My eyes sting, unwilling to blink. There's no way she's leaving me. Not after everything we've shared.

"Paige, I love you—"

"I know." Tears fall down her face. "I know you do, and I love you too."

"Then why are you leaving? What happened? I don't understand."

She looks around the kitchen. At the spot we shared our midnight snacks. Where we stood to make dinner as a family. Where I kissed her before she went to her room—before she stayed in mine. *Ours.*

"Talk to me so I can fix it," I say, the words rushing out. "Whatever it is, we'll work it out."

"Nate—"

"You were fine this morning. You left here happy, and we made plans for tonight. I'm supposed to be taking you to dinner right now, and you're in here breaking my fucking heart."

"I'm so sorry," she says, her words caught on her tears. "I'm so sorry."

"Then stop it. Stop it if you're sorry, baby."

I reach for her. When she pulls away, my heart shatters.

"This has nothing to do with you," she says. "Please understand that. I just ... I need some time. I need to think. My head is a mess, and I ... I don't want you to be upset."

My eyes bulge. "You don't want me to be upset? What should I do? Turn on the television and relax?"

"Nate, please ..."

"Do you want time? Will you consider coming back?" I take a

step toward her. "Dammit, Paige. I'll give you anything you want. Just don't end this for good."

She backs away, clearly struggling as much as I am. *So why won't she just stay?*

"Thank you for all you've done for me," she says.

"No. Don't say that. That sounds like goodbye."

"You are the best man I've ever known and I think you were made for me."

What?

None of this makes any sense. I just stand in front of her, speechless, and watch her disappear down the hallway. I don't go after her because I'm frozen in place.

She's leaving me.

But why? I consider every one of our interactions today, yesterday, last week. All I can conclude is that she was happy. Yet here we are, and she's wanting space.

"You are the best man I've ever known, and I think you were made for me."

So why the hell is she thanking me and leaving me? Leaving us?

She comes around the corner with her bags in her hand. "I love you. I want you to know that."

"You don't get to say that and then leave me with no fucking explanation," I say, my frustration turning to anger. "What else can I do? *Just tell me.* Don't do this, Paige."

Don't break my fucking heart.

"This isn't easy for me either," she says softly. "I'm just trying to do what's best for everyone."

"You are what's best for me. How is that a question?" I pause. "Are you saying that I'm not best for you? Is that it?"

"No," she says, the tears streaming again. "You're the best thing that ever happened to me."

I lunge toward her and take her face in my hands. Her body shakes, wracked with tears, as I press my lips to hers.

The kiss is wet and salty and tastes like goodbye.

When I pull away, I'm not sure if the dampness on my cheeks is from her tears ... or mine.

"I'll call you," she whispers. Then she bows her head and walks out.

She's given up on us. On the possibility of a family. On the possibility of forever.

And that shatters me.

Because we both know she's not going to call.

Chapter 31

Paige

I cover my face with my hands.

The light coming in the bedroom is on the wrong side. I reach over for Nate and get a fistful of sheets.

I scramble to sit up and then remember.

Breathing is difficult as the anxiety constricts its ugly head around my body. My head pounds from a mixture of overthinking, crying, and the tequila that Hollis finally let me have to help me sleep.

I grab my phone to check the time. My heart sinks.

Nate: I miss you.

I miss you too.

There are three missed calls from Kinsley, two of which I sent directly to voicemail last night. I just couldn't talk to her. She knows me well enough to see what I would have done with Marcie's words. *Self-sabotage.*

My feet hit the floor, and I stand, wishing I was being guided to the kitchen by a little boy *not* asking me for pancakes.

The thought makes me smile.

I walk down the hallway with tons of black and white pictures of Hollis and Larissa and other people I don't know. They all look so happy.

I take the stairs slowly and then across the dining room to the kitchen. Larissa is standing by the refrigerator.

"Good morning," she says softly. "How are you?"

"Do you have any coffee?" I ask, ignoring her question.

She grins. "I'll make some. Have a seat."

"You don't have to make it for me. I don't want to put you out."

"*Sit.*" She shakes her head and busies herself at the Keurig. "You are so much like your brother it's crazy."

"Really?"

She looks at me over her shoulder. "Yeah. You both deflect questions you don't want to answer. You always think you're bothering people. And you're hardheaded as all get-out."

I can't deny that.

She presses a button, and the machine makes a noise.

"So did a night of rest help you make sense of things?" she asks.

"I don't know. I didn't get a night of rest." I take a banana out of the fruit basket on the counter. "I just wish ..." *That I hadn't heard Marcie.* "I don't know. I wish a lot of things, I guess."

"You have to do what feels right to you, Paige. If that means giving yourself space until you're sure, then do that."

But I am sure. I want to be with him. I just ... can't.

"I just want to cause them the least pain, you know? Because if I'm being honest, I was going to walk out eventually. I do this self-sabotage thing where I ... implode my life? Keep me from having nice things?"

"Thinking you don't deserve them?"

Oof.

She hands me the coffee, her bracelet with a little succulent catching the light. "Hollis does this thing—he used to do it terribly, where he wouldn't buy himself anything. Like, *nothing.* The boy had a hole in his shoe and refused to get a new pair." She laughs. "He felt like he had to trade something to get the shoes or whatever it was. He had to write a song or finish a paper or do whatever it was to deserve the thing he needed or wanted."

I hold the banana and suddenly don't feel like eating it anymore.

"It's taken a lot of deprogramming to get him out of that head-space," she says. "Don't get me wrong—he still doesn't spend money. But he'll get what he needs, and he'll treat himself sometimes. And, of course, I spoil him."

I smile at her. "I'm glad he has you, Riss."

"I'm glad I have him."

"Even with his need for deprogramming?" I ask.

She leans against the counter and looks at me. "See? You see it as a negative. I see it as a positive."

"How?"

"All of that stuff in his head that makes him feel ... certain ways, whatever they are, from time to time? It's because of some really shitty people doing some really shitty things to him. *Yet he made it.*" She smiles brightly. "He made his way to me. He's the strongest person I know. And every day when I wake up, and I look over, and he's lying there snoring—because that man snores, let me tell you—I feel like the happiest person in the world."

That's because she has one of the very best men I know as her person. And Hollis is also one lucky man to have Riss and her family as his.

I think about what she said. It makes sense. And I'm happy for Hollis.

But Hollis isn't me.

"Thanks for the coffee. I'm going to grab a shower. Do you care if I take it to my room?" I ask.

"No. Heavens, no. Your brother eats and drinks as he walks around the house. He's a heathen sometimes."

I try to smile. I mean to. It's just hard to cut through my sadness.

I take my coffee and head upstairs. Once I get there, I check my phone.

Nate: I love you.

I love you too.

Me: Distract me.
Banks: Needy much?
Me: Banks. Please.
Banks: So there was this cat last night in the alley behind the house.

I lie on the bed and let Banks take my mind off the mess in my head.

Chapter 32

Nate

"I'm not in the mood, Dom. Don't start."

My brother closes his mouth. The amusement written on his face when I walked in is replaced with confusion.

"Good morning to you, too," he says.

"Do you want to talk about anything?" Troy asks.

I sit a few chairs away from Dominic instead of beside him like usual. I don't trust myself not to start swinging today.

I woke up—which is a joke because I didn't sleep—pissed. And sad. And lonely.

The same thought came rolling through my mind. *When was it over for her?*

Did she know this was coming? Did something happen yesterday? Was this always the plan?

Because it's not over for me.

She asked for space, and I'll give her that. She wanted time, and that's fine. As long as she comes back.

And I made no promises not to try to get ahold of her in the meantime.

Me: I had to make Ryder's pancakes this morning. Apparently, we do syrup shapes now. I had no idea. It resulted in a meltdown for Paige Stage. You are missed.

"Nate?" Troy says.

"Huh?" I look up to see Dominic and Troy staring at me. "What?"

Troy shrugs. "Are we gonna fight today? Talk? Not talk? What are we doing here?"

I don't know.

I could tell them Paige left me, but it feels so soul-crushingly wrong. It's like admitting she's gone. That we aren't together. That she's not coming back.

Fuck that. Fuck all of that.

"Let's fight," Dominic says. "I haven't kicked either of your asses in a while."

Me: I don't know how you have five brothers and don't kill them. I have one, and he might not make it to the end of the day.

Paige: Six.

My face lights up. A warmth floods my body, and I sink back into the chair. *She's reading my texts.*

Me: I'm making spaghetti tonight. Hope you are there.

Nothing.

Dominic sits up and slides a pen down the table. It hits me in the forearm.

"Hey," he says. "Talk to us."

"What do you want me to say? I'm in a bad mood."

"No kidding."

I glare at him. "Dom ..."

"Sorry I'm late." Ford comes into the conference room and sits at the head of the table. "What are we ...?" He looks up. "Okay. What's happening here?"

"Nothing," I say, pulling my gaze to Ford.

"Bad morning?" he asks.

"Something like that."

"Okay." He opens his black folder and gives each of us a packet for a concert we're going to work on. "I want to start with ..."

I stop listening. I can't force myself to care.

Chapter 33

Nate

hoever said time heals all wounds was a liar.
Granted, this is just the second morning since Paige was here, but that's beside the point.

I woke up this morning with the worst headache I've ever had. There's a gnawing, bleeding feeling in the pit of my stomach and, no matter how I move or what I drink, it's still there. It's from the loss of her. I'm not ignorant.

If I knew where she was and that she was okay and safe, and that someone was taking care of her, it would be better. Maybe.

As much as it pains me, it's almost worse that I can't be confident that she's okay. I had Shaye call her last night. Paige didn't answer but texted her that she was busy and wouldn't be working this week. She also requested that Shaye *please let someone know ...*

Fuck.

I'm torn from my thoughts by the little feet tapping the floor. Ryder's standing in the doorway, frowning.

I'm so sorry, my boy.

"Oh," he says.

My heart squeezes. I turn the stove off and move the eggs to a cold burner. *Please let me know what to say.*

This is what I was worried about. This is why I wanted to find someone ready to settle down. Yet even though Paige is gone, I don't regret having her here. Not at all.

She brought a light into our lives. She gave us a taste of what could be. *She showed me ... us what we were missing.*

I look at my son and, although I hurt for him, I know he'll be okay. He's strong. He's like me.

"Hey, buddy," I say. "Want some breakfast?"

"Where's Paige Stage?"

I take a deep breath. "She had some stuff to do."

"Is she coming back?"

My eyes close. *I can't lie to him.* "I hope so."

He shifts his weight from one foot to the other. "Her stuff is gone. I looked."

"She had to take it with her. What was she supposed to do? Go naked?"

He almost grins. *I wish I could too ...*

"Let's eat breakfast. You can come to work with me today if you want to. I'm just doing paperwork."

I hope this brings a smile to his face. He loves hanging out in my office and snacking on the chips and Sprites that the girls pretend to sneak into my office.

Like Paige used to do.

I move to get our plates, even though I'm positive neither of us has an appetite. But we have to keep going until I can figure out what to do.

"Daddy?"

My throat burns as I face him.

His bottom lip quivers. "She's not coming back, is she?"

"Ryder, I ..." I gather all of my courage.

How do I answer him when I have no clue if Paige will come back? How do I avoid breaking his heart? I go with honesty. "I don't know."

The green eyes that usually sparkle with mischief now blur with tears. The sight of it stabs me in the heart.

"Then we have to go get her," he says, his voice on the verge of panic. "We have to go, Dad."

I wish we could, buddy.

"Why are you standing there? Huh?" He stomps his foot, his face red with anger. "You can't just let her leave."

"It's not that easy," I say, my voice cracking. "She's a grown-up. We can't make her stay here if she doesn't want to."

"But she does want to. She loves me. I know she loves me."

"Ryder ..."

Tears flow does his little, rosy cheeks in rivers. "I will go find her if you won't."

"I'm trying. I promise you I am."

"Then try harder because she needs us. She needs us, Dad. She's probably scared wherever she is and we are just here eating breakfast. She'll think we don't love her."

I reach for him but he smacks my hand away. He's angry ... with me.

I wish I could explain it to him in adult language and make him see that sometimes things don't work out. But he can't grasp those concepts yet.

Damn it.

"Paige knows we love her," I say as calmly as I can, swallowing the surge of emotion welling in my throat. "I promise you that she knows that."

"She's counting on us, Dad. She thinks you're the best dad ever. She told me that." His eyes widen. "She said you're a very good man and you'll always keep me safe. You aren't like her dad."

My eyes burn. I don't rub them because I'm afraid I'll cry. I can't cry in front of him, even if my world is falling apart, because he needs me to be strong.

"I will keep you safe," I say, touched by Paige's words.

"Well, you love her too. So why are you just letting her be out there with monsters?"

Oh, my boy.

I grab him and lift him into a hug. He squirms, upset with me, but settles as I hold him.

I'm not sure who needs who more right now.

Ryder pulls away and takes my face in his hands. His breath smells like he ate a pudding in the middle of the night and his eyes look like he's just wrestled one of the monsters under his bed.

"Listen to me," he says, squishing my lips together.

He stares into my eyes like we're about to discuss the end of the world. Maybe we are—*the end of our world as we know it.*

"I'm listening," I say as clearly as I can.

He's undeterred. "You are the only one of us that's not scared of anything. You have to be the grown-up and be responsible. Okay?"

"Okay."

He leaves his eyes pinned to mine to drive home his point. *Like I don't already understand.*

I set him on his feet. He straightens his shirt and huffs back to the doorway.

"No work today. We're gonna find Paige," he says, storming down the hallway. "I'm tired of you being lazy about it."

He slams his door.

I exhale, wishing I had the strength to walk to his room and tell him to open and close his door properly. But who cares right now?

"There's nothing like being put in your place by a seven-year-old," I mutter, massaging my temples.

There isn't an easy fix to this mess. I can't respect her boundaries and give her the space she needs and still be happy. And like Ryder said, I don't think Paige can be happy either.

But why does she want space? Why can't she be here? Why did she tell me she loves me but she has to go?

It doesn't make sense.

I toss the eggs down the garbage disposal. *No one is eating this morning.* I start towards the shower when my phone rings.

My heart leaps in my chest, hoping it's my girl.

It's a number I don't know. Instead of sending it to voicemail, like I usually do, I take a chance.

"Hello?" I ask, holding my breath.

"Is this Nate?"

"Yeah. Who is this?"

"Hi, Nate. This is Hollis Hudson. Paige's brother."

"Is she okay? Is everything all right?" I ask, pacing the kitchen.

He sighs. "She's fine physically, if that's what you mean. Nothing has happened to her."

"Fuck," I say, blowing out a breath. "That's good to know."

There's a pause, a long moment of silence as the conversation switches gears. We go from the courtesy period to ... whatever he's calling about. And by the stretch of quiet, I'm not sure it's going to go well.

I stand next to the dishwasher and wait.

"We don't know each other well," he begins. "I've been in your bar many times. We have lunch there on the first Friday of every month. So we've met but never *met*, if you know what I mean."

"I do."

"But I'm going to cut the shit and talk to you like I know you, if that's all right."

Here we go. "Definitely."

"I'm standing in the middle of my backyard to talk to you so my sister doesn't hear me."

She's at Hollis's. Noted.

"She's a wreck," he says. "And I just ... This isn't my place to get involved. I know that. But I can't sit here and watch her torture herself."

"I don't want her doing that either. I don't ... I don't even know what fucking happened. Everything was fine. She left to have lunch

233

with her friends and the next thing I know, she's done. She's standing here in tears telling me she needs space."

Hollis groans. "I don't know how much to say without disrespecting her privacy. So, let me ask you this. Be honest with me. No games." He takes a breath. "What's your deal with Paige? What are you thinking? What are your intentions?"

I run a hand down my face and release a tight laugh.

"What are my intentions? I fucking love her, Hollis. This girl has my heart in her hands. My only intention is to make her happy. To give her a soft place to land. To give her the best life, a family, whatever I can, to see her smile every fucking day. All right? That's my intention here. Good enough?"

"So if you love her, if you know her, then you know some of the shit she's been through."

"Yeah. She's shared some of that with me. You two had a rough time of it."

He sucks in a breath and blows it out. The sound scratches through the line.

"Going through that kind of stuff—it has its way of hiding in your head. You wake up one day and you're twenty-one and think you're far removed from that shit. But then you try to live a life and there's a ... a *darkness* around every corner."

Damn.

"I'll be honest with you, and you can take this for what you will," he says. "When she said she was staying with you, I called a few people to see what was up. And I read some things about you."

I hang my head.

"I have an inkling that growing up wasn't easy for you either. And I heard what happened with your father."

My stomach twists.

"And I also heard that you tried to take the fall for your brother," he says. "That he was the one holding the gun when it went off and you tried to say it was you."

A lump settles in my throat. My eyes burn at the memory and at the fact that Hollis knows this. *How the fuck does he know?* I've tried to forget that entire night. But Hollis is right. It does cause a darkness to exist within you, waiting to rear its ugly head.

"The only people I'd ever take a fall like that for is Paige and Larissa. Because I love them," he says.

"Makes sense," I say, the words barely coming out.

"I think you and I love the same. Hard. Willing to die—willing to do anything for the people we love. Am I right?"

"Yes."

"And you love my sister?"

"Absolutely."

He sighs. "Then be a man and fucking fix this. *Do something.*"

Fuck. "I can't. She asked me for space and I promised her at one point that I would give her all the space she needed."

"She needs space, Nate. She needs not to feel pressured, not physical distance."

"I'm not pressuring her for shit, *Hollis*," I say, my irritation growing. "And I'm not the one that picked physical distance as the coping mechanism here."

"Don't blame my sister for this."

"I'm not blaming anyone but, reality check, I didn't do anything."

He makes a sound that tells me that if we were eye to eye, we'd be on the verge of fist-to-face.

I can't blame him though. He loves her like I do. We both want the same thing, the same result.

"We're getting off track here," he says, his voice more measured. "If you want to fix this, show her you want to fix it."

"And how do I do that and give her the precious space she's asked for?"

"No need to be a dick."

"No need to act like this is a fucking cakewalk, either. What do you want me to do, Hollis? Want me to come over and throw her over my shoulder and bring her home? Because I will. You have no idea how much I'd like to chain her to my bed until she comes to her senses."

"Easy there. We're cordial. Don't ruin it."

I roll my eyes, but he's right. My nostrils flare as I try to calm down.

"Look, she got scared," he says.

"Why? I don't know why. *Someone tell me fucking why.*"

"Talk to her. Don't let her ruin this for herself because that's what she'll do." He chuckles sadly. "She loves you. And I know from personal experience that she's going to run from that as fast as she can. It's in our DNA. It's some kind of abandonment response or some shit. But save her from herself, Nate. If you love her, save her. Don't let one mistake snowball into more."

I hold my head and try to mold his words into something actionable. *Can I do that? Can I just make this better? Even though she asked me not to?*

That's exactly what I want to do as long as it won't make things worse.

I look around the kitchen with no spoons in the sink, no pancake batter on the counter, or sugar on the floor.

Can it get any worse?

"I'm going to give you a tip and you can do with it what you want," Hollis says. "Larissa and I have an appointment at two o'clock. Paige will be here alone. That's all I'm saying."

For the first time since I came home and she wasn't here, a little hope flashes through me.

"You're a good man, Hollis."

"And I hope you're one too. Talk soon."

"Goodbye."

I shut my phone off and stick my head down the hallway.

"Ryder! Come here! I need your help!"

Chapter 34

Paige

"Hey," Hollis says, coming into the living room with Larissa at his side. "We have a doctor's appointment to check on the baby. We'll be back in a couple of hours."

I smile at them, even though I don't feel it in my soul. "Okay. Good luck."

"You okay?" Larissa asks. "I mean, I know you're not but do you need anything?"

"No." *Just Nate.* "I might run somewhere and grab a sandwich. I need a little fresh air and I don't know when I ate last."

Hollis swallows. "Oh, um, yeah. I have a box of shit from Coy being delivered today."

"You do?" Larissa asks.

"Yes. Papers and stuff. Could you hang around here until it comes? I'll order you food."

I wave him off. "Don't worry about it. I can order myself food."

"You don't mind waiting around here?" Hollis asks.

"My social calendar is packed." I wink. "Kidding. I'm happy to stay and get your important papers. But I might read them. Just warning you."

He laughs. "Go right ahead."

"Call us if you need us," Larissa says, eyeing Hollis out of the corner of her eye.

"Bye, guys," I say.

They wave and make their way to the garage. The door closes softly.

"And this is why you don't date men like Nate," I tell myself as I stand. "Because it freaking hurts."

I wander around Hollis's house, finally feeling comfortable in their space. The decorations are warm and there are pictures everywhere. It's been helpful to have so many things to look at while I don't sleep. Or eat. Or answer my phone.

The space I wanted isn't like I thought it would be. I imagined that I could take some time and think about things and probably talk myself out of falling in love.

I'm good at that. I can make myself believe anything.

Obviously.

But all I've done is think about Nate and Ryder and what could've been. I've been tempted every hour to pick up the phone and call Nate. To tell him I'm sorry for leaving. To tell him I'm scared shitless to marry him but if he wants to marry me, I'd rather do that than live with this hole in my heart for the rest of my life. Because I'm certain there will be no way to fill it with anything or anyone else.

Ugh.

I grab my phone and pointedly don't look at my texts. There will be messages from Nate and I can't look at them right now. I need to get my head together first.

It takes a moment to unlock my screen and pull up my favorites list. I press on my mother's name.

"Hi, baby girl," she says after the second ring. "How are you? I haven't heard from you in a couple of days."

"Oh, I'm fine."

"What's the matter?" she asks, her voice losing the cheeriness of a second ago.

I open my mouth to lie to her, to reassure her that I'm fine and change the subject to one of my siblings or her upcoming visit. But I can't. I need her.

"I think I screwed up, Mom."

"What happened?"

I groan. "I think Nate was going to ask me to marry him."

"Already?"

"Exactly."

"And how do you feel about that?"

I make a face. "That's it? *How do I feel about it?* Where is the bear mom that I'm used to?"

"I think the term is *mama bear*, honey."

"Whatever. You get the point."

It sounds like she turns a television off in the background.

"Sweetheart, I am ready and willing to go to bat for you. But only when it's necessary. You're able to handle your own business."

I snort.

"So, am I to assume you don't want to marry him?"

My heart squeezes so hard I have to move to ease the pain. "Not today." I stand up again, unable to sit still. "I'd be a horrible wife, Mom. I'd be an awful stepmom. I mean, I love them both but I'm not particularly domestic and, I hate doing laundry and—"

"Paige?"

"What?"

"What's the real reason?"

I stand next to Hollis's favorite chair and look at the ceiling.

"You are in the most difficult position you could be in." She pauses. "Loving someone when you're scared is terrifying."

You're telling me.

"To love someone, you have to open your heart and let light shine on the darkest places," she says.

"The gun went off. The sound was so loud. Mom screamed again."

"You have to trust that they have your best interests in mind."

"I want to know if you like it, if you hate it, or if it hurts. You have to communicate with me."

"You have to know that they will love you even when they see the worst in you."

"What else can I do? Just tell me. Don't do this, Paige."

The bridge of my nose burns with the rise of my emotions. *This hurts so much.*

"It takes a lot for someone to be that vulnerable, Paige. No one wants to show someone else their wounds. But that's what love is and, really, it's the only way to heal the things that hurt you."

I clutch my chest, willing the tightness to subside.

"Let me guess—you ran," she says.

"Yeah," I say around the lump in my throat.

"Oh, Paige. Honey ..."

"I thought that if I left now it would be easier," I say, my voice muffled by the tears threatening to spill. "Like dropping a class before you just fail it. Why wait it out and have the fail on your transcript forever?"

She chuckles. "You're going to walk away from someone you obviously care so much about just so you don't get hurt? But you're hurt now. So, what you're really doing is denying yourself the chance to be loved by what I assume is a good man, or else you wouldn't love him."

Fuck it. I cry. I let myself just cry. I don't try to stop the tears, even though I curse them in every way.

"I just look at Ryder, his little boy, and think that eventually he'll lay in his bed and miss me like I did my mom. Like I missed Hollis. That it will be this terrible circle of pain that needs to stop."

"But you're perpetuating the problem, Paige. Open your eyes. Where is Ryder now? Where is his mother?"

"She's dead."

"So you're willing to *not* be someone in this little boy's life because someday you and his father may not work out? Even though I've never seen you act this way over a man in your life?"

I sigh?

"You're letting fear rule your life. You're too scared of what might go wrong that you can't enjoy the good in front of you."

"Mom ..."

The doorbell rings.

"Hollis has a package or box or something coming and I told him I'd get it. I need to go."

"This conversation isn't over," she says.

I'm sure it's not.

"I'll call you later, okay?" I ask. "And don't talk to my brothers about this. Swear."

"I promise. I love you, honey."

The bell rings again.

"Gotta go," I say. "Love you, too."

I tuck my phone in my pocket and make my way to the front door. My head throbs from the intermittent crying for the last two days and my stomach gnaws at itself from not eating.

I'm such a mess.

The bell rings for a third time just as I grab the handle.

"For heaven's sake ..."

I gasp.

Oh, my gosh.

Chapter 35

Nate

Don't grab her.
    Don't cry.
    Don't drop the plate.
Speak, damn it!

She holds her hand over her mouth, covering the lips that I love to kiss. Her eyes are red and the skin beneath them dark. She stares at me in disbelief.

"You aren't answering my texts, so I thought I'd come over," I say gently, hoping my voice doesn't shake. "Ryder was afraid you were hungry. He made you breakfast."

I hold out a plate covered with tinfoil. She reaches for it slowly, almost as if she's not sure if this is happening.

Her fingers brush against my hand. I move my fingers towards hers without thinking and hers feel like they're going to lock on to mine. But they don't.

She pulls the tinfoil back and looks at the pancake. There's a heart on the top where the syrup that Ryder so carefully placed sank into the cooked batter.

Her lips press together, the plate shaking in her hands.

"Look, I don't know what happened or why you took off. I have no fucking idea, Paige. But you said you love me and that's all I really care about. That's why I'm here."

"Oh, Nate ..."

Her words are thick with emotion and I want to reach for her so badly. I crave it. I need it.

I need it for me and I need it for her.

"I thought I was doing all right," I say. "I thought I was loving you and taking care of you and giving you time to get comfortable. But if I didn't get it—if I didn't love you the way you need to be loved, then tell me so I can—"

"You love me just right."

Tears fill her eyes but don't fall.

"Did you do something then?" I ask. "Is there someone else?"

The thought of her being with another man makes me want to rage. The only thing that tempers the anger that flares instantly in my stomach is the small smile on her face.

"There will never be anyone else, I'm afraid," she whispers.

The hope I've been fighting to hold on to—the hope I've been praying for—floods me. I'm afraid to say anything. I don't dare move. I wait on her to expound.

"Do you want to come in?" she asks.

I nod and step inside.

She closes the door behind me. I look nowhere but at her. And as I see the fear lingering in her eyes, I make a decision that I should've made two days ago.

Change of plans.

"Here's what's happening," I say, planting my feet in place. "I won't let you ruin this for us. Not for me, not for Ryder, and not for you."

Her eyes widen.

"I've already given you my heart and I won't take it back," I tell her. "Not now, not next year, not in ten years. All right?"

Paige doesn't nod or speak or give me any indication that she understands. But I know she does. She understands exactly what I'm saying.

"I'm not a fortune teller than can show you some crystal ball and prove to you that we'll be together until I die. All I can do is tell you that I am done. I am yours. *You own me.*"

She covers her mouth, her eyes narrowing as if she's ready to cry.

I take a deep breath, ignoring the anxiety swelling inside me, and march on. Because it's all I can do and, I won't sit by another day and do nothing.

"I'm not rushing you," I say. "I'm not asking you for anything. I will never hurry you to do anything that you don't want to do because I have the next fifty years to wait, baby. And I will if that's what it takes."

Her hand falls to the side as a smile inches its way slowly across her face.

Thank God.

"Don't cry," I say. "There's nothing to cry about. Take your time and come home when you're ready. Ryder and I will be waiting."

I turn to go when she stops me.

"Nate."

I hold my breath, hoping for what feels like a miracle, and turn around.

She sets the pancake on a table by the door. Her hand trembles the whole time. Finally, she takes a breath, recentering herself.

"I'm sorry that I didn't talk this out with you," she says softly. "That wasn't fair. Actually, it was rude."

"Talk to me now. Remember, I can't read your mind."

We grin at each other, remembering the last time I told her that. *The night she gave me her body.*

"I went into your office the other day and walked on in like I always do, because I know no boundaries, and ... I saw the rings on your computer."

The rings?

What the hell is she talking about?

244

"I panicked. I'd had lunch with a friend and she'd gotten into my head because apparently, I'm not self-confident enough, despite the shit-talking I do, to ... *believe in me.*" She smiles sadly. "This was never about you, Nate. This was always about me."

"My boyfriend told me last night that he wants to propose to me and asked me to find a ring."

Motherfucker.

"Can we back up and go back to the rings?"

She cringes. "I know things have been going fast between us and they've been great. So I understand why you might've thought I was ready to be engaged and that's my fault if I put that vibe out but—"

"Hey, Paige," I say, fighting a smile.

"What?"

"I'd marry you today. Right now. I'm there. But that ring you saw on my computer? That wasn't for you."

She lifts her brows.

"Kira's boyfriend is proposing or something and, she and Shaye wanted to look at it on a bigger screen. So they came in and did whatever they were doing—driving me crazy, mostly—and I forgot to exit out of the website."

It takes a minute for her to process what I said.

Her shoulders fall forward. Her jaw drops. Her eyes go wide.

I grin. "Communication is key."

"Oh, my gosh. Are you telling me I've been freaking out for nothing?"

"Well, I wouldn't say for nothing. Now I know to maybe never propose."

She half-laughs, half-cries. "I'm so humiliated."

I can't help it. I laugh.

I laugh, even though she tried to ruin us. Even though she nearly killed me. Even though Ryder was heartbroken this morning.

I can do that because it's okay. *It's going to be okay.*

"What do I ..." she stammers. "I don't know what to say. I'm so embarrassed and you must think—"

245

"I can tell you what to do. And what to say. And I can share what I think." My lips twitch. "But I'd really like to hear it from you."

She pauses as if she's not sure how to respond—like she actually needs to think about it. *Is she for real right now?*

"Paige, for fuck's sake, I'm dying over here."

She taps her chin with her fingertip as if she's lost in thought. *Little minx.*

"Fine," I say, completely over this. "You're coming home. You tell me you love me. I think it's terrible that you carry so much fear over being happy, but I will try for the rest of my life to make you believe in forever."

She drops her hand and grins. "I was actually just thinking about make-up sex. I heard it's the best and I was wondering if you were going to make love to me or fuck me hard in the—*ah!*"

I pick her up and toss her over my shoulder.

"That's it. We're going home," I say, turning towards the door.

"My pancake! Don't forget my pancake!"

I roll my eyes and move her closer to the plate.

"You take it. I can't carry it upside down," she says.

I slide her slowly down my front, chest to chest, and capture her mouth with mine on the way.

Having her in my arms again, where she belongs, reignites a fire inside me that burned out when she left.

"Oh, crap! I'm supposed to be waiting on a package for Hollis."

"I think I am the package," I say with a grin. "Now, what about your stuff?"

She smiles as she looks into my eyes. "We can come back."

"Are you sure?"

"I have to show you how sorry I am," she teases, dragging a finger down my chest.

"I'm pretty fucking hurt. It might take a long time."

"Then we better get going."

"Okay."

I pick her up again. This time I hold her in my arms so I can see her face.

"You're never leaving me again," I tell her as we walk outside.

She closes the door behind us.

"I mean it," I say. "You can go into the other bedroom or I'll camp outside or whatever, but that's it. You're done running. That was your last hoorah."

I open the truck door and deposit her on the seat. She grabs my face with both hands.

"I kind of need a favor," she says, her eyes twinkling.

"Really? What's that?"

"Will you ask me to marry you one day? Not soon. Not now. But someday when I'm ready?"

I grin so hard it hurts. "I promise."

"Good." She drops her hands from my face. "But I don't need a big ring like that. I mean, *come on*. How is Kira even going to wear that on her finger? It was pretty, sure but ..."

I close the door mid-sentence and chuckle.

My girl is back. And she's here to stay.

Chapter 36

Paige

Nate squeezes my hand. Again.

The only time he hasn't touched me since he picked me up to carry me to the truck was the few seconds it took to walk around to climb in himself.

I'm not complaining.

"Where's Ryder?" I ask.

Nate chuckles. "That little shit is at home with Mrs. Kim, probably giving her hell." He glances at me. "He was pissed I didn't let him come with me."

I feel my smile in my soul.

"He put me *in my place* this morning," he says, shaking his head.

"Did he?"

"Oh, yeah. I mean, he told me he was going to find you. That I was lazy. That he was scared you were *out there with monsters*." He grins. "He likes you almost as much as I do."

That sweet boy. I truly hate that he was hurting, but I love how he fought for me too. *Just like his dad.*

I try to pull my hand away to scratch my arm. Nate clenches down harder. *I'll live with it.*

We drive towards Nate's house—*my house*—in the bright, early afternoon sunlight. The rays feel warm against my skin and I lift my chin to the sun to absorb as much as I can.

I feel terrible for what happened and how I handled it. But facing your fears for the first time is always hard, I guess. I'm just thankful Nate came to pick me up, literally, and carry me home.

We pull into the driveway and Nate stops the truck.

"Be ready. Ryder's probably going to be going a hundred—yup."

I follow Nate's gaze to see Ryder racing down the walkway towards the truck. I hop out just in time to catch him mid-jump.

"Paige Stage!" he yells, wrapping his arms around my neck. "I thought you left me forever."

I meet Nate's eyes over the hood of the truck.

My whole world has shifted, turned on its axis. I'm still afraid of forever. There's a voice in the back of my head that whispers that I shouldn't get comfortable. That the honeymoon phase will end. That I will wind up alone, crying in my bed.

But I've already done that and it didn't help.

Maybe the voice is right. Things will probably get hard. We may fall on hard times or, God forbid, one of us might get sick. But that could happen to me anyway. Besides, the thought of Nate and Ryder battling anything without me kills my soul.

They're my boys. Both of them.

"Forever?" I ask, holding him tight. "The only thing that's forever is the three of us. I'm really sorry I left, Ryder Spider. I hope you'll forgive me."

He presses a kiss to my cheek before I set him on the ground.

Nate smiles the softest, most tender smile I've ever seen on him. And out of all the things he said, and the pancake, and the fact that he came to get me—this is what binds my heart back together.

"I missed you," Ryder says, tugging on my hand. "I was afraid for you when you didn't come home. And Dad made breakfast and *bleh*," he says, sticking out his tongue. "And he only read me one story last night without the voices like you do."

I ruffle his hair. "I will read you three books tonight. Sound like a plan?"

He pumps his fists in the air.

Mrs. Kim comes out of the house and walks gingerly down the steps. Her kind face smiles.

"Mrs. Kim," Ryder says. "Look! Paige Stage Hughes is back!"

"Oh, no," Nate says, laughing. "Her last name is Carmichael, for the love of God."

I can't help it. I laugh. *Hard.* I laugh so hard that tears fill my eyes.

Mrs. Kim looks at Nate and winks. "Ryder, I'm going to the butcher shop. Do you want to go?"

"Oh, can I?" he asks. "I love it there. They have all these little candies and I'm always *really* nice and the ladies there let me have a couple."

"Ooh. Sounds fun," I say.

He starts towards Mrs. Kim but whips back around to me.

"You will be here when I come back, right?" he asks, his face dead serious."I'm only leaving you with Dad and, well ... ya know."

I giggle. "Yes, Ryder. I will be here every day when you come home."

There's a small scowl on his brow. He's not convinced. And that makes total sense. *He's been left before ... but never again.*

"Promise?" he asks. "I don't want to worry about this."

I crouch down so I'm at his eye level and take his hands in mine. "I promise you that you have nothing to worry about. I'm here and I will be here. *Forever.*"

He wraps his arms around my neck again and squeezes me tight. When he pulls back, he smiles.

"I love you so much," he says. "I'm glad you're home."

"Me too buddy. And I love you too. So, so much."

He marches around the truck towards Mrs. Kim, high-fiving his dad as he walks by. Nate and I laugh.

"Going with her," he says like a little man. "I'll be back later."

Mrs. Kim giggles and follows him across the lawn.

I saunter over to the man dressed in all black, who's waiting for me by the walkway. He holds a hand out to me.

"Well, what do we do now that we have a house to ourselves?" I ask, placing my hand in his as we walk onto the porch. "Probably have an hour we could kill. Two if Mrs. Kim really loves us."

"I have already made up my mind."

His smirk is so smoldering, so sinful, that I blush.

We walk inside and Nate shuts the door. The snap of the lock makes me jump.

His eyes are dark, his jaw tense. He grabs my hips and jerks me to him and kisses me with an intention that leaves little room for speculation.

"You, my lady, are going to get your wish," he says.

I already have it. "What's that?"

He reaches under my ass cheeks and hoists me up. I wrap my legs around his waist and kiss him with a passion that I didn't know I could feel.

We move through the house to the kitchen. He sets me gently on the counter.

He pulls back and grins.

"Now you're going to experience make-up sex," he says, unfastening his belt.

"*Ooh.* Okay. Tell me more."

"I'm going to fuck you until I feel better about you leaving," he says, unbuttoning his pants. "And then ..."

He lifts his eyes to mine. The look in them makes me teary.

The only way to explain it is love. It's relief and hope and a lifetime's worth of promises all rolled into a pair of beautiful green eyes.

"And then what?" I ask, my voice soft.

"And then I'm going to take you to the bedroom and show you how much I love you."

He brushes his lips against mine. They're soft and sweet—touching me so softly that I barely feel the warmth of his breath. It's unhurried, as if we're the only people that exist. Like we have all the time in the world.

I guess we do.

Slowly, he deepens the kiss, nibbling on my bottom lip. The bite sends a shot of energy to my core. His stubble from not shaving the last two days scratches my cheeks as he moves his head for a better angle.

I grab his face with both hands and pull him away far enough to see his eyes.

"Nate?"

"What?"

I smile the biggest, most real smile I've ever given anyone—and mean it. "I love you, Nate Hughes. Forever."

He cups my cheeks and grins. "I love you forever too."

Epilogue

P aige

approximately 1 week later

"Hollis, this is my mother ..."

My brother's eyes go wide when she pulls him into a very personal hug for a woman that just met someone—even if it is her daughter's brother.

"Sorry. She's a hugger," I say.

His grin makes my heart warm.

Mom pulls back and cups his cheek. "It is wonderful to meet you, Hollis."

"It's very nice to meet you too." He smiles like a little boy meeting an aunt that lives across the country for the first time. "I've heard a lot of things about you."

Mom loops her elbow through Hollis's and leads him across the room.

"Oh, I bet you have and I've heard a lot about you too. Tell me about yourself. We're family now," she says.

Hollis looks at me over his shoulder, amusement written all over his face. I shrug, making him laugh.

I venture into the kitchen where Nate is talking to my dad. And Ryder.

"Well, I like the '67 Yenko Camaros the best," Ryder says like he's a middle-aged man holding his Capri Sun. "There are 450 horses in that thing."

Dad looks at Nate. He shrugs.

"You're going to have to come to my house," Dad tells Ryder. "We have lots of car shows down there. I have a buddy that has a '67 Camaro Z28. Bet he'd take you for a ride in it."

Ryder's eyes grow wide. "Really? Can I go, Dad?"

Nate chuckles, looking a bit out of his element. I slide up beside him and rest my head on his shoulder.

Dad beams. When Ryder bebops off to find my mom, whom he's already nicknamed Nanna Banana—which made my mother's life, Nate turns to face me. Dad gives me a thumbs up.

I might cry.

"I need to call and make sure Murray showed up," Nate says before kissing the top of my head. "I'll be right back."

"No rush," Dad says. He waits until Nate is gone before he turns his attention on me. "Well, I'll be honest—I came here with my thumb on Banks's number."

I giggle.

"But you've really impressed me, Paige. I can't believe I'm saying this but I kinda like the guy."

"Dad," I say, swatting his shoulder.

His glass of tea sloshes in his hand as he chuckles.

"I'm very proud of you, Paige. You've turned into a hell of a young woman."

His compliment, which doesn't necessarily come easily, brings me a joy and comfort that I didn't know I needed.

The house is alive with voices and laughter. Ryder's giggle

streams over the top of the rest. It's not quite as chaotic as my parents' house in Florida, but it's full of love just the same.

Mom and Dad have loved me through my best *and* my worst moments. They've shown up when I needed them every single time. They've brought me in and loved me when no one else did. And now I have Hollis, Nate, and Ryder, filling places I hadn't known needed filling.

I am so incredibly happy. So wonderfully blessed.

Sometimes things like fear can be a habit more than anything else. You're scared because that's what you do. You are fearful because, at some point, someone told you that you should always look over your shoulder. Or that you weren't good enough. Or that your happiness will end.

It took a grumpy bar owner and his adorable little boy to show me that I'm more than my fear. I have love to give. I'm worthy of receiving their affection. And if you believe in yourself enough, life can be pretty sweet.

"Should we go rescue Hollis from Mom?" I ask Dad.

He makes a face. "Don't rob her of her moment. She's been talking about this for weeks."

I laugh.

"Come on," he says, nodding towards the door. "Let's step outside so I can tell you about this shit with Maddox. I can't tell anyone else."

"Ooh. Gossip. I love getting dirt on my brothers."

Nate

"Hello?"

I smile at the sound of Dominic's voice. I don't know why I called him—I don't need anything.

The evening air is crisp and cool as the sun dips behind the trees. It's calm and peaceful, just like me.

"Nate? I know this is you. I have you programmed into my phone."

I laugh. "Hey, what's happening?"

"Ah, not much. I'm currently trying to convince Cam to let me put a baby inside—"

"*Dom!*" Cam yells, cutting Dom off. He laughs.

"We're getting ready to go to Barrett's winery. Want to go?"

"I have a houseful of people or I absolutely would."

"Oh, that's right. Paige's people are there."

"Her *family*. But, yes, they are."

"How is that going?"

I walk around the backyard, sidestepping a baseball bat and tennis ball. *That's a window waiting to be broken.*

"It's actually going really well," I say. "Paige's mom is kinda huggy. Her Dad is pretty cool. We talked cars and just kinda shot the shit, I guess you could say."

"Are they still there?"

"Yeah."

"And you're calling me why?"

Good question.

I make my way back towards the house and stop on the stoop.

Dominic and I started life in a world of chaos. We fought hard to come out of it—sometimes literally—on top. We banded together when our mother took her life shortly after Dad died. We've relied on each other, pulled each other up when we were down, and encouraged each other to keep going.

And we did. We came out on top.

Dom now has Camilla, the only woman in the world that would be right for him, and she fucking adores him. He also has the Landry family at his back. They've enveloped him as one of their own.

I always knew I wanted a family for Ryder, mostly. But I never dared to want this. The woman of my dreams, a decent house, the best little boy in the world. And maybe, just maybe, an extended family that might welcome Ryder and me too.

It gets better. Life gets better. You have to scratch and claw your way sometimes and roll with the punches—that never goes away. But if you keep moving, remain hopeful, and never stop believing, you can overcome anything.

Dom and I are proof.

This feeling—I hope it never goes away.

"You know what?" I ask. "We did all right, didn't we?"

He must hear something in my voice. That, or he's a bit thrown by the question because he clears his throat.

"I don't think we did too bad," he says. "Not too bad at all."

"Yeah. Well, okay, I was just calling to say hello."

"You okay, Nate? You're good, right?"

I grin. "I'm the best I've ever been. I'll talk to you later."

"Later."

Just as I hang up, I feel a hand on my shoulder. I don't have to look to see that it's Paige.

"Hey," she says softly. "I wondered where you went."

"Just needed a bit of air."

She wraps her arms around my shoulders and nestles her face against my neck.

"Do you know what's funny?" I ask.

She hums against my skin.

"I always thought I needed to find someone to share my life with. But it was the opposite."

"What do you mean?"

I twist my head and kiss the side of her cheek.

"I needed to find someone that I couldn't live without."

She grins.

We stand together for a long while, watching the sun set over the horizon. Finally, as the golden hour ends and the sun drifts away, Paige releases me.

"If we don't get in there, Hollis might disown me," she says. "My mom won't leave him alone."

I take her hand and follow her inside.

"She keeps peppering him with questions and showing him pictures on her phone," she says, sighing. "He doesn't know who these people are. Why would he care?"

I tug her hand and stop her before we get through the mudroom. She gives me an inquisitive look.

"He cares because he cares about you," I tell her. "That's why I listened to her tell me her recipe for meatloaf step by excruciating step."

Paige giggles. "And, for that, I will always love you."

"Last night you said it was for the way I eat your pussy."

Her cheeks flush the prettiest shade of pink. "Well, that too. Now come on. Let's go see our family."

Our family.

I could get used to that.

Are you ready to read about the Carmichael family? Paige's family is ready to meet you in FLIRT.

Chapter One is next.

Or continue on with Sienna Landry's story in CRANK, the first book in the Gibson Boys Series. Check out Sienna and Walker here.

Landry Security Series begins in 2024. Pulse is available for preorder now.

Flirt - Chapter One

Chapter One
Brooke

WANTED: A SITUATION-SHIP

I'm a single female who's tired of relationships ruining my life. However, there are times when a date would be helpful. If you're a single man, preferably mid-twenties to late-thirties, and are in a similar situation, we might be a match.

Candidate must be handsome, charming, and willing to pretend to have feelings for me (on a sliding scale, as the event requires). Ability to discuss a wide variety of topics is a plus. Must have your own transportation and a (legal) job.

This will be a symbiotic agreement. In exchange for your time, I will give you mine. Need someone to flirt with you at a football party? Go, team! Want a woman to make you look good in front of your boss? Let me find my heels. Would you love for someone to be obsessed with you in front of your ex? I'm applying my red lipstick now.

If interested, please email me. Time is of the essence.

My best friend, Jovie, points at my computer screen. The glitter on her pink fingernail sparkles in the light. "You can't post that."

I fold my arms across my chest. "And why not?"

Instead of answering me, she takes another bite of her chicken wrap. A dribble of mayonnaise dots the corner of her mouth.

"A lot of help you are," I mutter, rereading the post I drafted instead of pricing light fixtures for work. The words are written in a pretty font on Social, my go-to social media platform.

Country music from the nineties mixes with the laughter of locals sitting around us in Smokey's, my favorite beachside café. Along the far wall, a map of the state of Florida made of wine corks sways gently in the ocean breeze coming through the open windows.

"Would you two like anything else?" Rebecca, our usual lunchtime server, pauses by the table. "I think we have some Key lime pie left."

"I'm too irritable for pie today," I say.

"*You* don't want *pie*? That's a first," she teases me.

Jovie giggles.

"I know," I say, releasing a sigh. "That's the state of my life right now. I don't even want pie."

"Wow. Okay. This sounds serious. What's up? Maybe I can help," Rebecca says.

Jovie wipes her mouth with a napkin. "Let me cut in here real quick before she tries to snowball you into thinking her harebrained idea is a good one."

I roll my eyes. "It *is* a good one."

"I'll give you the CliffsNotes version," Jovie says, side-eyeing me. "Brooke got an invitation to her grandma's birthday party, and instead of just not going—"

"I can't *not* go."

"Or showing up as the badass single chick she is," Jovie continues, silencing me with a look, "she wrote a post for Social that's basically an ad for a fake boyfriend."

"Correction—it *is* an ad for a fake boyfriend."

Rebecca rests a hand on her hip. "I don't see the problem."

"*Thank you,*" I say, staring at Jovie. "I'm glad someone understands me here."

Jovie throws her hands in the air, sending a napkin flying right along with them.

Satisfaction is written all over my face as I sit back in my chair with a smug smile. The more I think about having a *situation-ship* with a guy—a word I read in a magazine at the salon while waiting two decades for my color to process—the more it makes sense.

Instead of having relations with a man, have situations. Done.

What's not to love about that?

"But, before I tell you to dive into this whole thing, why can't you just go alone, Brooke?" Rebecca asks.

"Oh, *I can* go alone. I just generally prefer to avoid torture whenever possible."

"I still don't understand why you need a date to your grandma's birthday party."

"Because this isn't *just* a birthday party," I say. "It's labeled that to cover up the fact that my mom and her sister, my aunt Kim, are having a daughter-of-the-year showdown. They're using my poor grandma Honey's eighty-fifth birthday as a dog and pony show—and my cousin Aria and I are the ponies."

"*Okay.*" Rebecca looks at me dubiously before switching her attention to Jovie. "And why are you against this whole thing?"

Jovie takes enough cash to cover our lunch plus the tip and hands it to Rebecca. *Perks of ordering the same lunch most days.* Then she gathers her things.

"I'm not against it in *theory*," Jovie says. "I'm against it in *practice*. I understand the perks of having a guy around to be arm candy when needed. But I'm not supporting this decision ... this *mayhem* ... for two reasons." She looks at me. "For one, your family will see any post you make on Social. You don't think they'll use it as ammunition against you?"

This is probably true.

"Second," Jovie continues. "I hate, hate, *hate* your aunt Kim, and I loathe the fact that your mom makes you feel like you have to do anything more than be your amazing self to win her favor. Screw them both."

My heart swells as I take in my best friend.

Jovie Reynolds was my first friend in Kismet Beach when I moved here two and a half years ago. We reached for the same can of pineapple rings, knocking over an entire display in Publix. As we picked up the mess, we traded recipes—hers for a vodka cocktail and mine for air fryer pineapple.

We hung out that evening—with her cocktail and my air fryer creations—and have been inseparable since.

"My mom is not a bad person," I say in her defense, even though I'm not so sure that's true from time to time. "She's just ..."

"A bad person," Jovie says.

I laugh. "*No.* I just ... nothing I can do is good enough for her. She hated Geoff when I married him at twenty and said I was too young. But was she happy when that ended in a divorce? Nope. According to *her*, I didn't try hard enough."

Rebecca frowns.

"And then Geoff started banging Kim and—"

"*What?*" Rebecca yelps, her eyes going wide.

"Exactly. Bad people," Jovie says, shaking her head.

"So your ex-husband will be at your grandma's party with your aunt? Is that what you're saying?" Rebecca asks.

I nod. "Yup."

She stacks our plates on top of one another. The ceramic clinks through the air. "On that note, why can't you just not go? Avoid it altogether?"

"Because my grandma Honey is looking forward to this, and she called me to make sure I was coming. I couldn't tell her no." My heart tightens when I think of the woman I love more than any other. "And, you know, my mom has made it abundantly clear that if I miss this, I will probably break Honey's heart, and she'll die, and it'll be my fault."

"Wow. That's a freight train of guilt to throw around," Rebecca says, wincing.

I glance down at my computer. The post is still there, sitting on the screen and waiting for my final decision. Although it is a genius idea, if I do say so myself—Jovie is probably right. It'll just cause more problems than it's worth.

I close the laptop and shove it into my bag. Then I hoist it on my shoulder. "It's complicated. I want to go and celebrate with my grandma but seeing my aunt with my ex-husband ..." I wince. "Also, there will be my mother's usual diatribe and comparisons to Aria, proving that I'm a failure in everything that I do."

"But if you had a boyfriend to accompany you, you'd save face with the enemy and have a buffer against your mother. Is that what you're thinking?" Rebecca asks.

"Yeah. I don't know how else to survive it. I can't walk in there alone, or even with Jovie, and deal with all of that mess. If I just had someone hot and a little handsy—make me look irresistible—it would kill all of my birds with one hopefully *hard* stone."

I wink at my friends.

Rebecca laughs. "Okay. I'm Team Fake Boyfriend. Sorry, Jovie."

Jovie sighs. "I'm sorry for me too because I have to go back to work. And if I avoid the stoplights, I can make it to the office with thirty seconds to spare." She air-kisses Rebecca. "Thanks for the extra mayo."

I laugh. "See you tomorrow, Rebecca."

"Bye, girls."

Jovie and I walk single-file through Smokey's until we reach the exit. Immediately, we reach for the sunglasses perched on top of our heads and slide them over our eyes.

The sun is bright, nearly blinding in a cloudless sky. I readjust my bag so that the thin layer of sweat starting to coat my skin doesn't coax the leather strap down my arm.

"Call me tonight," Jovie says, heading to her car.

"I will."

"Rehearsal for the play got canceled tonight, so I might go to Charlie's. If I don't, I may swing by your house."

"How's the thing with Charlie going? I didn't realize you were still talking to him."

She laughs. "I wasn't. He pissed me off. But he came groveling back last night, and I gave in." She shrugs. "What can I say? I'm a sucker for a good grovel."

"I think it's the theater girl in you. You love the dramatics of it all."

"That I do. It's a problem."

"Well, I'll see you when I see you then," I say.

"Bye, Brooke."

I give her a little wave and make my way up Beachfront Boulevard.

The sidewalk is fairly vacant with a light dusting of sand. In another month, tourists will fill the street that leads from the ocean to the shops filled with trinkets and ice cream in the heart of Kismet Beach. For now, it's a relaxing and hot walk back to the office.

My mind shifts from the heat back to the email reminder I received during lunch. *To Honey's party.* It takes all of one second for my stomach to cramp.

"I shouldn't have eaten all of those fries," I groan.

But it's not lunch that's making me unwell.

A mixture of emotions rolls through me. I don't know which one to land on. There's a chord of excitement about the event—at seeing Honey and her wonderful life be celebrated, catching up with Aria and the rest of my family, and the general concept of *going home*. But there's so much apprehension right alongside those things that it drowns out the good.

Kim and Geoff together make me ill. It's not that I miss my ex-husband; I'm the one who filed for divorce. But they will be there, making things super awkward for me in front of everyone we know.

Not to mention what it will do to my mother.

Geoff hooking up with Kim is my ultimate failure, according to Mom. Somehow, it embarrasses *her,* and that's unforgivable.

"For just once, I'd like to see her and not be judged," I mumble as I sidestep a melting glob of blue ice cream.

Nothing I have ever done has been good enough for Catherine Bailey. Marrying Geoff was an atrocity at only twenty years old. My dream to work in interior architecture wasn't deemed serious enough as a life path. *"You're wasting your time and our money, Brooke."* And when I told her I was hired at Laguna Homes as a lead designer for one of their three renovation teams? I could hear her eyes rolling.

The office comes into view, and my spirits lift immediately. I shove all thoughts of the party out of my brain and let my mind settle back into happier territory. *Work.* The one thing I love.

I step under the shade of an adorable crape myrtle tree and then turn up a cobblestone walkway to my office.

The small white building is tucked away from the sidewalk. It sits between a row of shops with apartments above them and an Italian restaurant only open in the evenings. The word *Laguna Homes* is printed in seafoam green above a black awning.

My shoes tap against the wooden steps as I make my way to the door. A rush of cool air, kissed by the scent of eucalyptus essential oil, greets me as I step inside.

"How was lunch?" Kix asks, standing in the doorway of his corner office. My boss's smile is kind and genuine, just like everything else about him. "Let me guess—you met Jovie for lunch at Smokey's?"

I laugh. "It's like you know me or something."

He chuckles.

Kix and Damaris Carmichael are two of my favorite people in the world. When I met Damaris at a trade show three years ago, and we struck up a conversation about tile, I knew she was special. Then I met her husband and discovered he had the same soft yet sturdy energy. All six of their children possess similar qualities—even Moss, the superintendent on my renovation team. Although I'd never admit that to him.

"I swung by Parasol Place this afternoon," Kix says. "It's looking great. You were right about taking out the wall between the living room and dining room. I love it. It makes the whole house feel bigger."

I blush under the weight of his compliment. "Thanks."

"Did Moss tell you about the property I'm looking at for your team next?" Kix asks.

"No. Moss doesn't tell me anything."

Kix grins. "I'm sure he tells you all kinds of things you don't need to know."

"You say that like you have experience with him," I say, laughing.

"Only a few years." He laughs too. "It's another home from the sixties. I got a lead on it this morning and am on my way to look at it now."

"Take pictures. You know I love that era, and if you get it, I want to be able to start envisioning things right away."

"You and your visions." He shakes his head. "Gina is in the back making copies. I told her we'd keep our eye on the door until she gets back out here, so it would be great if you could do that."

"Absolutely," I say, walking backward toward my office. "Be safe. *And take pictures.*"

"I will. Enjoy the rest of your day, Brooke."

"You, too."

I reach behind me to find my office door open. I take another step back and then turn toward my desk. Someone moves beside my filing cabinet just as I flip on the light.

"Ah!" I shriek, clutching my chest.

My heart pounds out of control until I get my bearings and focus on the man looking back at me.

I set my bag down on a chair and blow out a shaky breath. "Dammit, Moss!"

He leans against the cabinet and smiles at me cheekily.

"We're going to have to stop meeting like this," he says. "People are going to talk."

Read FLIRT here.

Acknowledgments

Thank you to my Creator, first and foremost.

I had so much fun going back into the Landry world. Thank you to my readers for their love and support of this series. You made this book happen!

My amazing family certainly had to put up with a lot of days of me mumbling about this book. I couldn't imagine a better group of cheerleaders and supporters than my guys. Thank you for your patience, love, and for bringing dinner to my desk while I typed away. You are the sweetest part of my life.

While my parents aren't here anymore, I would be remiss if I didn't thank them. My mother's favorite series was the Landry family and I know she would be thrilled to read Sweet. I'm so grateful for your love and guidance. Also, I would like to thank Peggy and Rob for loving me like their own. I couldn't have dreamed up a better couple than the two of you. Thank you for loving my family ... and for loving me.

Thank you to Kari March for another beautiful, perfect cover. Sometimes I think that you know my brain better than I do. Your patience and willingness to humor my ideas is always so appreciated.

My assistant tolerated my craziness while writing this book. Many thanks to Tiffany Remy for sticking by my side and keeping things in order while I wrote.

There aren't enough words to express my appreciation, love, and respect for Carleen Riffle. You are amazing. I hope you know that.

There are many pieces of you in this book—and they're some of my favorite parts.

I put my beta readers to the test with this one. Big hugs to Susan Raynor, Jen Costa, and Anjelica Grace for their thoughtful notes and for not quitting on me.

I don't know how Marion Archer puts up with me and my madness, but she does and with a smile. (Or, I think she's smiling anyway. I hope so!) Thank you for your kindness and excitement over my words. I look forward to working with you every time.

Jenny Sims is absolutely amazing. I'm so grateful that you make space for me and my stories in your busy life. It's a privilege to work with you.

A huge shoutout to Michele Ficht for her eagle eye with proof-reading, as well as her friendship. You don't just clean up my words. You are a dear friend.

This book may not have been written without Mandi Beck. I owe you. Big. But I love you even bigger.

Thank you to S.L. Scott for her constant support and enthusiasm. Our conversations are the only thing that keep me going some days.

Brittni Van of The Smuthood is an endless source of energy, ideas, and fun. Thank you for working with me on this book—and for all the things you do and who you are. I adore you.

So many words of this book were written with Jessica Prince on Zoom. Without you, Jessica, I'm not sure I'd ever really sit down and work. Thank you for being the friend you are.

Thank you, too, for Team Harlee in Books by Adriana Locke. You got your wish. She lived happily ever after. Thank you for your endless (and I mean *endless*) enthusiasm for her story. I hope it was everything you wanted it to be.

And, last but certainly not least, thank YOU for picking up this book. I'm honored that you trusted me to entertain you for a little while. I hope you enjoyed the story.

About the Author

USA Today Bestselling author, Adriana Locke, writes contemporary romances about the two things she knows best—big families and small towns. Her stories are about ordinary people finding extraordinary love with the perfect combination of heart, heat, and humor.

She loves connecting with readers, fall weather, football, reading alpha heroes, everything pumpkin, and pretending to garden.

Hailing from a tiny town in the Midwest, Adriana spends her free time with her high school sweetheart (who she married over twenty years ago) and their four sons (who truly are her best work). Her kitchen may be a perpetual disaster, and if all else fails, there is always pizza.

www.adrianalocke.com

Made in the USA
Monee, IL
03 January 2025

76004846R00154